TEASER

A Corey Logan Thriller

TEASER

A Corey Logan Thriller

BURT WEISSBOURD

A Vireo Book V Rare Bird Books

Los Angeles, Calif.

THIS IS A GENUINE VIREO BOOK

V

A Vireo Book | Rare Bird Books
453 South Spring Street, Suite 531
Los Angeles, CA 90013
rarebirdbooks.com

FIRST HARDCOVER EDITION

Set in Goudy Old Style
Printed in the United States
Distributed in the US by Publishers Group West

10 9 8 7 6 5 4 3 2 1

Publisher's Cataloging-in-Publication data

Weissbourd, Burt.
    Teaser : a Corey Logan thriller / by Burt Weissbourd.
    p. cm.
    ISBN 978-1-940207-36-0

1. Homeless children—Fiction. 2. Runaway children—Fiction. 3.
Private schools—Fiction. 4. Seattle (Wash.)—Fiction. 5. Suspense
fiction. I. Title.

PS3623.E4593 T43 2014
813.6—dc23

For Dorothy Escribano

All of the characters and events in this story are imagined, as are many of the Seattle and Seattle-area locations. Seattle is, of course, real, though the author has created an imaginary landscape in and around Capitol Hill.

Special Acknowledgement

In creating the character of Teaser, I drew from Dr. James Gilligan's excellent book, Violence. *His understanding of violence, violent criminals ("the living dead"), and of the realities of prison life—that is to say of "the violence that prisoners routinely inflict on one another"—led me to understand Teaser.*

PROLOGUE

November 2011

STAR HATED WAITING. AIRPORT security lines made her arms itch and her stomach cramp. In the past year, Star had to visit her doctor twice. The first time, she had fled the waiting room after twenty-six minutes with hives on her forearms the size of wine grapes. Thirty-four minutes into her second visit the hives reached her chest, and Star upended a tropical fish tank sitting on a Plexiglas plank attached to the waiting room wall. "See how long your fucking fish can wait," she snapped at the stunned receptionist.

So the fact that she was waiting outside the gates of the Western Corrections Center—had been waiting for almost an hour—was like a very big deal, she was thinking. She'd done some downers, and she'd bought Milky Ways to eat in the car. And *Tomb Raider*, to keep her mind busy—smooth it out when it wouldn't slow down. She had her iPod, too, screaming out Liquid Red, a Seattle band she liked. And stuff to read. Star was rockin' on *Tomb Raider* when Teaser came out, slow, even lazy, moving like a jungle cat. He turned toward her, still pretty as a man could be. So fine, so fine it was unnatural. His long black hair was gone, but his eyes were the same. When you looked at him it just caught you up, like looking at fire. She felt something good inside when he found her eyes.

He was in the car then. She could feel his fingers touching her now, and she felt better. He was gentle, playing with her the way she liked. He knew just how to do it, Star was thinking. And then she was gone, riding the wave. "Thank you," she finally whispered.

She looked at him, watched his thin lips twist into a faint smile.

They were driving down Broadway when he finally asked, "You make the connection?"

"That red-haired guy you sent, Luther, he was a dick." She tensed up, turned enough to face him.

"You make the connection?" he asked again, so soft she could barely hear him.

"Yeah. Sure. There's two of 'em: big boss Maisie and Aaron, her itchy Chinaboy." She watched him smile—nice—with Teaser, she wasn't always having to explain what she meant. "They're like little puppies." Star took a bite of a Milky Way as he turned down Pine. "Tease, they like how I move...silky smooth."

"Perfect." He continued west toward the water. "I've got something going."

She knew he would, he always did. "Tell me." She watched him looking out the side window, like he was somewhere else. Teaser was the only one she could wait for—he slowed her down. Something about the way he was with her. He was the only one who could do that.

He pulled over and stopped, quiet, still looking out. Star saw a building, a lighted window. "We're going to take this girl to the moon," he whispered.

CHAPTER ONE

COREY LOGAN WAS ONLINE, checking out VampireFreaks.com/Gothic Industrial Culture. One of the kids she was looking for was a "Goth," and Corey was trying to figure out just what that meant. She was reading about New Orleans, the vampire and voodoo mecca of America.

She turned away from her screen, setting her boots on the window sill. Through her window she could see a Japanese container ship slowly bearing down the shipping lane past downtown Seattle.

Corey could just shut down her lovely face, make it hard and lifeless. When she didn't, her face was like some kind of barometer, giving an instant reading of whatever was brewing inside. At the moment she was thinking, on the edge of something. The corners of her mouth had turned up, just a little; the fine lines around her pale grey eyes had disappeared, and the patch of freckles that spread across her nose had crept onto the gentle rise of her cheeks. She relaxed when she was thinking. She just liked it. Her husband, Abe, guessed it was her time in prison. Corey thought it began earlier, during the long days at sea. Her smile, when it came, was open and warm.

Her boots shifted as she tilted her head back, and the scar running from her ear to her collarbone made a thin pink line. Corey was thinking about her son, Billy. When she'd called earlier Billy was upstairs, "getting it together," an expression, she'd discovered, that covered almost any activity. She imagined him at his computer, checking out some edgy web site, listening to music, and texting his friends.

On the phone, she and Billy had worked out the timing and the driving for his school's eleventh-grade family night dinner. It was a potluck, which Corey hated because it meant she had to bring something that other people would eat. Last time she'd come empty-handed, and a mother from the parent organization had explained to her that "potluck" was a Native American word for sharing.

The buzzer was too loud, and unexpected. Corey went through the empty reception area. The half glass door said: Corey Logan, in big block letters. On the glass she saw a woman's shadow. The buzzer rang again. Who was that?

"Coming," she called to the silhouette on the glass, then she opened the door. In the hall a skinny, teenage girl was staring at the floor, using her middle finger to twist a knot in her flaming red hair. She wore over-sized black sunglasses. "Annie, what...?"

Annie toed the hardwood floor.

"Come in."

Annie sat down, took off her sunglasses. There were cuts on her hands, forearms, neck, and face, and sticky mats of blood in her hair. One of her eyes was blackened. "He found me," the girl said.

"Luther?"

When Annie nodded, ever so slightly, Corey felt pressure inside, like she was overheating. Her skin was cold though, clammy. She sat beside Annie, taking her hand. Corey was a detective who was hired out exclusively to find runaways—on one condition: once found, the runaway became the client. And once found, Corey worked with these young people to make sound decisions about their lives. Usually, they had a reason to leave home, and though returning home was always an option they considered, it was not necessarily the goal.

Annie liked living with her mom when her uncle wasn't around. But she couldn't live there if he was stopping by. So she ran away ten days before Uncle Luther was released from prison. When Corey found Annie, four weeks later, she checked in with Luther's Community Corrections Officer (CCO) who confirmed that Uncle Luther had rented his own room in one of the few buildings that still accepted registered sexual offenders. Corey had talked several times with Uncle Luther and his CCO about staying away from Annie under any and all circumstances. Luther had convincingly promised Corey and his CCO that he would do that.

His CCO had vouched for him and agreed to monitor, and, because of these things, Corey had worked with all of them so that Annie could live at home. For just an instant, Corey let down her guard, and her face turned haggard.

Annie took a series of quick breaths, then she leaned over in her chair. When Corey touched her shoulder Annie melted back into the chair, her cut hands covering her face.

Corey put a pillow behind her head, then she gently took off Annie's shirt. She could see purple bruises on her arms, a bone-deep cut across her left elbow. She lifted Annie's T-shirt. There were welts snaking across her back. A broken rib pushed out the skin under her left arm.

Corey kissed Annie's brow, undone.

❖

ABE STEIN WAS READING a file as he sat at the big oak table he used as his desk. He was six feet tall and weighed two hundred and twenty-five pounds. His short salt-and-pepper hair was tousled, his closely-cut beard needed a trim, and behind his old table, he looked puzzled. Blackened pipes and his pipe-smoking paraphernalia held down scattered piles of papers. An abandoned Diet Coke can sat beside a stone ashtray. His favorite tweed sport coat was rumpled, and it had a hole in the pocket where a hot ash from his pipe had burned through.

He reread a portion of the file on Theodore "Teaser" White. Abe was a psychiatrist, and he often evaluated prisoners. Still, this file was unsettling. Something had gone wrong for Teaser in prison. He'd become more unstable and, Abe sensed, even more dangerous.

Lou Ballard, a police sergeant built like a pear, sat in the worn leather chair across from Abe, waiting for him to finish.

Abe looked over at Lou. "This guy doesn't belong on the street."

"This guy did his time," Lou replied.

"I know that. But suppose 'Teaser' wants another little girl?" Abe was soft-spoken, and he chose his words carefully. He tapped the open file on his desk. "Suppose it's what he likes?"

"What are you suggesting here?"

Abe studied a spot on the ceiling. "Make him get help. Put him in a program."

"I can't do that. He's already out. And he doesn't want to be in a program."

"Talk to him." Abe leaned forward, focused. "Lean on him. Be yourself."

Lou snickered. "I'm the one's supposed to be the hard-ass."

Try diplomacy, Abe chided himself. He and Lou helped each other often, though they rarely agreed. Making it Lou's idea sometimes made it easier to find common ground. Abe lit a pipe, tossed the match into a wastebasket beside his desk. "Why'd you send me the file?"

"His CCO red flagged it. I've dealt with Teaser, so it came to me. There's weird shit in there, so I thought of you." He sat back, smiling meanly.

Abe nodded, oblivious. "The self-mutilation?"

"Right. How about pulling out his own damn toenails?" Lou cracked his knuckles. "He told the doctor he couldn't feel anything."

"He was disturbed when he went in. I'd say prison made it worse. Teaser needs help."

"And be still my bleeding heart." Lou shook his head. "Doc, he's in for drug possession with intent to deliver—not some psycho-crime."

Forget diplomacy. "A plea bargain. Before the girl ran away, Teaser was charged with rape of a child in the second degree. This girl, Holly, she was twelve and she was pregnant." Abe set his pipe in the stone ashtray. He thought about what to say. "Lou, he was having sex with her for three months. She was eleven when he took her off the street. In prison he says he stopped feeling things. According to the file, Teaser's unusually bright. What do you think he's capable of now?"

Lou pointed at the smoke rising from the fire in Abe's wastebasket. Abe stood, frustrated and surprised, as always, by his own absent-mindedness.

Lou laughed out loud, a gravelly sound.

The phone rang. "Abe Stein," he said, pouring the remains of the Diet Coke onto the fire set by his tossed match. "Oh no..." Lou shook his head, watching the smoke. Abe whispered something then hurriedly cradled the phone. "Gotta go," he muttered and tapped Lou on the shoulder on his way out the door.

Fifteen minutes later Abe ran up the wide stairs of the old hardware building just south of Pioneer Square. The paramedics were packing up when he burst from the elevator, running toward Corey's office. Annie was on a gurney being wheeled out the door. Abe took her hand, squeezing gently. Annie smiled at him, a thin, sad smile. The lines in his face deepened as he watched her being wheeled out.

When the last paramedic had left, Corey put her arms around him. "It's my fault."

"Our fault."

"You said it could happen."

"Could, not would. A possibility."

"He found her on the Ave, brought her to an abandoned building in the trunk of his car. She jumped through a locked window to get away."

He held Corey close. He knew how troubled she'd been about bringing Annie home. How she'd labored over that decision. He'd encouraged Corey to meet with Luther and his CCO to work it out. He stepped back, trying to get his bearings. The price for their mistake was too high.

"The police are there now," she said quietly. "Mom is saying Annie fell. She swears Luther didn't do it, that he was out with her."

"Let's make sure Annie's safe, then we'll deal with them."

"Abe, I blew this. It's—"

He touched a big hand to the small of her back. "She's still alive, babe. Let's do what we can for her."

❖

BILLY'S ELEVENTH-GRADE FAMILY NIGHT was at 5:30 on Queen Anne Hill. Abe and Corey agreed to meet there at 6:00, after his last appointment. She'd pick up Billy as planned.

Corey cancelled a meeting and went to check on Annie at the hospital. She stayed at Harborview until Annie was sleeping soundly, safe and settled, then Corey called her lawyer, Jason Weiss.

She told him about Luther and Annie. When she asked him to get a court order to keep Luther away from the battered girl, he said, "It doesn't often work."

"I'm going to talk with him," she replied. "I need a starting place."

She could picture him, thinking about it, rubbing his right ear lobe between thumb and forefinger. "That could work," he admitted.

Some time later, she didn't know how long, Corey made her potluck purchase, then she went home to pick up her son.

Billy was brooding. When she pulled up, he was sitting on the front porch bench looking up at the clouds. On the way to the truck he just stared at his phone scrolling through old text messages, shrugging noncommittally when she asked how he was doing.

Now he was leaning against the window of their black pick-up, staring at the faces on Broadway. They lived on Capitol Hill, and Corey was coming south on Tenth, anticipating the soft right past the Harvard Exit Theater, toward Lake Union. At the last moment she veered left, following Billy's eyes down the busy street.

Broadway wasn't picturesque, like the waterfront, or old, like Pioneer Square. It was, however, Broadway, and it was, in its way, a Seattle phenomenon: quirky street life, hip stores, the "hot" spots, the fringe. Corey drove slowly, trying to see it through his eyes. Wild hair colors. Pierced body parts. Cross dressing. Ethnic restaurants. Gay bars. Straight bars. Edgy clothing stores wedged between fast food franchises. Tourists. Tattoo parlors. Homeless people. A fancy market (the QFC). Sex shops. Smoke shops. A trendy mall. Dick's Drive-in. College kids. Street kids spanging, asking for spare change. Suburban kids. City kids. Cruising. Drugs scored at ice cream parlors, pizzerias, hamburger stands.

Much of her work led to this odd adolescent mecca. She found runaways and this was one of the places they ran to. And though she knew the kids, knew every shop and every stoop, Broadway was still as foreign to her as the mountains on the moon. Growing up, she worked summers on a fishing boat, and after school at the wharf, canning fish. As a teenager Corey didn't have free time. Billy smiled, a girl with blue and green streaks in her hair was blowing bubbles. "You're awfully quiet," she said. "Something wrong?"

"Mom." It came out ma-umm.

"Okay. Sorry."

At the light, a woman in rags pushed a shopping cart full of garbage in front of their car and into the QFC parking lot.

"I can't reach Aaron."

"What do you mean?"

"He's not responding when I text. I call, I go straight to voicemail, which is full. He's not at school. Two days now... Today I couldn't find Maisie."

"Won't Aaron be there tonight?"

"Un-unh, I don't think so."

"And that's okay? It's his house."

Billy shrugged. "His dad stays out of stuff, unless Aaron says fireman instead of firefighter."

"Easy—"

"Sorry. He's just so serious...his mom's in New York."

She turned down Denny, thoughtful. "His dad's pretty high up at Olympic—"

"Yeah, a dean."

"Just what does he do?"

"Tries to figure out what's going on, I guess." Billy tapped his thumb on the seat. "If there's a problem, he decides what's okay. Like where you can use your phone. Or if something's racist."

"I see...I could ask him about Aaron tonight."

"That'd be okay. Don't talk about me."

"Hmm-hmm." It was quiet until Corey asked, "Storm game tomorrow night?"

"Cool."

At Seattle Center they turned up the hill to Aaron Paulsen's family's home. The Paulsen's house was a series of glass and metal planes, cleverly assembled to form cleanly-articulated, overhanging rooms with sweeping views. From the front door Corey looked south, toward downtown. Cream-colored clouds and flat skyscrapers were etched in a hard, blue sky. A sunset played streaky pink off the vast reaches of glass. The islands to the southwest were fir-green mounds floating in the dark waters of the Sound. The snow-capped Cascades circled behind the city to rest against Mount Rainier, glistening pink in the sunset. Corey turned away from the view. Backlit by the cream and pink striated northern sky, the Paulsen's dream house was a little chilly.

"What'd you bring?" Billy asked.

"Sweet and sour pork." She raised her eyebrows, a question. "From Chungee's."

He put his arm around her. "It's okay, mom." At the door, she leaned against her boy. They had the same lithe, athletic bodies, though he was half a head taller; the same black hair, though hers was cut short, and his was tied back in a pony tail. She wore form-fitting jeans and a sweater. His jeans were older. He had a tear in his left back pocket and a hole at his right knee. Billy's T-shirt was from a rock concert at the Gorge. Some group she didn't know.

She glanced up at her teenage son fidgeting on the doorstep, his arm draped around her. Along with Abe, he was the person she liked best in the world. Billy's arm dropped to his side as the door opened.

Inside, modern art mixed it up with French Provincial furniture. The potluck offerings were spread across a vast pine table. She saw lots of pasta and vegetable casseroles. Corey finally set her Chinese take out alongside a fancy platter of spinach lasagna.

Billy found a friend and disappeared into the basement. Corey looked around for someone she knew. After more than a year with these people, she still felt like she had to work to keep from making a mistake. Near the window one of the soccer moms, Susan Hodges, a single mother who had a big job at Amazon, was talking with Aaron's dad, Toby Paulsen, the dean at Olympic and their host at the potluck. Another mom she didn't know was listening in.

"Hey, Corey," Toby called as she came over.

He wore a brown corduroy sport coat and old grey Dockers. Shoulder length brown hair framed a thin face. Toby was serious, the descendant of Danish school teachers. The one time she'd seen him angry, Corey remembered him as stern, rather than fierce—more kindly reverend than Viking. Toby shook her hand. "Nice," he said, noticing the tattoo on her wrist.

"This?" She raised her wrist, showing off a bracelet braided with red, turquoise and black strands. "I was seventeen."

"Ahead of your time."

Hardly. "I didn't mean to interrupt," Corey said, wanting to talk about other things.

"You're not," Toby assured her, then looking at the two women he had been talking with, "I'd like to hear how Corey feels about this."

"About what?"

"We're considering a presentation on bisexuality." Toby adjusted his bifocals, attentive. "Maybe a bisexual support group."

"A what?"

"A group at school to read and discuss issues. Bisexuality is a viable option for the young people in this community," he explained.

It is? She hesitated. "You sure you want my opinion?"

Susan nodded.

"Of course," Toby added.

"I was in prison. In that community, there was a bisexual *action* group. I put a fork through a woman's cheek to stay out of it."

"Uh...I'm sorry," Susan said. "I didn't know."

"It's okay. Listen. These kids have enough trouble with regular, old-fashioned—"

"Regular?" Toby frowned.

"Uh...gimme a break here, Toby."

The other mom excused herself and went to the buffet.

Toby hesitated, made a steeple with his fingers. "Corey, how well do you understand homophobia?"

"C'mon, I don't care who these kids have sex with— so long as they come to it fairly—"

"Fairly, yes—"

"Because they want to, not because they think it's a viable option."

"Isn't that Abe?" Susan interrupted, pointing out the window.

Corey's husband was getting out of a burgundy-colored '99 Oldsmobile with freshly-painted white trim. Abe was looking at the sky, scratching his salt-and-pepper beard, trying to figure something. The car was driven by an elderly Chinese.

"Who's driving?" Toby asked.

"Abe doesn't drive," she explained. "That's Sam, his driver."

"Why doesn't he drive?"

"He sideswipes parked cars. Abe's often pre-occupied." As if to make her point, Sam took Abe's arm, steering him around a puddle.

"I see," Toby said.

She changed the subject. "Where's Aaron?"

"He's staying with his grandmother while his mom's in New York."

"Billy's been trying to find him."

Toby wrote the number on a napkin.

"Thanks." Corey took the napkin, then saw Abe. "'Scuse-me."

Abe was near the metal front door. She waved, caught his eye. He was getting an earful from several parents. His half smile—Abe was drifting—made her feel better. Corey saw him take out his pipe, a sure-fire crowd disperser. She hurried over.

Abe's bearing changed. He put his pipe in his jacket pocket, straightened up, then wrapped his arm around his wife's slender waist.

Corey leaned against him, relaxing a little.

❖

STAY COOL IN YOUR mind, Teaser was thinking. He was working the grill at the Mex drive-thru. Sweating. His eyes were watering and burning from the smoke. He had to keep this job. It was part of the plan. So he had to pay attention to his boss, Raoul, who thought cooking freeze-dried greaser food for minimum wage was some kind of an honor.

While he grilled chicken and vegetables for the fajitas, he was getting ready. Going over the list in his head. Taking his time about it. He had four things left to do today. And everything had to be perfect—just so. He thought about Maisie. He could picture her now. He'd watched her from the shadows. Invisible. He'd learned to be careful. Finally. And he'd learned that if you were careful, if you took your time, your time would come.

Just like that, Raoul was there with a spatula, turning the soft, shriveled-up green peppers right in front of him, yelling in his ear about how he had to pay attention, take pride in his work. Teaser could feel the heat, inside. The drive-thru cook telling him to be careful? His thin lower lip slid between his teeth as he numbed up. Teaser looked at Raoul, said "Sorry, sir," then nodded at everything.

On his break he stepped outside. Under a tree Teaser stuck the point of a plastic toothpick under his thumbnail. He watched it disappear under his skin.

Later he pressed on his nail, wondering how to let the bad blood out. When he raised his thumb it caught the moonlight, and he thought he saw a little blue line.

❖

THE LOGAN-STEINS LIVED ON 14th Avenue East, near Roy. After serious negotiating—Corey wanted Ballard, a port-oriented neighborhood; Abe favored downtown, or anywhere close—they compromised on Capitol Hill. It was an older residential area ten minutes from downtown. Capitol Hill had a mix of grand old homes, wood-framed houses, stucco, brick—apartments, condos, commercial—a little bit of everything. It was also a comfortable mix of families, seniors, students, and singles and couples of every sexual orientation. Fifteenth Avenue East, with its busy stretch of neighborhood shops, markets, and restaurants, parted the hill at its highest point. Five blocks below, Broadway was an artery, pumping life through the Hill. Pike Street, a trendy, though still-funky, commercial and nightlife center, ran down the south slope. Part of Capitol Hill's charm was the tree-lined residential streets so close to the shops, the cafes, the fringe theaters, the lakes and the leather bars. Volunteer Park, with its cruising gay men and pick-up frisbee games, fronted some of the oldest mansions in Seattle.

Their street was quiet, mostly three and four-bedroom Victorians, with a sprinkling of condos. At their corner the rundown stone mansion was often for sale. They piled out of the pick-up at 9:00 p.m.

"You got homework?" Abe asked Billy.

"Not much."

And then they were home. The Logan-Steins' traditional, wood-framed house had been built in 1927. The day they bought it, Corey insisted that it be repainted. She chose grey, then forest green trim. Inside, the walnut woodwork was kept as perfectly as the trim on her 1930s hardtop wooden yacht, the *Jenny Ann II*.

"Sit," Corey said to Billy. She lit a fire in their fireplace, then sat on the stone hearth facing him. "What's a bisexual support group?"

Billy frowned. "Mom, you didn't start in on that, did you? It's like Toby's new big thing."

"Why?" Corey asked, confounded.

"Why what?"

She took a measured breath. "Nevermind. You still like Olympic?"

"It's okay." Billy shrugged. "You picked it."

"When I got out of jail, you were failing two courses in public school. Most days, you weren't showing up. We needed to do something. We couldn't get you into Northwest, or University Prep. Olympic was new. They meant well..." Corey let it go; she was rationalizing.

"And now he's getting good grades and showing up," Abe pointed out.

"I'm not bisexual, mom. I don't have a boyfriend or a girlfriend. And I still miss Morgan. Okay?"

Corey held back a smile. "Okay...have you heard from her?"

"Just an email, maybe two weeks ago. She loves New York City. She's not coming back for Christmas. She didn't ask me to come out there either. I'm sure she's got a new boyfriend."

"Did you respond to her email?"

"Not yet."

Corey bit her tongue, pretty sure that Morgan was still Billy's girl. A mom's intuition, she was well aware, but she knew what she knew. And, she knew to stay out of it. Corey changed the subject, "Oh, here's Aaron's phone number." She handed him the napkin. "He's at his grandmother's."

"That's weird." He shrugged. "I'll try again." Billy loped up the stairs.

Corey watched him, silently offering thanks that family night came just once a year.

❖

"Cor, why are you so down on Olympic?" Abe asked after Billy was in his room upstairs. He was facing the fire, comfortably settled into their worn couch.

Corey came over, unsure how to answer. She sank into the couch beside him. Just thinking about this made her tense. Eventually she turned. "I'm worried, I guess, that something's not working at that school."

"What are you thinking?"

She wasn't sure. "Okay. At Olympic they have like their own very demanding little world: character contracts, a social justice club, anything and everything to get into an Ivy League college. And in this world, everything is supposed to be a certain way. Fine. I could live with that," she hesitated, "except they don't get it about kids." She took another moment. "I mean teenagers are supposed to bounce around. They're confused... You and I expect that." She watched him nod; sure, of course. "At Olympic, the adults expect the kids to be, I dunno, fully formed..." Corey just stopped, unable to fathom this. "Since when are kids supposed to know what to believe, what to eat, even— for Godsake—how to feel?" And leaning in, "When I was growing up, I didn't know anything." She made a rueful face; it was true. "What I did, I learned to start with what's real. Including the bad stuff. They start with what they think something should be. It's the opposite of what I do. I think that's the problem—I'm not like them. And I don't want my son to be like them either."

"People who send their children to private schools aren't all the same—"

"Okay, maybe it's me. I'm different. I mean I think it's fine if Billy goes to a community college. I don't really know what a start up is. And I like hot dogs. These people make me feel like I should apologize for those things." Corey sat back, frowning.

"Cor—" Abe brought her back.

"Sorry. Bear with me. I'm starting to get this. What I think is that at Olympic, they hand down all these ideas about how to be, they tell these kids what they *should* feel, then they leave them to work it out on their own. I mean they made Billy sign a contract about being a good person, told him 'bisexuality was an option,' but no one notices when he's lonely or low. It scares me. There's no safety net. No regular, reliable, grounded conversation. The grown-ups come on so righteous, so certain of where these kids need to go, what they need to be, and then they don't even see it when a kid feels bad."

Abe was looking at the fire. "What's worse," he turned, "I'm afraid the kids know that."

"Yeah, they do. He's my son, Abe. No one in my family has ever gone to college. His grandmother raised me on a fishing boat..."

"How old were you when she died?"

"Seventeen. Same as Billy. And don't start that psycho mumbo jumbo with me."

"Right."

"Toby asked Billy to volunteer at a shelter in a church on Broadway. He said it would look good on his college applications. When he was locked out of foster care, Billy used to sleep at that shelter. When I explained that to Toby he said, 'Not to worry. The *take away* from Billy's time in foster care and Juvie is that it will help *his story* for an Ivy.' His words—no kidding." She took Abe's hand. "Billy won't tell his friends we go duck hunting. And he eats tofu burgers. I didn't know what tofu was until he started at that school."

"Your son is just like you."

"You think so?"

"Forget what he eats. Watch how he thinks, how he handles hard things—in every important way, he's his mother's son."

"Huh," was all she said. Corey leaned against him, pensive, wondering if this could be true. She loved the idea, but she couldn't stay with it. She closed her eyes. What was bothering her? Something more about Olympic. It took a moment to get at it. She was worried, she realized, that these people would make Billy feel ashamed, yeah, like the things she'd taught him were old-fashioned, or even silly. And then, without meaning to, they'd come between her and her son, break the connection they'd built so carefully, when things were at their worst.

From the day he was born, she knew what Billy was feeling. But before Billy turned thirteen, his dad disappeared, and drugs were planted on her boat. At her trial a man warned her that Billy could disappear too. In prison she learned violence. It was part of life. Twice she hurt people. It made her feel out of control, stunned by what she could do. When she came out of prison, twenty-two months later, she and Billy had become strangers. Billy said he'd decided that bad things just happened to him.

Here it was, less than two years later, and she, Billy and Abe talked to each other. Checked in. Worked things out.

She glanced up at Abe. Billy was in private school, and Abe thought he was just like her. Her face softened. What a nice thing to say. And it was partly true.

She put her arm across his chest and held him. After a while she whispered, "He's your son, too."

❖

STAR'S EFFICIENCY APARTMENT WAS in a red brick four story building on Regent, a block and a half east of Broadway. The street had small, run-down, wood houses wedged between newer, cheaply-built apartments and older buildings. A spattering of commercial spilled over from Broadway. From her third floor unit Star could see Alden's Hair Salon and a used bookstore.

She had one large room with an alcove. Centered on the floor was a king-sized mattress with a baby blue blanket. Beside it there was a Coors lamp and a side table made from two cinder blocks and a piece of plywood. Star kept her bureau against the wall. Her beat-up laptop was on the bureau. In the little kitchen alcove she'd squeezed in a table and two stools. One wide window faced the street.

An empty wine bottle stood on the side table next to a mirror with two lines of cocaine. A half-smoked joint still smoldered in the ashtray, surrounded by cigarette butts. Star, Aaron, and Maisie were on the mattress, naked. Maisie was on her back. Aaron lay beside her, kissing her. Star's hands were on Maisie's thighs, spreading her legs. When Star lowered her head, Maisie gently pushed Aaron away. He watched, flushed, as, moments later, Maisie began to tremble. She seemed to relax as her body rocked in orgasm, her second. It was quiet for a moment, then Maisie put a hand behind Star's neck. She slowly guided Star's head toward Aaron. Star took him in her mouth. Aaron closed his eyes, leaning back on his hands. After he reached orgasm Aaron fell back onto the mattress beside Maisie.

Maisie leaned in, her short, brown hair pasted by sweat to her forehead. She was intense and sensuous, her adolescent breasts still growing. Maisie ran her tongue along her upper lip, not at all self-conscious, savoring her post-coital feelings. This was new for her and she loved it. Gently, she ran her forefinger along Aaron's eyebrow then across his cheekbone to the stud in his lower lip. He turned toward her. Aaron was Chinese, adopted at birth. His eyes were brown, steady. His features were sharp, chiseled into his round face. A bright red Z zigzagged through his short, black hair down the left side of his head.

Maisie smiled, sweet and sultry. "We missed family night," she said.

CHAPTER TWO

COREY STOOD, ANTSY, RAISING her binoculars from the window sill. She was waiting to hear back from Luther's CCO, trying not to think about Annie. Her office was in an older building overlooking Elliot Bay. In its heyday, the stone building had been a hardware emporium. She turned to face the Sound. From her seventh floor window she could just see the southern tip of Bainbridge Island, deep green against the grey sea and sky. When she was fourteen, Corey harvested sea cucumbers off that shore. It was the last innocent time she could remember.

In 1987 she turned fifteen. While her girlfriends were smoking dope, drinking, and partying, she was canning fish. After her mother died in '89, she lived alone on their boat, the *Jenny Ann*, doing whatever she could for money.

The phone rang. It was Luther's CCO. The guy explained that Luther had his own room on Bentley, which she knew, and that he had an alibi, which she already knew, too. His CCO went on, detailing Luther's post-prison routine.

"You screwed up," she interjected, matter of fact.

"No, lady, you screwed up. That girl wasn't my responsibility." He hung up.

She stared at the phone.

Yesterday she had filled him in. Even if it was Luther—which he doubted—he had sixty clients; there was only so much he could do.

Corey took a walk—no place special—over to Madison, up to Broadway. She tried to imagine how frightened Annie must have been to jump through a closed window. Annie had once told Corey how her Uncle Luther was an *unhuman*. She said he was way dead and full of worms and every time he touched her she died.

She thought about Annie's chances. Abe said that when things went badly, she was too hard on herself. She wasn't sure. Corey sat on a bench in front of Seattle Central Community College, watching the kids drift by.

❖

"I'M WIRED," MAISIE SAID. "Like I can't slow down." She wore worn jeans, and a white, hand-woven Mexican blouse.

Abe sat at his desk, watching her, waiting. Maisie had large, sea blue eyes. Her lips were full and her smile alluring. She was thin, delicate, growing into a sensual woman's body—an intense, unwieldy business. Abe sensed that she was keenly aware of her nascent sexuality, though unsure how to manage it. Maisie fidgeted, anxious, running a hand through her short, brown hair.

"Sometimes things start to spin," she said. "I told Verlaine. The sixties-stoner stepdad wants me to take Prozac."

He almost smiled, caught himself. "Do you want to?"

"Are you like kidding or something?"

Abe wasn't sure where this was going. He'd first seen Maisie three years ago when her mother remarried. Her stepfather was fifteen years older than her mom, and he was her boss at Microsoft. Maisie didn't approve and she withdrew from family life. At that time Abe had prescribed a very low dose of an anti-depressant, and after just a few sessions, Maisie was back at the dinner table. He'd had little or no contact with her until six weeks ago when she called to announce, "My parents say I have to see someone and you're it." Since then he'd seen Maisie five times.

"So sometimes things start to spin," he repeated. "What would you like to do about this spinning?"

"Well, I skipped flute yesterday, and today I cut Spanish. My mom was totally pissed when I missed flute."

"Why did you skip flute?"

"I was getting it on with Aaron." Maisie touched the gold ring in her eyebrow. "We met this really cool girl. She's got a place near Broadway, and she lets us come over."

He waited before asking, evenly. "Does your mother know why you missed flute?"

"I think she picks up on it. It's like she can smell sex. She can't be exactly satisfied in that department.

I mean Verlaine wouldn't even know if he got her off. Un-unh." Maisie raised her palms—she knew that much. When Abe didn't say anything, she leaned her forearms on his desk then rested her chin on them. "I saw Billy today. Why don't you call him Will? I think Will's better than Billy, don't you?"

"That's up to him."

"I wish you were my dad."

Abe didn't respond.

"I mean Will's so together, and I'm so, I dunno, what's the opposite of together? Apart?"

"Does Billy—"

"Will. Hey, does he know you see me?"

"Not from me."

"Does anyone know, except us, and the dot com deadheads?" And solemnly, before he could ask, "Devoted fans of the Grateful Dead."

When Abe still looked confused, she added, "Duh— the Microsofties—my so-called parents, okay?"

"I haven't told anyone."

"What about your wife?"

"No, she doesn't know."

"Our secret, huh?"

"Until you say otherwise."

"Cool." She sat back in the brown leather chair. "Now, can we talk about something personal?"

"Sure." Abe waited, watching her drum her fingers on the arm of the chair. He liked Maisie, liked her quickness, her directness, liked how she was more and more open with him. He could help her, he thought, if they could learn to rely on one another. As far as he could tell, she didn't have this with any adult.

The drumming stopped. "I tried some cocaine," she volunteered. "Afterward, we got it on, the three of us."

Why, he wondered, *is she being so provocative?*

"And?"

"Is that crazy or what?" Maisie closed her eyes.

"I don't know. Here, with me, you often say something shocking, then measure my response. Did you expect something terrible to happen?"

"Won't it?"

"Not necessarily." Abe waited until he had her full attention; this was important. "The drugs worry me, though."

"When I'm stoned I sometimes do things in my mind. But this was different. I really wanted to try it. Do something just really hot." She found his eyes. "I mean so hot just thinking about it would get me going. In class, at the dinner table, anytime."

He watched as she folded her legs up under her in the big leather chair. Abe thought Maisie seemed more edgy than excited. She closed her eyes again, unaware that her face was flushed. He understood her desire for intensity. He hoped he could help her find it in less worrisome ways. And without drugs. "What did Aaron have to say about it?" he asked.

"He got off on it, I can tell you that." She opened her eyes, smiled at him coyly.

Abe ignored it. "Did you talk with him about it?"

"I told Aaron it would help me see if I'm bisexual. I knew I might be. I mean I got really excited in the tenth grade when I was into pregaming–"

"Pregaming?" Abe furrowed his brow, a question.

"That's when you make out with another girl before going to a party." Maisie pursed her lips, touched them with her fingertip. "You know–like warming up."

Abe sat back. "I've never heard of that."

She smiled again. "Does it freak you out?"

"No, I don't think so. But the drugs do worry me. I'd like you to stay clear of them. Can you do that?"

She made a face. "Even weed?"

"Yes."

"I'm addicted to grass."

"I don't think you are."

"What about cigarettes?"

"They're okay, for now."

"And if I can't?"

"I know a good program. You'll have to live there until you clean up."

Her mood shifted, Abe could see it change her face. She laughed. "No way." When he didn't respond, Maisie squinted, tense, then snapped, "No fucking way."

She was keyed up now, almost speeding. Abe waited until she wound back down, wondering if her desire for sexual intensity was related to managing her own mercurial feelings. "Maisie, you're sixteen. This is important."

"I just changed my mind about you being my dad."

"Try staying clean until I see you again."

"Whatever." She stood.

"Listen to me, Maisie. I think I can help you figure out what you want—not what your parents or your teachers think you want—what you really want. And then we can figure out how to get it." He let that sink in. "It's difficult work, and drugs make it much harder, if not impossible. I'd like you to stop taking drugs. That's the one thing I'm asking you to do. I'm going to set up weekly lab screenings until you're clean. Can I count on you to do that?"

Maisie flipped him off as she left.

❖

"EXCUSE ME, PLEASE," JASON Weiss, Corey's lawyer, said into the phone.

"It's family that's dropped by." Then he was up and at the door, smiling wide, taking Corey's hand. Abe had asked Jason to represent Corey when she was in trouble almost eighteen months ago. Jason had helped her, earned her trust, and he and Corey had become friends.

Jason Weiss was a sole practitioner. His practice of law flowed loudly, and effortlessly, from his large office in the Maritime Building. Two stacks of papers always sat on his desk: favors owed, favors due. He spent his days matching them. His generous figure spilled out of an expensive charcoal suit. He wore a silk tie every day.

Jason put up a finger. "Corey, you missed the last two Sundays at Jesse's. She's worried."

Corey didn't respond. Talking about her mother-in-law was like touching a tar baby.

"So have Abe call her." Jason rubbed his ear lobe between thumb and forefinger. "Make something up."

"Soccer? Allergies?" Corey took a candy from a bowl on his desk. "She checks. I swear to God."

"She—" Jason stopped. He raised his palms. Jesse was, well, Jesse. "The court order you wanted for Luther Emerson. Done." Jason handed her an envelope.

"Thank you."

"Be careful," Jason added, then he touched her arm. "So...brunch. Pick a Sunday. She's been in therapy over a year. She's getting better..." He nodded, solemn. And finally, when she didn't respond, "Abe's dad..." He raised his eyebrows. "My best friend...since childhood."

Corey made a funny noise—part laugh, part aagh! Jason was incorrigible, and, she knew, a rare friend.

Jason rubbed his earlobe again. "You know what it is, a mitzvah?" And before she could answer, "It's a good deed."

Corey pursed her lips. Her freckles bunched on her nose. "I have to talk with her?"

❖

WHEN BILLY WAS SIX he'd taught his mother to skip a stone over the water. He'd worked with her every day until she skipped one five times. Then another. Two

years later Billy dragged Corey to her first Sonics game.
It was love at first sight. And he'd taught her about
basketball in the same deliberate way. When the Sonics
left for Oklahoma City after the 2007-08 season, Corey
and Billy started following the Seattle women's team,
the Storm. Corey liked the women's games more than
the men's. When Billy asked why, she thought about it
before saying, "they share the basketball."

It was a thing they did together, just the two of
them. They'd asked Abe to come but as he put it,
"Basketball makes me nervous. I can't run, I can't
jump. In high school, I had the lowest vertical leap in
King County."

Now, whenever Corey went inside the Key Arena
she felt old. Espresso, fajitas, sushi, frozen yogurt. The
plush upholstered seats sparkled under bright, white TV
lights. Where were the greasy burgers, the beer-stained
wooden seats, the smoky yellow lights? Gone the way of
the cheap seats, she supposed.

Corey sat back. Billy was already screaming about
a bad call. At halftime, New York's Lady Liberty was
leading by three.

"I found Aaron," Billy offered at the half, between
bites of Mexican pizza.

"Where was he?"

"Some girl's apartment. Off Broadway."

Corey's antenna went up. "What about Maisie?"
Aaron and his girlfriend had been together almost nine
months, a long time for Aaron.

"She was there, too. I mean Maisie and Aaron were there together. You see, Maisie met this girl a while back and they got friendly. She and Aaron have been cutting classes, hanging at the girl's apartment. I think they go at night sometimes."

Corey turned to face him.

"I know what you're thinking, but it's only weed."

"Only weed? Have Aaron and Maisie done other drugs?"

"Not Aaron. I don't know about Maisie."

"What's your guess?" Corey asked.

"Chill, mom, just let me talk to you."

"Chill?" She bit her tongue. He was talking to her, even though his friends thought talking to your mom was really weird. She and her mother had talked—she remembered wild, wonderful late-night conversations, mostly at sea. Had it been so complicated? Probably. Certainly. She touched Billy's arm. "Okay. Tell me about Maisie."

"Her mom and dad, they have like, I dunno, this agenda for her—flute, poetry readings, she dances in the Nutcracker every Christmas, she feeds the homeless Sunday dinner. Maisie's always tired, and whenever she breaks loose, she parties. I mean she smokes at breaks because it's a break, you see what I mean?"

"Yeah. I'm surprised. People seem to like her parents."

"That's part of her problem. They're like poster parents for Olympic—Microsoft millionaires who still talk the sixties. Verlaine even has sixties cred—Woodstock, the Yale student strike committee..." He sighed. She noted his resigned, that's-my-world face.

"I didn't get that." She watched her son. "What's worrying you?"

"This girl, Star, they called her, because of this tattoo on her thigh. She stopped by to see them at Blue City. She's twenty, at least, and she's weird. You know, cool, on—always moving, high energy—but, at the same time, a little off." Billy made a puzzled face that reminded her of Abe working on some idea. "If you know what I mean."

Corey nodded, unsure what he meant, but aware that, like Abe, Billy would get there in his own way.

"And I think she has tracks on her arm. I mean there's a tattoo there now—some kind of flower thing—but the little knots are there on the vein, underneath. I wouldn't have noticed if you hadn't told me what to look for."

There it was. "Can I ask around about Star?"

"Alright, yeah. But, you know, stay out of it, okay?"

"I'll try." This was a thing she was getting good at: being "in it" and "out of it" at the same time. "Stay away from her place, will you?"

"Yeah. Sure."

Corey touched his hand for just a second. "Thank you, Billy, for coming to the game with your mom."

The halftime was over, and they were on their feet for the fast break.

"Mom, from now on, could you call me Will?"

"Will?" She read the look on his face. He wasn't kidding. "Uh, yeah. Sure."

❖

THE FRONT DOOR OF Luther's apartment building was gated, the kind of accordian gate often seen covering pawn shop doors and windows. It was almost 11:00 p.m. when Corey and Abe went around back, past several men smoking on the back door stoop.

The apartment was in a seedy four-story building on Bentley, several blocks north of Pine. Pine ran parallel to Pike, and the Pike-Pine Corridor, as it was called, was attracting artists, night-life, small businesses, and real estate developers. The Bentley Building was a single-room-occupancy building that still rented to sex offenders.

They took the stairs two at a time. Corey gently guided Abe around a hole in the third floor landing, then banged on Luther's door. She was tense, bracing herself for god-only-knew-what. The door swung open. The air inside was stale, somehow fouled. Abe shone a flashlight across the tiny apartment. No one home. She was almost glad. There was an unmade bed, a card table, a chair, and a small TV. Dirty dishes and half-empty soup cans filled the sink.

Abe's light stopped on a tattered porn magazine. "Let's wait out back," he suggested. He, too, was readying himself. She could hear it in his voice. Abe was more anxious than she, but he'd worked hard and learned to manage his fears. He was better at that than she was. Abe did what he had to, even when it scared him.

At the rear entry the men were still smoking. These guys had probably done time. The building housed men in drug and alcohol rehab and work release programs, as well as sex offenders. "We're looking for Luther Emerson. Muscle-bound, red-headed guy," Abe said. "We'll pay twenty for a conversation." Abe held out a ten. "There's twenty in it for him. And a deal. No cops."

One of the men nodded. The ten disappeared, and the three men faded into the night.

Abe and Corey sat on the stoop, helping each other wait. They went over again what they knew about Luther. He was Annie's uncle. Uncle Luther started raping Annie when she was eleven. Annie told a teacher what was happening when she was twelve.

Luther had lived in this building since he was released—untreated—from the Western Corrections Center three months ago. Annie ran away ten days before he was released. Abe emptied several pockets onto the stoop before finding matches, then lighting his pipe.

They listened to city sounds, sitting back to back, tense. They'd talked this through, carefully weighing the risks, and finally decided that they had to do this—someone had to brace Luther, put him on notice. It could make a difference for Annie. Still, there was danger.

They shifted subtly when a harsh voice came out of the alley, "What you want with me?"

One of the three men reappeared. Abe stepped down, handed him another ten, then signaled for him to leave. When he was gone, Luther ambled out of the shadows. The red-haired man had muscles bursting from under his sweaty T-shirt.

Corey stood slowly, pointed a finger at him. "Remember me?" she asked, somehow right there, ready.

He just stared at her.

"When I found Annie, you promised—no, you swore—that if I brought her home to her mother, you'd stay away from her. Your CCO backed you up. I trusted him, and I trusted you. This morning you kidnapped her off the Ave, then whipped her with your belt. You would have raped her if you could. I can't have that. Ever again."

Luther lit a cigarette. The light from his match showed a large purple birth mark, like a stain on his cheek. "Un-unh," he muttered in a raspy voice. He shook his head, no, then he stepped closer.

Corey took a document from her jacket pocket. "This is a court order. You go near Annie—anywhere, anytime—you're back inside."

"She's mine."

"Not anymore."

Luther took the document, lit it on fire, then unfolded a curved skinning knife. He cleaned his thumb nail with the blade. "I need some money." He turned the knife toward Abe, moving behind him, positioning himself so Abe was between them.

"Easy, big fella," Abe said, soft, reassuring. Abe turned, handed Luther a twenty-dollar bill.

The big man stepped closer still, knife near Abe's throat, rubbing his left thumb and the first two fingers of his left hand together.

"Don't make another mistake here, Luther." Corey unholstered the gun at the small of her back, showed it. "You touch him, I'll put you down." She found his eyes.

Luther fixed her eyes in a fuck-you prison glare, then grabbed Abe's hair and touched the knife to his throat.

Corey blew off Luther's right kneecap. It happened so fast Luther never took a step. He spun, buckled, then fell to the ground, writhing.

Corey looked at him, feeling the rage wash over her, like lava, unstoppable. When it passed, she felt empty and lonely. In prison, where violence was as quick as a night shadow, she'd learned to push through these awful feelings.

Luther wasn't finished with Annie, she knew that.

She took a slow breath, aware she was pumping adrenaline like she was snake-bit. Guys like Luther lived in this never-ending macho horseshit soap opera. She hated it. Corey twisted the .38 into his ear, drawing blood. She twisted again. "If you ever get near Annie again, I'll kill you."

CHAPTER THREE

O N SATURDAY MORNINGS, THROUGHOUT the fall, Billy played soccer for Olympic. The phone rang as they were leaving for his game. Corey made a face when Abe asked for a minute, then went to his study.

It was Amber Daniels, Maisie's mom. Abe had barely said hello when she started right in.

"Maisie's not telling me anything," Amber explained. "She likes upsetting me."

He didn't respond.

"How is she? Why did she miss flute? She said you knew."

"I can't answer those questions. I'm sorry."

"Of course. You're right. I just don't know how to manage this. She won't tell me where she is, or what she's doing. I'm worried."

Like Maisie, Amber was quick, and direct. "How can I help?"

"Would medication help?"

"Help whom?" he asked.

"Maisie. For what it's worth, I'm taking enough Wellbutrin to bounce around most of the day."

He wondered if the Wellbutrin, a stimulating anti-depressant, was making her anxious. "I don't think Maisie needs medication."

"Good." Amber waited. "Abe, I'm having a bad time with Verlaine, and with Maisie. The medication makes it hard to think. I'm stuck in the middle."

Stuck and speeding. He thought about her choices. "For now, the middle may be better than the alternative."

"Doesn't feel better...she hates me."

"Do you want to see someone?"

"I'd like to get off this damn medicine."

"Call Shelly Katz. She's in the book. She'll work that out with you."

"That would be good. Uh-huh."

Was that why she called on a Saturday? Unlikely. Abe had a bad feeling. "Amber, what did Maisie do?"

"Well...she backed Verlaine's new BMW through the garage door."

He smiled, just barely, relieved she hadn't backed through Verlaine. "That's not so bad," Abe finally said.

"Are you serious?" Amber was pretty loud. "He'll want a heart to heart."

He gave it a second. "How about this? There's this body shop," he thought about how to put it, "where they know me pretty well."

Billy and Corey were in the truck, impatient, when he came running up.

❖

IT WAS A FAMILY tradition to stop at B&O Espresso for coffee and pastries after the soccer game. This particular morning, the conversation was especially lively. Billy's team had won. Billy, the goalie, had not been scored on, and he was feeling good.

When the Logan-Steins arrived home at 11:30, Sergeant Lou Ballard was rocking on the bench swing on their front porch. A listless, misty rain came and went, leaving the sidewalks slick and gunmetal grey. The damp fall breeze scattered leaves across their lawn. Before his parents reached the porch, Will was off, headed for the Blue City Cafe.

"What's up, Lou?" Abe asked.

"Nice. I come calling on Saturday, and you don't even ask me about the wife and kids. No sociability here."

"Lou, you don't have a wife and kids," Corey said.

"You miss my point."

"Okay. How are you, Lou? You want to come in for a drink?"

"Love to." Lou stood, smiling meanly. He always wore a tie. Every hair was in place.

Corey brought him a Diet Coke.

"What's up?" Abe asked again, watching him carefully.

Abe was trying to figure Lou's mood, Corey could tell. Abe and Lou went way back. Lou had helped him when she was running from Nick Season. Later, Abe had helped Lou make sergeant. Still, Abe couldn't read him. No one could.

"You know Luther Emerson?" Lou asked.

"You know we do." Corey led him into the living room. They all sat around the river-rock fireplace.

Out of habit, Lou took in the room, then his hard eyes settled on Corey. "He's dead." Lou just tossed it out, letting it hang there.

His eyes never left Corey as she turned it over. Her face was blank, lifeless, though her stomach was churning. This day was turning sour as vinegar. She worked to go slow. "How?" she eventually asked.

"He was shot in the knee, then his throat was cut."

"Where and when?" Abe was standing now. Corey saw that he was worried.

"In the alley, behind the pervert palace. Last night."

"Is that what you call the building on Bentley?" Abe asked.

"And what do you call it, the Inn for Sexual Felons?" Lou cracked a knuckle.

Corey knew to ignore Lou's wisecracks. She looked at Abe; he nodded, just barely. "We saw him last night," she said. "I shot him in the knee when he went after Abe with a skinning knife. We left him twisting in the grass behind his apartment building."

"You didn't phone this in?"

"Did he phone it in? If you were me, with my history, would you phone it in? I'm telling you the truth. So knock off the cop shit. Okay?"

"Cop shit is what cops do. I should run you in for failure to report a crime."

"Back off," Abe said, meaning it. "And what—"

"I'm okay." She touched his arm, pleased to be the "good cop," for a change. She'd tell her story. Lou wanted it, even if he didn't know how to ask. "Lou, the man kidnapped his niece, beat her 'til she jumped through a window. I called you that afternoon. You said Luther's sister swore she was with him the whole time, that there was nothing you could do." She paused. "Someone had to help Annie. So I filled in his CCO, and I managed a court order to keep Luther away. You can check that out. I was delivering the news when he went after Abe with his knife. Luther was hurt, but he was okay when we left. I called 911 from a pay phone on Broadway. You can check that, too."

"You leave a name?"

Corey shot him an are-you-kidding look.

Lou snorted. "He's not okay anymore. I'll need a statement. Come in Monday."

"Fine." Corey leaned back in her rocker, her lips pressed into a tight line. Something wasn't tracking. Lou knew she didn't kill Luther. What was he after? "You got any ideas on this?"

"Maybe the sister, but I doubt it. She's got two gals swear they were with her. I called Western. The warden says that in prison, Luther looked after a guy. His pal got out a couple days ago—"

"Luther was dumb as a fence post," Corey interrupted. "No way he was doing anything on his own."

Lou adjusted his belt, irritated. He turned to Abe. "His pal inside was Teaser White."

"Teaser?" Abe asked, plainly frustrated. "Teaser? Why didn't you say that?" And to Corey, "Lou sent me copies of Teaser's file documents. According to the file he's uncommonly bright. Something happened to the guy in prison. He stopped feeling pain. What I read worried me."

Corey stopped rocking.

Abe pressed on, "He's smart, he's dangerous—"

"It's the law," Lou snapped. "Don't start—"

"C'mon Lou..." Corey interrupted, feeling antsy, unsure just why. "You know anything else about him?"

"Not much. Teaser's 33. No priors. At Western, the guy played it smart and careful. Still, he loses it." He turned to Corey. "One night, he drove a ten penny nail through his forearm. Another time he burned some symbol into the top of his own head." Lou shook his head, *go figure*. "Teaser refused any kind of treatment."

"You talk with Teaser?" Abe asked.

"We tried to make him for it. He's got a story. So far, it checks out."

She tapped her thumb on her chair. "Teaser?" Corey squinted, pursed her lips.

"Don't know where the name comes from."

She watched the sergeant, sipping his Diet Coke, quietly waiting. She thought about Lou, his nature. Her eyebrows inched up. "Are you asking for my help, Lou?"

Lou shrugged. "Let's just say I'm not bringing you in on a Saturday."

"I find kids, I'm not a cop."

"Holly—the twelve-year-old girl he got pregnant—she needs finding."

"That's not what I do. That's police work."

"From here, it looks like you do pretty much what you want."

"From where—"

"Corey," he interrupted. "Just before he got busted, Teaser was connected with a kid that nearly died. No one could make him for it. She was yours."

Corey's face went hard, like a mask. "Jolene?" She felt suddenly wary, right at the edge of something awful.

"Stay away from him, Corey. That's police work."

"Jolene?" she asked again.

Lou nodded.

Her face melted. Jolene was the second runaway she'd been hired to find. She'd hit it off with her, tried to help her. It ended badly—she found Jolene wired to her bed. She'd been whipped with a red-hot coat hanger. Days after Corey found her, Jolene disappeared. When Jolene OD'd in a Denver whore house, six months later, she had Corey's phone number in her wallet.

"I'll help," she said.

CHAPTER FOUR

"JIMMY WANTS TO TELL you something, honey."

Maisie and Aaron were lying back on the mattress, smoking a joint, touching each other and giggling. Star was fixing lines of cocaine on a little mirror, humming a song, while Teaser—who had introduced himself as Jimmy Dubonnet, after the wine—just sat there on the floor, watching them in that way that only he could. Maisie thought he was twenty-nine, or even thirty, and she was pretty sure he could make her come by looking at her. Incense was burning on the fridge. Jimmy—Teaser—reached over and touched Maisie's arm. He was five nine and sinewy, with finely drawn features and large black eyes. His movements were graceful, even feline, though his torso was sculpted by prison time on the free weights. Jimmy wore jeans and a beaded necklace over a black T-shirt. A blue stocking cap covered the top of his head. His head had been shaved, but below the cap, you could see where his black hair was starting to grow in. "Jimmy wants to tell you something, honey," he repeated.

Maisie sat up. "What's that?" She watched him watching her, liking his intensity.

"Let's rock and roll," Star interrupted, then snorted a line. She passed the mirror to Maisie. Aaron was looking at Star, who wore only a black bra and panties. The star tattooed on her inner thigh was dark blue.

Aaron turned. "C'mon, Maise, you don't need that," he said.

"Aar, you don't have to whine." She took a line, like she knew what she was doing. She handed him the mirror, watching him.

He fingered the silver stud in his lower lip. "Unh-unh," he said.

Jimmy pointed a forefinger at Maisie, cocked his thumb, found her eyes. "Jimmy's going to blow your mind."

Maisie smiled, sure he could do that. She hoped he'd at least get her off.

Star ran her hand along Aaron's thigh. She kissed his ear, then his mouth as she touched him. She lay beside him on the mattress. Maisie watched as Star took off her bra.

Maisie turned to Jimmy, who was still watching her. "How old are you?" he asked when she leaned back.

"Seventeen," she lied.

"I think you're sixteen," Jimmy said, then he gave her a slow drawn-out smile.

Maisie turned back toward Aaron and Star. Star was straddling him now, rocking back and forth and making little noises. Aaron held her large breasts. Star's blond shoulder-length hair swirled around her head in slow rhythmic circles. Her face was angular, flat and smooth, like a model's, only now she looked older.

Maisie watched Aaron approach orgasm. She loved the way his face got so serious just before he came. This time, though, it pissed her off, even though she knew it shouldn't.

Maisie turned back to Jimmy, whose eyes were still on her. "Jimmy's going to tell you something. Jimmy's going to rock your world."

Maisie took another snort of coke, then she took off her sweater, exposing her small, firm breasts.

Jimmy ran his slender forefinger along her cheek. "Listen up, little one. Jimmy knows your daddy."

Maisie pulled away. "Verlaine?"

Jimmy moved behind her, soft and smooth as a jaguar, putting his arms around her bare chest. "Shh, honey, shh. Your real daddy."

Maisie couldn't speak.

"Jimmy knows your natural daddy, little one."

"How do you know about me?" she asked, leaning back against him.

"Your daddy knows you. He talked to Jimmy about you. He loves you. You're his sweet baby girl."

"I don't understand," she whispered, letting this wash over her.

"He said to tell you that he saved your three-legged brown bear, and the little red and blue blanket with the white stars and the chewed-up corners."

"Oh God."

"When I get to know you better, I'll take you to him. He's afraid of stepdaddy Verlaine, so you can't say a word. That's all Jimmy's going to say about it now."

"Take me to him, please." Maisie lay her cheek against his chest. *Her real dad. Just the two of them.* She remembered how he used to sing her to sleep. Thinking about that was like being in a lovely, soothing dream.

"Soon, little one, soon."

❖

COREY AND ABE WERE thinking their own thoughts, off in their own worlds.

Corey was back on Annie, wondering why she'd ever listened to the CCO. She was, she knew, too trusting of the people in charge, too easily influenced by their authority. And that got her thinking about Olympic, where the people in charge were confusing her. At Olympic, the kids learned that they were privileged, and—here's where it got confusing—that because of their privilege, their experience was not quite as hard, not quite as "real," so they were subtly encouraged to seek out more "authentic" experiences. *What,* she wondered, *was that?*

She came over and sat beside Abe on the couch, wanting to be close. The day had caught up with her. He wrapped his arm around her, folding her in.

It was quiet then, for a long time, until he kissed her, tenderly. Their kiss progressed to something eager, even urgent, when he carried her up the stairs. Usually clumsy, Abe was now as sure footed as a mountain goat. Soon, Corey and Abe were intertwined on their king-sized bed. They were improvising, and it was a slow, sweet business.

When they were finished, they lay back, her head on his shoulder.

Some time later, she wasn't sure how long, Corey softly said, "I feel better." And taking a slow breath, "Yeah." She paused, musing. Another breath. Then, out loud, "It's maybe eighteen months now, we've been doing this. And you keep pleasing me." She raised up on an elbow. "You know, no one ever did this for me. Ever. With Al—" she looked at Abe. Al was Billy's dad, her former lover. Stuff like that didn't get to Abe. "It was good for me, max, one out of three times. And I thought that was, you know, as good as it gets."

Abe was quiet, lightly running his fingers along her back.

"Say something," she said.

"And what if I couldn't please you?"

Corey thought this over. "Well, I guess that would make you, sexually, what's that Olympic word? You know, that PC word for fucked up..."

"Challenged?" Abe offered.

"That's it. So that would make you sexually challenged..." She kissed his ear, then whispered, "That is to say—useless."

"That's what I was thinking." The lines in Abe's face softened.

She sat up, turned to look at him.

He raised up on an elbow, finding her eyes. "How could I ever be the man I'd like to be if I couldn't please you?"

She drew her hand across his chest. "That's nice."

He sat, kissed her slowly, then lay back on the bed, kind of dreamy.

For a long time, Corey sat there, watching him think. She loved how nothing about Abe was quite what it seemed. Corey made a funny face, to see if he'd notice. He didn't. She did feel better. She should have stayed in bed this morning, unplugged the phone.

"There's something we need to discuss," he finally said, interrupting her thoughts. He glanced out the window. His bushy eyebrows were almost touching. "It's complicated, though, because it concerns a patient."

She leaned toward him. "Confidentiality?"

"Right."

"Shit."

Abe looked up at her. "I'm seeing someone who knows Billy."

"Who?"

"You're not supposed to ask." He touched her face. "The thing is, they're doing drugs, and I'm worried about the whole set up. There's an older girl involved."

"Billy—Will—told me about Aaron and Maisie. They're hanging out with an older girl that scared Billy. Sounds like she is or was an addict."

"Is Billy with them?" Abe asked.

"He's at Everyday Music." When Abe furrowed his brow, puzzled, Corey said, "It's that used CD store on Tenth. After, he was going to find Aaron."

"Let's find Billy," he said, already on it.

"He won't like it," Corey pointed out. She imagined Billy with Aaron, Maisie and Star. Not today. Un-unh.

They reached for their clothes at the same time.

❖

THE BLUE CITY CAFE was west of Twelfth Avenue between Pike and Pine. The old Victorian home had been converted to commercial space as the area changed. The owner of the café had a hunch and she signed a long-term lease. That first year she ran a coffee counter. She waited, she watched, and she figured out that more and more kids were going to be drinking more and more exotic coffees. She traded her Formica coffee counter for cheap oriental rugs, her Folgers and doughnuts for a state-of-the-art espresso machine, homemade cookies and fruit bars. The coffee counter reopened as the Blue City Cafe, with live music on Saturdays. Her sense of where the area was going was pretty much prescient.

Since then, the cafe had taken over the house. Most of the space had become an over-sized, laid-back living room, with small groupings of sofas, dark oak tables and chairs, exposed fir posts, and fir mullions on the windows. In the back, against the living room wall, Aaron and Maisie were deep in conversation, ignoring their lattes.

"Come down, Maise," Aaron was saying.

"I am down. He knows my real dad." She sat back. Just saying it gave her a rush. "I mean it."

"How?"

"I don't know. He just knew things about me. About when I was little."

"This is too crazy."

"I think it's like fate, you know. Maybe Jimmy's a messenger, sent to get me off the twenty-four-seven Olympic treadmill."

"And maybe we're going too fast here."

"It wasn't too fast to get it on with Star."

"I was stoned."

"Kind of groovin' on great big breasts, huh?" Maisie smiled when Aaron blushed. She watched him, so pumped about seeing her dad she wasn't even jealous anymore.

"C'mon, hey..." He turned away.

Maisie kissed his neck, his ear, then she whispered, "You are so cool. And I think it's so awesome, the way we went for it."

"Yeah. Yeah, it was..." He turned back, cracking the window, then offering cigarettes. They knew they were violating the no smoking ordinance, but here in the back, it wasn't often enforced. Aaron lit her Marlboro, then his. "Did you think it was kind of weird, the way Jimmy just watched?"

"I liked it." She took a slow drag, remembering. "I think he's waiting."

"Maybe. I guess. What about us?" Aaron asked.

"We're good. We're just experiencing some real life here. It will make us better."

"I'd rather be with you than with anyone."

"Thank you." She gently ran her finger along the bright red Z in his hair. Sex made him act older, she was thinking. And after, he always looked good. "Me too."

"Maise, we're doing great, yeah, but here's the thing— I'm not liking the coke, and I don't know about Jimmy." He let the words hang there, met her eyes. "I mean he's really nice. But there's something about the guy, the way he's always out there, like he's circling or something."

Maisie closed her eyes, frustrated. She let go of his hand. "How many adults do you know who aren't middle class? I mean really know. I'm not talking about the ones who work for your parents."

"Some." He shrugged. "I dunno."

"C'mon, Aar. We live in this cocoon. I mean, we are groomed like thoroughbreds and sooo protected. I've been prepping for my SATs since the fourth grade. The adults we know actually believe that going to an Ivy matters. My parents check the value of their stock options every day. They worry about getting a window table at Canlis. These people aren't like that. They've done some living. Hard times. Risk taking. Real life."

He exhaled smoke through his nose, uncertain. "It's cool, how easy it is to be with them."

"Yeah," she smiled, liking this better. "And they don't seem so, I dunno, moralistic. Like Verlaine, always doing the hard thing."

"Do you think they actually know your real dad?"

"Jimmy says he'll take me to him."

"When?"

"Soon. I think he wants to be sure I won't tell Verlaine."

"Can we talk to anyone about this?"

"No way." Maisie mashed her cigarette butt on the open window sill. "Maybe after I meet him. For now, let's just hang in. Show Jimmy he doesn't have to worry."

"What worries me is that they found you. Maybe meeting Star was no accident."

"I've been thinking about that, too. " Maisie waited. "You remember that sixties Italian movie, *Theorem*, the one Verlaine made us watch with him because it was 'a game changer.'" Maisie made her *what-a-scuz* face—eyes wide, lips pursed, tip of her tongue out.

Aaron grinned. "I do remember the movie. Yeah. Kinda strange but sexy."

"That's the one. Okay. You remember how the guy comes out of nowhere—a mysterious stranger known only as "the visitor"—no money, no family, no past, no nothing. And before he's done, he gets it on with every member of the family, male and female. And he changes all of their lives. Jimmy and Star remind me of that guy. What if my dad sent them?"

"It's possible, I dunno."

"What if he did?" And what if her weird life changed for the better because of it? "What if my dad did that?" she asked, again.

"Maybe he did," he turned to face her, "but until we know for sure, Maise, let's go slow. Let's be careful. I mean it's okay if you want to be with them, and you can do what you want when it comes to sex—you know that's our rule. But the coke turns me off."

"If you hang in with me, I'll stay away from the coke. I need you for this. Don't ruin it." She touched the nape of his neck, suddenly worried. "Okay?"

"Okay, yeah." Aaron turned the thin, gold ring in his left ear. "Hey, there's Billy."

"Will," she corrected him. She sat up, waved Will over.

"What's happening?" Will sat down in a big lounge chair.

"Real life," Maisie laughed.

"Are you high?"

"Coming down," Aaron explained.

"You been at Star's?"

"Uh-huh," Aaron said.

Will saw their faces change. Maisie was up and in the ladies room before Abe and Corey got through the door.

"What are you doing here?" Will asked. He was standing, physically separating his parents from his friend.

"Looking for you," Corey explained. "How are you, Aaron?"

"Okay. Yeah. Fine." Aaron stood, shook hands with Abe. "Gotta check on Maisie. She's not feeling too hot. Give me a sec?" He was off to the restrooms. Abe and Corey sat.

"Sorry, Will," Abe said. "But we wanted to talk with your friends."

"It's really embarrassing." He was still standing. "I wish you weren't here."

"Will, I'm sorry, but we were talking about Aaron, and Maisie, and Star, and we started to worry," Corey explained. "Look, is it alright with you if I talk with Aaron and Maisie? I want to check out this Star person, make sure she's okay."

"I'd guess they're long gone, mom." He sighed, frustrated. "They split."

"Right. Stupid of me. Billy, do you have Star's address?"

"Mom, back off, okay? Just leave me alone." He went toward the door, two steps, then turned back. "And call me Will."

❖

MAISIE HAD HER HAND stuck in the back pocket of Aaron's jeans and his arm hung over her shoulders. Aaron's fingers lightly brushed across her left breast as he walked her to her front door. Across the street, in the shadows, Teaser was watching, invisible. He liked the big, old wooden house on Federal, liked it more than the rutty Chinaboy's shiny, new one. He chewed on a plastic toothpick, the kind he used because it didn't break up into little splinters. When Aaron and Maisie kissed on the doorstep, he turned away. He looked back at them, and they were still doing it. He felt the dryness in his throat. Teaser ran his tongue between his teeth. When he watched Maisie, he thought he could actually feel his scar.

❖

"DINNER," MAISIE'S MOTHER, AMBER, called out, pressing the intercom button to Maisie's room. "In the garden room, honey." Their house was grey, with white trim and a white porch. It sat back from the street, on Federal, several blocks north of Aloha. Maisie could walk to Olympic— down to Tenth then north to the campus. Their home was built in 1921, and it had six bedrooms. Maisie's was on the third floor, as far as possible from everything.

"Gotta go," Maisie said to Aaron. "I'm going to find out tonight. Whatever it takes. Think about tomorrow. You and me at Star's, all afternoon. Think about that." She punched off her phone.

The garden room was named after the perennial garden that swept around the southeast corner of the house. The room had a country feel: pine farmhouse table, exposed beams, walls of windows with small panes separated by freshly painted white mullions. Tonight Amber was serving coq au vin. She was forty-eight, and plainly the source of Maisie's sexual allure. Amber was a classic, Jewish beauty: full-breasts, black hair, fine features. When she relaxed, Amber was radiant. She wore a long denim skirt and a colorful peasant blouse. Verlaine had been Amber's mentor, almost nine years ago, when she came from Stanford's Symbolic Systems program to manage a project at Microsoft. They were married in 2008.

"How was school today?" Verlaine asked. He was young-looking for sixty-three, with a rower's muscular upper body, wire-rimmed glasses and curly, grey hair.

Verlaine wore a grey herringbone jacket over a black cashmere turtleneck sweater.

"Fine," Maisie muttered, caught herself, and thinking of her mission, took a friendlier tack. "We're reading *Oedipus,* maybe we can talk about it later?"

"*Oedipus,* yes. Anytime, Maisie."

"That'd be great. Listen is it okay if I stay out late with Aaron Wednesday? Thursday's a holiday, we're going to a party and—"

"No problem," Verlaine said, putting a hand on Maisie's forearm as he turned toward her. "Just remember how we roll, babe—a designated driver and safe sex."

Maisie winced, barely keeping her tongue in her mouth. He was such a scuz. "Do we have to talk about that?"

"Your responsibility?"

Maisie nodded.

"Do Aaron's parents approve?" Amber asked.

"Isn't that between Aaron and his parents?" Maisie asked, a little too sharply. Since her mom had started on the psycho meds, as Maisie called them, Amber's ideas sometimes popped out before she thought about them. Maisie hurried a smile.

Verlaine smiled back. "I'm sure they've worked it out." He tasted the coq au vin. "It's wonderful." He bowed his head toward his wife.

Maisie saw her moment. "Mom, I've got a question." She hesitated. "I need you to help me with something."

"Of course."

"Could you tell me more about dad?"

Verlaine set down his fork. "Sure."

"My real dad." Maisie felt the adrenaline kick in, just saying it.

Amber put a finger in the air before Verlaine could speak. "What do you want to know?"

"Everything."

"I see," Amber said, folding her napkin, working to slow down.

Verlaine sat back, crossed his legs.

"How about who he is? What he does?"

"I don't know that, Maisie." She looked at her daughter. "I'll tell you what I can. A lot of it you know already. All of it is ancient history." Amber's face softened then reformed in an earnest expression. "I met Dave in San Francisco. I was a graduate student at Berkeley studying computer systems and theory. Dave was a gifted computer programmer working at the computer science center. He was, well, a charmer, in a *bad boy* sort of way. Smart, good looking, and sensitive when he wanted to be. Dave was a risk-taker. He, well, he just swept this aging Jewish intellectual right off her feet. I was already thirty and, at the time, Dave was pretty much irresistible." Amber shrugged.

She looked over at Verlaine, who was watching Maisie, his steepled forefingers touching his upper lip, before continuing, "Anyway, over time, Dave grew more and more frustrated with his work. He wasn't well-paid to begin with, and when he developed an early pattern recognition program, he deserved a bonus and at least some kind of an acknowledgement for his accomplishment. Instead, his boss took the credit. He got into a fight with his boss, they were shouting at each other in the hall. His boss threw a punch, then Dave broke his boss's nose. His boss swore that Dave threw the first and only punch. They fired him from the school, which made him virtually unhireable. He taught martial arts off and on—Dave was big, and good at karate—but he couldn't make a go of it. Then he drifted from job to job. Before you turned four, he was dealing drugs. At first it was just marijuana, but soon he was dealing whatever he could get his hands on."

"Whoa. You never told me this." She thought about it, gently pulling at the ring in her eyebrow, a thing she knew irritated Verlaine. At least it explained why Verlaine wanted her head shrunk. He was afraid she was a bad seed. Nice.

Verlaine uncrossed his legs, pulled his chair forward. "Perhaps we should have," he offered.

Amber frowned. She wasn't sure. "In any case, it gets worse," she said. "Dave was arrested. He was in jail for more than a year. When he came out, he was cynical and mean. He went back to dealing, with a vengeance. We started fighting a lot, and somewhere along the way, he developed a drug habit. I took you and moved out. Less than a year later, I took the job in Seattle. We lost touch after that. When I got the divorce, I made contact through a friend. Dave was hiding from the police. That's all I can tell you. I haven't heard from Dave in, oh, it's at least nine years."

"Do you have any idea where he lives?"

"No. He could be anywhere. Why, honey?"

Maisie looked at Verlaine. He needed stroking. "It must have something to do with reading *Oedipus,* don't you think?"

"I was wondering that myself," Verlaine said, smiling at his step-daughter.

❖

ON SUNDAY MORNINGS COREY often cooked pancakes at a downtown outreach program. On her way out, she stopped at Billy's door, which was cracked open. She watched him, sleeping soundly, his youthful face carefree.

She was worried, she realized, about Billy and his friends.

CHAPTER FIVE

THE "CAMPUS" OF THE Olympic Academy covered almost two acres, on Tenth. The centerpiece was the arts and humanities building, a five story, 50,000 square foot affair. The outside of the building was teal green, with over-sized windows strategically placed to reveal classrooms, a dance studio, the wood shop, and a group of Plexiglas teachers' offices. Inside, the supply lines were Plexiglas so a person could trace the wiring, plumbing, heating and so forth. All except the sewage lines, of course, which were painted sea blue.

Corey arrived at 9:50 a.m. Monday morning for her 10:00 a.m. parent conference with Will's advisor. The design committee had probably specified relaxed and welcoming, but they'd ended up with specially-milled, wide-planked, hardwood floors, stone water fountains, ancient Asian tapestries, and stark white, space-age security panels. Corey found the place stiff and self-conscious. She stopped, confused by a poster for a film series with admission restricted to people of color.

Will's advisor's office was on the fourth floor. Through his Plexiglas walls, she could see Tom Gleason, a history teacher, grading papers. She watched him—so serious—before she knocked.

"Hello, Tom."

"Nice to see you." He shook her hand. Tom had long black hair, a neatly trimmed mustache, and a kind face. She liked his colorful hand-woven tie, worn without a jacket. He was openly gay, no nonsense, and, Corey thought, easy to talk to.

"Can I let my hair down a little—off the record?" she asked.

"Depends."

"I want to talk about a couple of Billy's friends. I don't want them to know—or Billy to know—that we talked."

He scratched his head, weighing this. "I can do that."

"Here's the deal. I'm pretty sure Aaron Paulsen and Maisie Daniels are doing drugs. It may be just marijuana, it may be more than that. The thing is, they're lying to their folks."

Tom nodded, just barely.

"The drugs by themselves aren't the problem. They're hanging out with an older girl—Will said 'at least twenty'—and I think she's been into the hard stuff. Look, I trust my instincts on this. Something's wrong."

He looked at her, making a decision. "Let's ask Toby to join us."

Corey hesitated. "If you think it'll help." It couldn't hurt, she reasoned. At least it would get his attention.

Tom receded to a corner when Toby Paulsen arrived. He leaned against the Plexi wall, a watcher. Corey understood that.

Toby paced the floor in Tom's cube, listening to Corey's concerns. When she was finished, he turned to her. "Corey, I spoke with Aaron last night. He and Maisie are in love, he was articulate and sweet about that. And yes, they may have cut some classes, but that's something I know how to handle. He's a responsible young man, and he's old enough to manage his own love life. Even make a mistake."

She looked right at him. He didn't get it. "Toby, please... 'Letting them make mistakes' doesn't work with opiates."

Toby raised his bony fingers, a give-me-a-chance gesture. "Aaron promised me he wasn't doing anything more than a little weed. And last night, he promised to lay off that, too. I believe him."

"Maybe." She hesitated, wanting to get this right. "But Star's streetwise, and there's a reason she's hanging out with sixteen-year-old, private school kids. Maybe it's sex, maybe it's boredom—"

"And maybe she's just lonely," Toby interrupted.

"You're not understanding..." Corey stopped, started over. She tried to be really specific. "Please consider this. Young drug users, especially the girls, are exposed to unspeakable horrors on the streets. Aaron, Maisie, and Billy could be marks to her—a way at food, or money, or god-only-knows what. And that's all they'd be. Even if our children had the right values and the best intentions." She watched him, thinking about it, frowning.

"I have a suggestion. Before we get too worried," Toby sat on the edge of Tom's desk, "I'll talk to Aaron again about all of this. Okay?" He touched her arm. "I'll ask about Star. And I'll insist that he stay away from her apartment if she's doing drugs."

She wasn't sure why Billy's dean couldn't really hear her. It bothered her—Toby wasn't stupid. "Fine, but what if Aaron lies?"

Toby spread his arms. "I'm sorry. I'll do the best I can." He checked his watch. "I have an appointment."

Corey's pale blue eyes widened. She was working hard. Really trying. And Aaron's dad, the dean, didn't have time? She bit her tongue. After a beat she stepped forward, inches from Toby's face. "Toby, suppose these kids are not as well put together as you'd like them to be?"

He didn't respond.

"Okay. Can you at least promise me that you'll keep them safe. Don't let them go to her apartment. Find out who she is. Take whatever steps you can to make sure that your son and his girlfriend don't get hurt...and please keep Billy—Will—out of it. Will you do that?"

His face turned grim. "Corey, these young people are very capable...I know your intentions are good, but over-protectiveness can easily, unknowingly, become stifling, or even evolve into paranoia. Have you thought about talking to someone?"

Corey just stared at him, disbelieving. Stuck. Her mouth was getting dry. She wanted to hit him. She didn't want to ruin it for her son.

Tom busied himself, re-adjusting his tie. Corey touched his shoulder on her way out.

❖

"THE GUY COULDN'T HEAR me. Picture this alien saying, 'I'm here to eat your children' and Toby keeps saying, 'Welcome to Olympic'," Corey said, still angry. "And what does it mean when he says 'over-protectiveness can easily become stifling'?"

Abe was sitting, watching her pace in front of their fireplace. Abe scratched the back of his head, looking glum. "He said that?" he finally asked.

"Just before he asked if I'd thought about," she raised a forefinger and middle finger from each hand above her head, scrunching them to mimic quotation marks, "'talking to someone.'"

"Did you provoke him?"

"What kind of a dumb-ass question is that?"

Abe grinned. "Sorry."

"He didn't like what I had to say. But what difference does that make? It was true."

Abe rubbed the top of his ear with his thumb. "You had to say something. Aaron's his son."

"He was so full of himself. So sure he knew everything. He thinks I'm paranoid. Is that what I am?" she asked, looking at him, suddenly anxious.

He looked up at her. "No, you're nothing like that."

"Okay. Thank you," she said, then Corey turned to watch the fire.

Abe stood, aware she was still upset. He made a grumbling noise.

Corey looked back at Abe over her shoulder. "I almost hit him."

"Cor, he's Billy's dean..." Abe barely suppressed another grin. One time she'd hit Billy's baseball coach. Billy had just turned eight. She came late for a game and he wasn't playing. She finally found him stuck way up a tree, crying because he couldn't get down. The coach had sent Billy up there for missing a fly ball, told him to play look out. Two grown men had to pull her off the guy. Abe loved that she'd done that.

Will walked in. "Is this about me?"

Abe said "Yes" and Corey said "No" at the same time.

"Great. I saw you at school, mom."

"Parent conference."

"Oh...yeah. What's up?"

Corey hesitated. Abe turned to stoke the fire. This was between them.

"Okay. Look, I talked with your advisor about Aaron and Maisie. I told him about Star. I had to. I'm worried about them."

"Jesus, mom. Are you crazy? I have a life you know."

"I made them promise to keep it—"

"Them? There's more than one?" Will asked, agitated.

"Well, he called Toby in. We got into it." She shrugged, *no big deal*, hoping to reassure him.

Will just stared at her, then he stepped back, cracking his knuckles, one after another.

"I had to, Will. I'm sorry if it makes things hard for you." She watched him turn away.

Will faced the fireplace. Finally he turned his head just enough to see her. "Just because you know every hard case on the street doesn't mean that everyone on the street is like that."

"You're right." She tried to explain, "But you don't take chances with your son and his friends."

He turned to face her. "Is that up to you? Why can't you leave things alone? Why do you have to mess things up for me? You know I'm seventeen, and I do just fine without you. Okay? Okay?" Will slammed the door on his way out.

Her shoulders sagged. She got a log to put on the fire.

Abe watched her stew. Billy was right, he reflected, and so was she. There was a fine line between too fearful and streetwise. It was hard to find that line at Olympic, harder still to walk it. It was their job to help him do that anyway.

She looked at him, leaning against the mantel, watching her. "So?" she eventually asked.

He looked into their fire, then back at her. "I'd say he'll be mad for about a day then carefully sort it out." His brow furrowed until his eyebrows almost touched in a "V." "He'll get it, too, even if he doesn't like it."

Corey poked at the fire, idly now. "Okay, my way of solving problems is maybe one-of-a-kind and hard for a teenager to understand. I get that. But I'm trying to get this right."

He stepped beside her, close. "You are getting it right."

❖

NIGHTIME. THREE THINGS LEFT to do. Teaser watched the girl. Right there. Trolling for tricks on Aurora. He knew he'd find her. Before anyone else even looked. His thin lips turned up. He cruised by again, the royal blue Mustang catching her eye. He slowed, opened the door. She came right in. When he turned, she gasped, reached for the door. He held her hand, firm. She made little noises. His stomach was getting hot. He could feel Loki, rising. Teaser worked to keep him down. He took out his buck knife, Little Buck, and pressed it to her thigh, as he put a finger to his lips.

"Teaser?" the girl asked, quieted.

"Loki," he whispered.

She started crying when Little Buck made the thin red line. Follow the plan, he reminded himself. Lucky for her he was the most careful man in the world.

CHAPTER SIX

COREY GOT TO THE Ave before 9:00 a.m. The fall air was blowing cool, moving toward cold. Even so, University Way was already humming. Kids, including homeless and transient teens, hung out in front of ice cream parlors, fast food stops, clothing stores, even the old movie theater. Shopkeepers were opening up, sweeping away leftovers from last night's street life.

Corey was looking for Johnny Boy. This fall, JB's "squat" was in an abandoned garage, not far from the Ave. Johnny Boy was a student of housing options for street people. He knew the ins and outs of every youth center, every shelter—what time you had to show up, where they had the best food, what nights, and so on.

Corey had a lead on Holly Park. Murray, the director of a shelter on Broadway, had suggested she talk to another girl from Bremerton who might know Holly. What he knew about this girl was that she had a fire-breathing dragon tattooed on her chest, and that she hung on the Ave. JB would know where to find her.

When she arrived at JB's squat, he was standing shyly at the garage door. Johnny Boy was seventeen, a skinny, fair, blue-eyed boy with long brown hair. He'd spent four years hustling on the street. Corey had helped him in little ways whenever she could. A year ago she got him started selling Real Change, a paper largely written and sold by the homeless. Now he was washing dishes at a restaurant on the Ave. "She's cool," he said to two others who were sharing his squat.

Corey told him about the girl with the fire-breathing dragon.

"That'd be Flame. She's been stayin' at Digger's." Digger, he explained, had scored a basement room in an abandoned building.

Corey waited in the alley when Johnny Boy went down the stairwell. He pried open a boarded-up window to get inside. The alley smelled of urine and feces. These kids were lucky to have shelter. Okay, she got that. What she didn't get was why any child in Seattle had to live without windows, or plumbing.

She was frowning when she saw Johnny Boy coming up the stairs. He was leading a tall, blond boy with blue streaks in his hair. Flame, JB said, was just waking up. The blue-streaked boy knew Holly Park.

"Where is she?" Corey asked, stepping over an old pizza box in the alley. She held out two dollars.

He pocketed the money. "She split. Last night."

"Where?"

Blue Streak shrugged.

"Why?"

Another shrug. Corey held out another dollar.

He took the money. "Some wacko shit about Loki—whoever the fuck that is."

"Loki?" Corey first saw the name Loki when reading about 'Goths'. She had found the Norse myth. Loki was cunning, changeable, a deceiver who could take many forms. "In myths, Loki's an evil god, a trickster," Corey explained.

"Cool," he said.

She watched him picking at a scab on his arm. "Tell me about Holly?"

"She was weirded-out. I mean really scared. She was trying to get her shit together before she got away. She kept saying this name, Loki. It didn't make sense."

Flame came up the stairs, a little bleary eyed. Corey was surprised to see that she was African American, but the fire-breathing dragon was exactly as described. "You the one wants to know about Holly?" Flame asked.

"Yes."

"Will you pay?"

Corey touched Johnny Boy's shoulder before he could say anything. "Five."

"Five's cool."

The tall boy with the blue streaked hair held out his hand for more, but Johnny Boy escorted him back down the stairs.

Corey took out a five, watching Flame wake up. "When did you know her?"

"Summer before last. We hung together before she got scooped up by her sugar daddy—"

"Teaser White?"

"Teaser, yeah. That man got her pregnant then cut her cold. That's when she got into the shit."

"What was she like?"

"That girl was really messed up. Her old man used to jump her, and Teaser wasn't right. One time she told me how he cut her arm, watched her bleed. She told me he got off on that."

"What happened between them?"

"When she got pregnant, Teaser fucked her up pretty bad, then turned her out. She stayed with me a couple nights. Holly said when she told him about the baby, he just freaked out. It didn't matter that she didn't want it. It was like she'd tripped his crazy switch."

"When did her father find her?"

"I dunno, it wasn't much later. She was less than two months pregnant, and cracked out of her skull, when her old man dragged her off the street. Made her do the cold turkey. Made her snitch on Teaser. She ran away, had this gal we know do a back-room abortion, then Holly left Seattle. Six months later she was back on the street. Shit, by the time she was thirteen, she was half-dead."

Corey believed that. She'd bet Holly had tried to be brave and resourceful. She never had a chance. Between her father and Teaser, it was a wonder she turned thirteen.

"Do you know how she met Teaser?" Corey watched her think about that. Flame seemed tough and clear-headed, easy to like.

"All I know is one day Holly's at the shelter, hustling like the rest of us. The next day, she's gone. No big deal, you know? Say a week later, when I see her, she's got this brand new coat. And she gives me money, too. That's what I know."

An old, sad story. Corey knew the rest.

Corey gave her the five dollar bill. Holly had disappeared by now, she knew that, and Lou would be disappointed. Still, the money was well spent—she'd gotten a glimpse of Teaser, a bone-chilling snapshot. Even before prison, he was hanging by a thread.

❖

ABE SET DOWN THE phone, concerned. Maisie had not shown up for her lab work. He'd set up the appointment then called her to confirm. She'd forgotten...or ignored it. Treating kids was complicated, more art than science. And he didn't make many rules. But he'd learned that to have a working relationship with an adolescent, he had to set reasonable limits; that when he did draw a line in the sand, he had to mean it. No drugs. No violent or abusive behavior. That was about it. He scratched his beard. Maisie hadn't forgotten. Something was wrong.

CHAPTER SEVEN

"HOW DO YOU KNOW my dad?" Maisie asked Teaser, aka Jimmy Dubonnet. Olympic had an open campus, and Aaron and Maisie had left at noon. Maisie was sitting on a pillow set against the wall in Star's apartment, smoking a joint, feeling kind of breezy. Her colorful wrap-around skirt had risen above her knees. Star took the joint from Maisie and sat beside Aaron on the mattress. She wore headphones and was tapping three fingers of her left hand to music that only she could hear. Jimmy was meditating, naked from his waist to his watch cap. He wore the same beaded necklace around his neck.

"Jimmy?"

Jimmy ignored her, staring at the wall, chanting some kind of Indian mantra.

Maisie studied his sculpted torso. He was a total turn on, she decided. "C'mon, Jimmy."

Jimmy lit a match and held it under his palm.

She could smell burning flesh. "Is that some kind of trick?"

He showed her the burn on his palm. "Black magic."

"Does it hurt?"

"No." He brought her fingers to his burn. "Like a hot stone."

She gently touched his flesh. "Crazy."

Jimmy turned toward Maisie, lit another match, held it in front of her.

"Please, Jimmy, I need to know this stuff."

When the match burnt out, he let it drop, then leaned in and gently lay his fingertips on each of her bare thighs. "And so you shall, little one, so you shall."

"So I shall when?" She sat up, close to him now.

"When Jimmy decides the time is right." He ran his finger along her cheek, then gracefully eased behind her and began massaging her neck. Star was watching from the mattress, where she and Aaron were rolling another joint. Star was still tapping to her music. "For now, I will tell you that your father is well. He's a computer programmer..."

"Yeah, he used to do that." Maisie stretched her arms, relaxing as he worked on her shoulders. "You have the best hands, Jimmy."

"He lives for the day he will see his daughter."

"Really?" Could that be true?

"His eyes light up when he talks about you."

"Tell him I can't wait to see him, too. Okay?" She lay on her stomach. Jimmy's slender fingers lifted her black sweater, working now on her bare back. She felt really

good. Lately, just thinking about her dad gave her this
sweet, mellow buzz.

"I will."

Star came over, handed Maisie the joint. She took
a long pull then groaned as Jimmy's fingers dug deeper.
Jimmy declined the offered marijuana.

"Aaron, you want another drag?" Star asked, moving
her head now to the music.

"I'm cool." He lay back on the mattress, humming
something.

"Too hard," Maisie told Jimmy.

"Sorry, little one," he whispered in her ear, rubbing
the sore spot softly.

"Jimmy, please, when can we see my dad?"

"Soon. He wants to know his world is safe."

She sat up, thinking this over. "You mean like
I won't tell Verlaine?" She frowned. "I don't tell that
hipster wannabe anything."

"Your father must know that there's no danger.
From Verlaine, your mother or anyone else."

"What can I do?" She touched his knee. "How can I
help?" *This could be so big*, she was thinking—it was like a
second chance for her with her dad.

"How long is your school break?"

"Thursday—Thanksgiving—through the weekend."

"I want you to tell your parents that you are going
away with someone. Make a list of who's going to be
away that you might go with—at least three families.
Bring it tomorrow."

"Okay, but Verlaine will check."

"Leave that to me. I'll give you a phone number. I'll help you."

"What about Aaron?"

"Aaron can come, if you'd like."

"Yeah. Great."

Aaron was sitting up now. "This is getting too complicated."

Jimmy looked at Maisie. "Perhaps we should wait?"

"Hang in with me, Aar, okay?"

Star put her hand on Aaron's thigh, still moving her head to the music.

Aaron fell back on the mattress. Star handed him the joint.

"If you do as I say, he'll come to see you." Jimmy had both of his hands around Maisie's. His large dark eyes locked onto her hopeful blue ones. "No one can know he's in Seattle. Not your mother, not Verlaine, not any of your friends."

"I promise." Maisie ran her finger along his cheekbone. When she had his attention, she took off her sweater, then her skirt. Today, she wore pink bikini bottoms. She led Jimmy to the mattress, beside Aaron. "I'll take care of him," she whispered to Jimmy. Maisie stepped close to him. "You take care of me."

Jimmy leaned over then whispered in her ear, "I'd rather watch you, little one." He stepped back.

When Jimmy nodded, Maisie unzipped Aaron's pants.

❖

COREY WAS WAITING ON the porch when Will came home from school. He kicked a neatly raked pile of leaves before he trudged up the porch steps. "Hey," Corey called. "I'd like to talk with you."

Will ignored her, heading for the door.

Corey took his arm. "You have reason to be angry. I get that."

He turned. "You screwed it up for me, Mom. Totally. Aaron said his dad pulled him out of class, really weirded out. Toby was asking all these questions about him and Maisie. And he knew all about Star. Aaron wanted to know if you talked with his dad. I had to tell him." Will leaned against the porch rail, looking away.

"I'm sorry," she said. For a second she wished she was different: one of those blow-smoke-up-the-dean's-ass-type moms who knew how to work the system, get what they wanted.

"He's really pissed. He wants to know why you can't mind your own business."

"I see."

"No, you don't see. Or you wouldn't be all over my life."

"Will, I may have made a mistake, but I'm not stupid. Just hear me out. Okay?"

He looked away. "Isn't it a little late for that?"

"Look, I should have talked with you first, but I'm not like your dad. I don't usually think about what I'm going to say—or do—before I say it or do it. Sometimes things just come out of my mouth. Sometimes they just don't. This one got ahead of me. I had to make a tough call. I decided it was important for Aaron and Maisie to be safe. Even if it made you angry. I'm running on instinct here." They'd talked about that—how, for a long time, her instincts were all she had. He'd remember those conversations. Perhaps they'd help him see her side.

Will was quiet.

She leaned against the porch rail, next to her son. She tried another tack. "Aaron is lying, you said as much." She hesitated, watching Will stew. "Now I'm going to tell you something that will make your dad angry, but you need to understand all the pieces. Abe didn't tell me this, but I think Maisie's his patient."

"What?" Will hit his palm against a near post.

"He said something about seeing someone you know who he thought was running around with an older girl drugs, sex, the whole deal. He wouldn't tell me who it was. He's really worried though. You know how he gets."

"Mom, listen to what you're saying." Will's voice rose in pitch when he was frustrated. "I mean you're like totally over-reacting. Remember the first time you got drunk or smoked weed or stayed out all night? You didn't die from trying new things."

"That's true. But—"

"Let me finish. You're worried because Aaron's cutting class and lying. That's normal for Aaron." Will looked down at his mom, spread his long arms. "Look, let's forget that Maisie's therapy's private. Let's forget

that your work makes you spooky about everything...
can't you just please leave my friends alone?"

Will could be tenacious as a pit bull, like Abe. It
was getting to her. She held her temper because it was
Billy. "Abe's worried about Maisie. I'm worried about
Star. That's not over-reacting." Her tone was firm. She
knew what she knew.

He frowned, pensive. "Okay...if I can find out exactly
where she lives, will you check her out then back off?"

"I'll check her out. If she's okay, I'll back off." It
seemed fair, though she felt beaten down. "Just don't
hang out with her, okay?"

"I'll try and get the address from Aaron. One way
or another, I'll get it. And mom, just stay out of my life
until I do."

Corey raised her hands, hoping for a truce. Billy
ignored her, turning and going inside. She ran her fingers
through her hair, irritated. He needed some room.

She watched a cloud, counted to ten. When she
heard Will banging around inside, she sat on the porch
swing. She rocked back and forth, settling down, wishing
Abe was around.

CHAPTER EIGHT

"Y OU DIDN'T SHOW UP for your drug test," Abe said.

"Did you, like, think I would?" Maisie asked. "You know you're not the boss of me. I don't have to do what you say."

"That's true. Still, I called your parents and recommended the drug program. Your dad suggested we get together after his meeting tonight, talk it over."

"I'll run away first."

"Why's that?"

"Man, you are so out of it. I've got things to do." She crossed her legs, adjusting her skirt to cover her lower thigh.

"What do you mean?"

"C'mon. I'm smoking some weed. That's all."

She was wound up again. And she had this testy, impatient edge. "I asked you to stop."

"You can't make me do anything."

"No, I can't. But I'm still your doctor, and I'm still recommending the program."

"Why?" Maisie stood, drumming her fingers on his desk. And louder, almost shrill, "Why would you do that?"

"Because the drugs scare me. And because I told you I would if you didn't do as I asked." And, because it was getting harder to reach her. Something had subtly shifted. It was important to make contact, he wasn't sure if he could.

"And you're a hard guy, huh?"

"What do you mean?" He tapped the contents of his pipe into a large stone ashtray, leaving ashes on his desk. Abe weathered her scornful look.

"I mean you think that if I don't do what you say, you've got to make me—or I won't respect you, or some shrink rules-of-the-road shit like that."

"That's not me." He watched as she leaned back against the edge of his desk. "What I do think is that you're smart and complicated. You've been pushed, and you've succeeded, in this very demanding, rarified world. But as I listen to you, I'm beginning to realize that your parents, and most of your teachers, don't really know you, or what you want—"

"Duh."

"I'm sorry if it took me too long to see that." And he was. It had taken too long. It often did.

Maisie sighed, turned away, her fingers working again.

"Please hear me out." Abe paused, listening to her drumming fingers, aware he wasn't getting through. "I think your parents make you do things because they think they're good for you, or because they fit some picture they have of a girl your age, and these things may not be what you need or want. I'm not like that. I'm only going to ask you to do one thing: give up drugs. It's the only condition I have. If you do that, we'll make every other decision together."

She stood, turned back to look at him. "How about the decision to see you at all?"

"That's up to you."

"I quit."

Abe watched her leave. He was sure he'd had a real, albeit fragile, connection with Maisie. In their way, they'd each worked at that. It was broken. He sat back, troubled and confused. Abe clenched his fist then spread his big fingers—once, then again—only vaguely aware of the slow, regular motions. The game had changed; the stakes were higher. He didn't know why.

❖

"WHY IS IT THAT teenage boys fuck like jack rabbits?" Star asked.

Teaser was sitting in the corner, a trace of a smile on his face. He was poking at the burn in his palm with a nail. "Doggies get stuck inside. Swell up so big they can't pull out. You can teach him that."

"No way. You teach him."

Star noticed him poking at his burn and took his hand. "Please don't, baby," she said, concerned. "I'm so glad you're out. I missed you every day. When you were inside, I didn't know what to do. I couldn't sleep at night—I was bored, crazy bored, but my mind was always racing..." Star shook her head, bit down on her lower lip. "I played my games, did my projects on the web, and listened to my music all the time. I even listened to my seventies music..." Remembering that, and how she missed him, Star offered a little smile. "Now you're out, and it's like I got all my good energy back. You slow me down, smooth me out. I'm ready to rock and roll... Baby, how long do we have to wait?"

"They got their eye on me. The Man, he stops by my rat hole room. Day and night. The Man makes me check in. Keep a log. Everytime something goes down, Mr. Fat Fuck Man asks me all the questions. That's why I can't stay here. That's why I double back. That's why we can't go anywhere together. That's why I work the grill at that punk, greaseball drive-through."

"Tease, I need more time with you. I'm getting jumpy—you know how I get." She knew he did, too. He once told her not to worry about the rashes, or the cramps she got from waiting, that everyone had some out-of-control thing like that. It didn't help. "Tease, I don't mind playing sex games with rich kids," she explained. "I'm down with that, for you. I mean, I understand you've been inside, and, okay, whatever you need. If it's baby pussy you want, I'll find it for you. Just say the word... And you know I can take care of the bossy, sixteen-year-old princess and her fucking pet jack rabbit for as long as you want." When he didn't respond, Star made a sad-little-girl face. "I know you got something goin', baby. Just tell me what we're waiting for, okay? And baby, tell me when you can start staying over?" When he was with her, at least she'd sleep.

"Soon, sweet Star...soon...not to worry, not yet."

Star touched his cheek, tenderly. "You're smarter than anyone on the street. You can score at will. I mean you're so fast, and this is already old. C'mon baby, what are we doing here?"

He took her hand, then ran the nail along her palm, thumb to middle finger. She pulled her hand away, blood trickling between her thumb and index finger. "Don't hurt me, baby."

Teaser took a drop of blood with his fingertip, brought it to his lips. "I won't hurt you, ever."

She offered her hand. He kissed the bloody spot. "When are you going to tell me?" she asked.

Teaser kissed her hand again. "We're going to the moon. Star's going to the moon."

"Please baby. You know how I feel about waiting. I mean I don't mind if you jerk them around with that Indian Karma crap. I mean they think you're the shit, and that's cool. But explain what's happening in words I know. Please?"

Teaser slid behind her, began massaging her temples. "Not to worry Star light, Star bright." He spoke softly, near her ear. "This little girl, the one who thinks she knows everything..."

"She does like to be in charge." Star laughed. And, she had to admit, she liked playing them—it was a good project. At least it kept her mind busy.

"This little girl who likes to tell people who to fuck—" Teaser stopped abruptly, the corners of his mouth turned down.

Star waited. When he didn't go on she asked, "What about her?"

"In prison, I shared a cell with her true daddy. The man was a freeze-dried, brain-fried mother fucker. He's been inside for five, and his, like, hobby: it's doing research on his lost little girl. I swear to God. He researched her stepdaddy too. On his computer. Did he ever. Mr. Verlaine Daniels. Verlaine. I heard about Verlaine most nights. Verlaine's a big-shot Microsoft guy. He's worth maybe eight mill. We own, say, two of that. You and me."

"Oh no, T, that's too heavy."

"Babe, since I'm in the joint, I see this picture. I see the beach. I see white sand. A hot, red sun. Cool blue waves. I see our beach. Do you see that? Our sand, our sunshine, our waves? Do you see that?"

She hesitated. "You and me, on the beach?"

"I see this white house with orange tiles on the roof."

"A house on the beach? Our own house?" It was sinking in now, making the small of her back sweaty. Her heart was beating faster too, she could tell. She'd bet she could sleep at night, just listening to the waves.

With his finger, Teaser traced the cut on her hand, then he clicked his tongue, a soft, rhythmic sound. "It's our beach."

"Teaser, do you know what you're saying? It's like my dream come true."

"Now how are we going to get close to dream come true without heavy?"

"But they're watching you."

"Teaser made just one mistake." He shook his head, sad, then he whispered softly, "Teaser didn't know his baby was too old." And mostly to himself, "Teaser's baby bred a baby, and Teaser didn't know. Teaser's baby bred a baby, and Teaser let her go." He took her hand again. "That's the past. And the past is over. In prison I became the most careful man in the world. I did that. I'm never going to put you in danger, Star of Wonder."

"I love you for that."

"So we go slow. Tippy toes."

❖

Corey was sitting by the fire, re-reading the section about Loki in the *Dictionary of Norse Myth and Legend*. He was a shape shifter, the master of lies and deceit, the most dangerous god in the Norse pantheon. Loki produced three monstrous offspring—Hel, the goddess of death, Jormundgard, the evil serpent so huge that he stretched like a ring around the whole earth, and the most dangerous of the three, Femrir, the Fenris wolf who swallows Odin. Eventually Loki and his evil progeny prevailed over the gods and the world. This terrible age of destruction, the Ragnarok, or the end of all things, was marked by bloodshed throughout the world, brothers slayed brothers, parents went to war against their own children. During Ragnarok, a ship sets sail from the realm of the dead carrying the inhabitants of hell with Loki as their helmsman.

She looked at the fire. Billy—Will—was upstairs, doing his homework, and, she'd bet, texting two or three friends at the same time. She knew he was still mad at her. Maybe she was hovering too close. She didn't know. She called his name.

Will slogged down the stairs.

She waited until he stopped at the landing, arms resting on the banister. "I'm sorry if I get too close to your stuff," Corey offered.

Will shrugged.

"I am." She stood, touched his arm.

She was going to say more, but he grinned then turned up the stairs. She watched him, taking the steps two at a time.

Corey sat in her chair by the fire. She remembered a moment they'd had when they were on the run. She'd just told him she wanted to change their name. Start again. Everything.

Billy had leaned against her. After a while he'd said, "No kid would ever believe the things we've done."

❖

SNOW FLURRIES SWIRLED AROUND his father's Volvo as Aaron drove north on Broadway, toward the Blue City Cafe. He'd had a call from Maisie, who was panicking about rehab, and he'd lied to his father so he could meet her. It was, he decided, a good reason for a lie.

It was colder than it ought to be, he was thinking, when he saw a parking place. Parking was always a problem on and around Broadway, and a space was rare. Aaron had been driving, however, for barely six weeks, and parallel parking made him nervous. He chose a parking lot on Pike, closer to the cafe.

Pike was quiet. The cold weather was keeping people inside. Aaron walked west, preoccupied. Mostly, he was thinking about lying. What was a real lie? Was it a lie when you said one thing and did something else? His dad did that all the time without even knowing it.

There was another thing. His dad was smart, he knew that. But how could such a smart guy understand something so well at a distance, then miss that same thing right in front of his own nose? Like when his dad gave these lectures about all the subtle ways we exclude people because of racial differences. He really saw how that worked. And he was right. But he didn't even notice it when everyone treated Josey Tompkins like shit—no one would talk to her or eat lunch with her—because she was new and fat. Or when Henry Lewis didn't get invited to class parties because he was geeky and liked country music. Stuff like that happened at school all the time, and no one ever said anything. Maybe it didn't seem important enough. It was important to Josey and Henry though.

Aaron had worked out his own philosophy. He'd discussed it with Maisie and with Will. He believed it was okay to lie if you knew it, if you were doing it for a good reason, and if you weren't hurting anyone.

The Blue City Cafe looked warm and welcoming. It was 7:30 p.m., and the cafe was busy, serving an older crowd. Maisie was in the back, hunkered down deep in a soft, low couch, sipping a latte and staring at the wall. Even when she was sulking, or speeding, Maisie was so hot. And when she looked at him, there was this new, kind of tingly sexual energy between them. So just seeing her picked him up, made him forget his dad.

Aaron sat beside her, kissing her, tentative. She responded tenderly, and it became a slow, sweet kiss. "Waiting long?" he asked when their lingering kiss ended.

"Oh Aar, what am I going to do? I mean just when things are going good," she tensed up, her face fell, "the fucking sky falls in."

He gently rubbed her neck, hoping to slow her down. "What's the deal with this program?"

"Stein wants me committed to some kind of live-in drug rehab deal. Verlaine went for it. My mom's kinda checked out, so she just went along. I'm supposed to meet them all at 8:30 tonight. Pack my bags or something." Maisie was touching her fingertips to each other—thumb to thumb, forefinger to forefinger.

"This isn't tracking. I mean it's not like you OD'd or anything. Can't you reason with him? I mean tell him you're clean, and you'll take a test next week?"

"I tried that."

He frowned, unsure how to help her. He wanted to help; he knew that much. "You want to stay at Star's or something tonight?"

"I called Star. She's coming here."

Aaron took her hand, still working on calming her down. When she was calm, he knew she saw things really clearly.

"I'd die in some reform school drug program," she said. "I mean those kids are hardcore..." She looked at him, anxious. "We're talking strung-out junkies, not some high-strung private school babe who's, I dunno, just trying new things..."

Aaron gently massaged her neck. She took his hand.

Aaron squeezed her hand. "There's Star," he said and waved her over.

"This sucks," Star said as she sat down across from them. She wore torn jeans and an old leather jacket. Aaron liked the way her breasts filled the tight jacket. Star was squeezing a little rubber ball in her left hand. Squeeze, relax, then squeeze again.

"What does Jimmy say?"

"He says stay cool. Not to worry. Today's Tuesday. He says there's no way you could see your dad before Thanksgiving anyway. Don't run off. If you do, they'll be looking for you, and it won't be safe."

"But I can't face some kind of rehab program." Maisie's voice was tense. "The people in those programs, I dunno, I'm not a junkie."

"Jimmy said tell them you'll go, but ask them to wait 'til after the Thanksgiving weekend. Make up some shit about how you want to spend the holiday with your family. You can ditch them, can't you?"

"No sweat."

"You think Stein will give you 'til Monday?" Aaron asked.

"Maybe. Yeah. I think I can do that."

"Jimmy says he'll try for Thursday morning."

Maisie handed a piece of paper to Star. "Here's three families."

"I don't think that will work now. Jimmy says to meet at the apartment tomorrow, Wednesday afternoon. He'll have an answer."

"That's cool. What do I do if they make me go tonight?"

"Honey, in this state you can sign out of drug rehab. No problem."

"Are you sure?"

Star smiled, a sad, sweet smile. "I've been in those junkie programs-"

"You have?"

She put the ball in her jacket pocket. "I've got to go. See you tomorrow." Star was up and gone.

"I think I fucked up," Maisie muttered.

"What do you mean?"

"I wasn't too PC about drug programs. How was I supposed to know she was a junkie?"

"She doesn't care. Listen, you want me to be there tonight?"

"Would you?"

"No problem." Maybe they'd make love, after. Sex helped him feel better. And lately, he thought about it more than ever.

"Thank you, Aar." She put a hand on the inside of his thigh, pressed her body against him.

❖

COREY WAS SQUINTING AT the fire, her freckles rising to the bridge of her nose. She was back on Billy, brooding about his friends, reminding herself how hard it was to think like a teenager, let alone be one. She made a face; thinking like one was what she did, much of the time. Abe said she had a knack for it. Whatever that meant.

People still asked what she did, exactly. Her mother-in-law had once bought a travel agency for her to run, so she'd be in a real business. When Corey politely declined, Jesse snapped, "If you like kids so much, why don't you have more of your own?"

Abe had handled it. Something soft—very Abe—suggesting she had the sensitivity of a bottom fish.

Her mouth was dry, her lips a tight line. Corey was worried. Aaron and Maisie were overconfident. And hard to read.

She put another log on the fire. The only good thing in this whole deal was that Abe was Maisie's doctor.

CHAPTER NINE

MAISIE AND AARON, AND Maisie's parents, Verlaine and Amber, were waiting in the library, sitting around the walk-in fireplace, when Abe arrived. Verlaine let him in, then showed him to their library. The ceiling was twelve feet high, and three of the four walls were books in floor-to-ceiling mahogany bookcases. The fourth wall was an authentic Nantucket walk-in fireplace. He'd had it built in the old style, Verlaine told Abe, warming oven and all. He stopped to adjust a framed photograph on the mantel. In the photo, he and Amber were with Bill Gates. When he was satisfied, Verlaine steered Abe toward a cherry-colored leather chair beside the carefully-laid fire.

"Dr. Stein, I wanted to be here," Aaron said, after greetings were exchanged. "Is that okay?"

"That's up to Maisie."

"I really want him here," Maisie said.

"No problem," Verlaine added.

"Dr. Stein," Maisie found his eyes. "Look, I'm sorry for what I said about quitting. But I have to say, I don't know why I'm seeing you in the first place."

It was quiet. Abe waited, unsure how to handle this. The ground was shifting again.

"Maisie, there's hostility, cutting classes, and now, regular drug use," Verlaine explained.

"What do you mean regular drug use? You're stoned more than I am."

Verlaine stood. He looked at Maisie. "Let's start over. Okay?"

"Why? What I said was true."

"I'm really trying, but that kind of hostility is why you're in therapy."

"So therapy's punishment," Maisie snapped. "Nice—"

"Please," Amber implored.

Abe began to get his bearings. Amber was in the middle; she'd been right about that. But Maisie was stronger than Verlaine, and it seemed to Abe that the middle had pretty much drifted to Maisie's corner. And Maisie used it to get what she wanted.

Verlaine had his back to them now, using a pair of tongs to rearrange the fire.

"I'm going to recommend several things," Abe said, clear, at least, on what he'd like to see happen. "First, Maisie should enter the drug rehab program as soon as possible. When she completes it, I'd like to see you as a family—"

"You mean all of us?" Verlaine asked, turning toward them.

"That's exactly what he means," Amber said.

"Why?"

"Because I think it would help Maisie, and, hopefully, help the family deal with problems more easily." And help me keep this from unraveling any further.

"Why can't we do this before I go to this program?"

"They're separate issues. You have to get off drugs and stay off. Then we can deal with whatever problems are out there."

"Dr. Stein, I'd like to ask a favor. Thanksgiving is the day after tomorrow. Can I start this program next Monday?" Her voice was shaky. "I mean, I'd really like to be with my mom and dad for the holiday." She looked at them. "It would give us a chance to talk." She looked away, nervously twisting a lock of hair. "That would help me, you know, be ready."

"I don't think that's a good idea," Abe replied. He loosened his tie. Maisie was in charge here, insidiously, and it was part of her problem. Someone in her family would have to stand up to her, then ride out that storm. He could help with that. He couldn't make them do it though.

Maisie looked to Verlaine, hopeful.

"Abe, aren't you being a little too rigid?" Verlaine asked, trying to respond. He was still standing. "Can't we give her the holiday, let her start the program on Monday?"

"This is not the kind of thing that should be postponed," Abe said to Amber and Verlaine.

"Could you explain why?" Amber asked.

"I'll try..." He looked at the ceiling, pensive, then back at Amber. "Okay. To begin with, you have to remember that sixteen-year-olds are still learning to manage their impulses. Setting reasonable limits can be difficult for them. That's why it's illegal for sixteen-year-olds to drink or gamble or buy handguns," *or flirt with cocaine*, he wanted to add, though he couldn't. "I believe Maisie needs someone else to set limits for her. Right away. She's taking dangerous risks, and I worry that she may be putting herself in harm's way. I don't know specifically how, and she's not saying, but I think she needs a safe place to slow down."

It was quiet. Maisie was fidgeting, holding back tears, then she said, strident, "You're not helping me—"

"I understand Dr. Stein's point of view," Aaron interjected, taking her hand, "but there isn't anything dangerous happening. And if you give her a chance to get ready over the break, I promise—I guarantee—she'll stay away from any and all drugs over the holiday."

"I guarantee that, too," Maisie added, looking at her mother, teary now. "Please, Mom?"

Abe saw Amber's expression soften. Maisie and Aaron seemed to have an unerring sense for what Maisie's parents wanted to hear. And Amber and Verlaine so wanted her to like them. It made him tense up, apprehensive about something he couldn't even specify.

"Can't it wait until Monday?" Amber asked Verlaine, putting on a little pout. "Thanksgiving is a family holiday."

Verlaine looked at Maisie, who met his eyes. "I don't see the harm in waiting, especially if she's off the drugs," Verlaine said. "I'm sorry Abe, but that's our decision."

Abe looked up at Verlaine. His own face was drawn. "It is your decision. But I'm asking you to please reconsider."

Verlaine put a hand on Abe's shoulder, basking in Maisie's approval. "I think its better for our family to wait."

"No, it's not." They had to hear this. "I'm not sure what these young people are involved with. But I'm sure that you're being manipulated. And although you may think you're showing Maisie how much you love her, in fact, you're only confirming that you're easily deceived—"

"Why are you doing this? What's wrong with you?" Maisie was on her feet, tense and teary. "My dad does this good thing for me. A nice thing." She wiped her eyes. "And you try and ruin it. I thought you were supposed to be helping me."

"I'm—"

"Well you're not!" Maisie ran from the room, crying.

Amber followed her up the stairs. Aaron waited at the foot of the stairs, nervously, for Amber to be finished.

"I'm sorry Abe, but I think you'd better go now," Verlaine said.

"I'll arrange for her admission on Monday morning." Abe got up, frustrated. He'd learned that he couldn't make parents put their children first. It was hardest when the parents needed to be seen a certain way, and when they avoided conflict. The muscles in his back and neck were tight. He wanted a drink. "I'll show myself out. Enjoy your holiday."

❖

TEASER WAS CRUISING BROADWAY, checking out old hangouts, taking in the street life. The street was his, a place where he could move, a tiger in the tall grasses. That was the thing about prison, you could never disappear. Even at night. Especially at night. *Living dead.* He took a deep breath, trying to keep calm. Just thinking about prison made him numb up.

He tried thinking about the future. The gagging sensation in his throat eased up. He went over the plan again and again. Every little thing had to be just so. There was always something unexpected—like the scarred prison bitch who had shot off Luther's kneecap—and he had to be able to turn those problems into opportunities. Sow's ears to silk purses, his mother liked to say.

The present was hard. He hated the rat hole he'd rented. It was a tiny room in the beat-up Bentley Building. The address was necessary—he had to register—part of his plan, but he missed his condo. No one knew about the condo except Star. His safe house. His sanctuary. Soon.

He saw Marie Claire's. Still there, good. It wouldn't last much longer. The kids who came for tattoos, smart phones, and street action weren't buying $400 pants suits, or antique mahogany tables from Java. The fancy little store was what he wanted though, perfect for Star's present. She deserved one, the way she'd kept it together—clean, no junk. And he knew how hard it was for her to be alone. How her motor wouldn't ever stop or even slow down. How it was always overheating. So he wanted to buy her something special. He pinched his

arm, hard. There was no feeling at all. He tried the back
of his neck. Nothing. His face went blank. He wanted to
feel something when he bought Star's present. He felt
the frustration, then, coming on. Slow down, easy, he
told himself. Little by little. Maybe he'd feel something
after, when he gave it to her.

He chose a $1500 silver necklace. He knew it was
right as soon as he saw it. The necklace was the kind of
thing that didn't have to scream out how it was fancy,
and beautiful. It just was. He had the eye.

They wrapped it, just the way he asked them to,
eyeing him a little funny when he paid all cash. The lady
with the hairdo like a beehive tried to make small talk.
When she wouldn't shut up, he took his stocking cap
off, just for a second. The beehive bitch didn't say much
after that.

He'd have to take Star here, buy her some fancy
clothes. She'd like that.

Walking out, he was back on the plan, thinking
about how he'd handle Maisie and her pussy-whipped
Chinaboy. Teaser smiled, thinking about what he'd do
tonight, then tomorrow. He went over the steps, in order.
He fingered the torn burn on his palm. No feelings, yet.
By the time he got to Pine, he was at the part about
Maisie, and he could feel the scar on his tongue—just
barely—when he ran it over his lower front teeth. Maybe
tonight he'd sleep.

❖

COREY STORMED INTO THE bathroom, waved the evening paper at Abe. "Did you see this?" He was trying to trim his beard, working on the line under his chin. "Your mother's behind this. Her mission in life is to send me back to jail."

"What are you talking about?" He set down the razor, turned to her.

She grabbed his arm, sat him on the old four-poster bed, spread the story out in front of him. The headline said, "Mayor's task force asks, why so many sex offenders?" then, "demands new dispersion ordinance after slaying."

"You see who got slayed?" And before he could answer, "Luther Emerson—Annie's uncle, the guy I shot—that's who got slayed."

"Agh." He rubbed his neck.

"And who runs the mayor's task force on neighborhoods?" She paced, red-hot. "No one on that committee wakes up without your mother's permission."

"Okay. Right. I'll deal with it." He tried to think clearly. His mother made him crazy, too.

"Deal with it? How can you possibly deal with it? I promise you, I'll be hearing from Lou Ballard within the hour. He can't cut me any slack on a front page deal."

"She didn't know—"

"Right," Corey snapped. "And—"

"And I see Sergeant Ballard outside," Sam, Abe's driver, interrupted, in the room after feigning a knock. "Car out back, we go now."

"It's okay, Sam," Corey said, trying to reassure him. "He's here to see me. He won't ask for your papers."

"We go now. Okay? Yes?"

"I'll handle it." Corey put a hand on Sam's shoulder. "Don't worry."

"Don't worry? In this backward country, everyone needs a psychiatrist."

Abe made a deep disapproving noise, which made her smile.

Corey watched Sam scoot down the back stairs, then she leaned against the window, collecting herself. She heard Abe, still grumbling about something, near the front door.

There was Lou, coming onto her porch.

❖

"No one else knows. That's the only thing we got going for you." Lou was pacing in their living room, a Diet Coke in his hand.

Corey sat in the rocking chair. Abe was deep in the old leather couch facing their fireplace. An intricate, multi-colored rug from Turkistan covered the hardwood floor in front of it. Corey looked up. "I didn't do it. Isn't that going for me?"

"Always the smartass," Ballard snarled. "When the mayor's task force shines a spotlight on it, I can't cover for you. Lieutenant Norse is top gun on this." He watched Corey's face shut down.

She started rocking. "Lieutenant Nor—"

"I'm not finished," Lou raised his Coke can into the air, "the lieutenant remembers you. And *you*," he pointed his Coke can at Abe, "the loco shrink shot Nick Season." Lou scratched his bald spot. "As you may recall, Lieutenant Norse was Nick Season's choice for chief." When Abe grimaced, Lou grunted, almost a laugh. "He doesn't care who pulled the trigger, then or now. Norse's a politician. Here's your problem. Norse hates your mother." Another grunt. "*Hates her*," he repeated. "He believes she black-balled him." Lou cracked a knuckle, punctuation, then turned to Corey, serious. "Jesse went to war, quietly, when Nick turned out to be dirty. She served her revenge ice-cold. Jesse did every last thing she could to nail Nick's people. None of the rats got off that sinking ship. Not even Jim Norse." His eyes turned beady. "The first thing in this whole deal that Lieutenant Norse is going to like is that you shot Luther Emerson. He's going to like that like crazy."

"Corey didn't kill him. You know that," Abe said, matter of fact.

"What I know doesn't figure into this."

"You know us," Abe said slowly, not letting him off the hook.

Lou grunted. "Read my lips—this is politics, not police work. I can't help with politics. That's real." Lou seemed genuinely regretful. "I hate politics..."

Abe turned to the fire, irritated. He found Lou's "realism" too cynical, too clear cut. He was even angrier, he realized, that his mother cast such a long shadow. Still, they had a problem, and Lou was here, in his way, trying to help. "I'll talk with my mother," Abe finally suggested.

"And what's she gonna do? Give the lieutenant a taste of what she gave Nick?" Lou laughed out loud. It didn't matter no one else found it funny. "You over-analyze-everything types need some kind of retreat about hate. Jim Norse was riding Nick's coattails. Norse was about to make Captain. He was on track for Assistant Chief. When you took Nick down, Lieutenant Norse was instant dog shit. And he still can't shake Nick's stink. He holds your mother responsible for that. The lieutenant hates your mother. You can't change it, you can't treat it. It's like a vampire hates the daylight."

Abe watched Lou's stoney face, looking for he didn't know what.

Lou pressed on. "He calls her the 'rich, liberal cooze' (his word) 'who led Nick around by his johnson' (also his word) 'straight to his grave.'" He showed his palms, finished.

Corey's face was lined, pensive. "This isn't making me happy, Lou."

"Good. Because I'd say we've got three days, max, before I arrest you."

Abe stood, ignoring Lou. Thinking about Nick never helped. Lou was right about that.

Corey was brooding. Abe knew the look on her face. She was back in prison, hard as a diamond.

Abe opened the door, uneasy. "Go home, Lou," he said.

❖

ABE STAYED AT THE door, watching Corey.

She was pacing in front of the fire, reminding herself that she'd found a way to understand her past that she could work with. The problem was to hold on to that. Keep it clear. So what if her history, and her directness, often made people wonder? She'd learned to live with what other people thought. She felt the soft pressure of Abe's sizeable hands. He didn't care what people thought; he usually didn't even notice.

Corey turned, held him, grateful he was there.

CHAPTER TEN

T DAWN, TEASER LIKED to walk. Prowling, he called it. Night was the worst time. Dead time. Waiting for sleep. After 10:00, he had to stay in the rat hole room, in case the fat man came. He had to, even if his throat tightened up and his mouth turned salty. Prowling reminded him he was out. On the street, he knew who he was, who he could be.

This morning he'd walked Pike to the Market. Teaser smiled. The market was up and running, moving fast. He liked to smell, then to touch, the crabs, the squid, the mussels, and, particularly, the fresh fish. Today, he couldn't really feel the squid, though he could smell the fish, especially the herring. After, he'd woven along the Sound. Through downtown. Over to Pioneer Square. Off the square he'd stopped at his secret place. He checked the phone, the voicemail. Then he phoned Star, told her it was on for two-thirty. As planned.

Four hours and twenty-two minutes more. Outside again, he saw the rain coming down, but he didn't feel wet.

Back on the street he went south, toward Safeco Field. He liked the stadium, liked the way the metal roof moved. Sleek steel girders gliding through space. The old stadium, the Kingdome, had looked like an ugly breast. He went north, then east, toward Capitol Hill. As he walked Teaser pictured Maisie. Daddy's girl. Something maybe stirred inside, almost a tingling. Sweet.

Four hours. He'd go to Federal, past Maisie's house, her school. Killing time.

❖

MARGE, THE PROPRIETRESS OF the Blue City Cafe, loved the holidays. It was the one thing that gave away her true, non-hip self. When the harvest baskets appeared on the coffee tables, the cut-out turkeys popped up behind the counter, and the Blue City featured pumpkin pie, street kids knew to stop in at closing for a Thanksgiving treat.

Maisie and Aaron were at a table in the back, side by side on their favorite sofa, sharing a cigarette. "Tom Gleason's worried about us," Aaron said, referring to Will's, and his own, advisor. "He offered to help."

"What for?"

"He knows something's up. Will's mom really threw a scare into my dad, and I guess Tom was there."

Maisie groaned. "She's like this witch. And I think my shrink's under her spell." Her knee was going up and down.

Aaron gently put a hand on her knee, trying to help her unwind.

"I think she's just worried about Will."

"Why?"

Aaron gently pressed her knee as he explained, "She lost him once. You know that."

"Uh-huh, I get that. Uh-huh," she said, softly, enjoying his touch. "What's the deal with her? Will said she stabbed someone in jail. With a pencil. In the neck."

"I'm not sure. Corey's from the dark side...she's been into stuff you wouldn't believe." Aaron paused. "Tom's a different kind of deal, I'd feel really bad if we let him down."

"How can finding my true father let Tom down?"

"I don't think it will. I just want to be sure that that's what we're doing."

"That is what we're doing." And when it's done, maybe the so-called grown-ups would cut her some slack.

"We meet Jimmy and Star in half an hour. Suppose... huh." Aaron stopped.

Maisie waited. She could tell when he was planning something. She liked the way he looked, cool and serious. He was cool, she thought, and he really wanted her to like him.

He took a drag, still considering, then looked right at her. "Can you think up some question that only your true father could answer? Something that Jimmy will have to ask him to get right. If he gets it, that will prove your real dad's going to meet us."

Maisie drank coffee, weighing this. "It might piss Jimmy off."

"So what?" Aaron asked. "Your dad's being careful, and so should we. If he really wants to meet you, he'll understand."

"Okay. Yeah." Maisie's expression slowly changed to something like delight. "Aar," she blurted out. "I've got just the thing." It made her feel good, too. In charge.

"Okay...great." He smiled, took her hand. "I've got to say, if we find your real dad, and make a connection, that would be like, incredible."

"Count on it." A look passed between them. It was part sexual promise, part a special understanding. They were after something real—the indisputable truth, the genuine article—and nothing else would do. "You know, when they get it, they'll have to stop hassling me. I mean, really stop. And maybe let this drug thing go."

"One thing for sure, they'll know you have reasons for what you do."

"You'd think they understood that, with all their so-called high-powered connectedness. And where does their know-it-all certainty about what I should be come from, how have they earned that? It's funny, I'd at least tell my mom stuff if they weren't so, I dunno, predictable. I mean safe sex and a designated driver," she made a sour face, "is that supposed to make me feel grown up? I don't think so. I knew that in third grade." She stood, ground out their cigarette. "Let's split."

Maisie held onto Aaron's arm as they made their way down Broadway. Maisie's long, red scarf was easy to spot in the crowd. Across the street, Will followed.

❖

COREY WAS BACK ON Teaser. Stuck. She watched a fancy sailboat cut across the ferry lane. She thought she heard the ferry blasting its horn. Teaser had an alibi, some guy his CCO had talked to who confirmed he was with him in Tacoma. Still, she thought Teaser was the key to this. She turned away from the window.

Corey had two people on Broadway, one on the Ave, and one on Pike, keeping an eye out for Star. Nothing else she knew to do. She forced herself back to her work.

It took a minute, but before long Corey was focused on her next appointment, a lawyer representing the parents of a child she'd found: a fourteen-year-old boy who wouldn't come home. The boy had his reasons, too. Corey considered how to back off this lawyer. How much to tell him. Why did she like this sad, difficult work? Like it more than anything she'd ever done?

She remembered when Abe had convinced her to go back to work. It was pretty simple at first, fixing up other people's old wooden boats. Within a month she was finding special order items. It turned out she was good at finding things, especially in and around Seattle. Then Abe asked her to help him find a patient who'd run away from home.

Corey discovered that missing children moved her in unexpected ways. She turned, watched the sailboat getting smaller. It was something she rarely talked about. What it was, she thought, was how this work connected her to her past. She knew how it was for these kids. She could talk to them, help out in little ways. And the kids liked that she could be who she was, coming from where she'd come from.

There were five to ten thousand homeless youth and young adults in Seattle every year, one thousand on any given night. They couch surfed; they squatted in empty houses and abandoned buildings or in big clumps of bushes at the U; they stayed in shelters, parks, on the street, or under I-5. Sometimes they stayed with adults, or older kids, in return for sexual favors: survival sex, it was called. The kids commonly hung out on Broadway, at Westlake Park, or on the Ave, spanging. They gave each other street names—Peanut, Eightball, Twist, Shadow—and often looked out for one another. Relationships were always shifting. Drugs were often part of life: using, selling for dealers then getting paid in drugs to feed a habit. And there was always danger. The girls prostituted themselves at Seattle Center, or on Aurora Avenue, or wherever worked. The boys did the same, near the Federal Building, at bars, malls, and so on. It bothered her that so many people didn't get that the drugs and prostitution usually began *after* these young people left home. She frowned. Even more troubling, these kids were always vulnerable. During a three-month study, two-thirds of the boys and one-third of the girls had been physically assaulted. Still, they came. Corey knew that for most of them, there was no chance at home.

Finding these children was mostly intuitive for her. The hard part was earning their trust. If that happened, she was likely the only adult they trusted.

She worked no more than five cases at a time. That was her rule. So far, of the eighteen kids she'd searched for, Corey had found twelve. Four were still open, and two families had given up on her. Of the twelve she'd found, three were back with their families, two were in juvenile detention, or "Juvie," two were still on the street, three were working and living on their own, Annie was in a shelter, recovering, and Jolene had taken her own life. Jolene was still hard to think about.

The phone rang. The lawyer was running late. As she set down the phone, she was back on Jolene. Jolene was one of her first cases. A week after she found her, Jolene wasn't at any of the usual places, so Corey went looking for her. When she'd broken into her room, Jolene was wired to the bed. Someone had whipped her with a red-hot coat hanger.

She was wild, ranting about Satan. She kept screaming in this hoarse voice how *He* owned her. Something about how Satan was her man, when she was eleven. Corey fingered her scar and sighed. Apparently, two years later, Jolene needed money to feed her habit, and she knew where Teaser kept his stash. At the hospital, Corey had asked Jolene if she wanted payback. She laughed, this loud, crazy laugh. She said she wanted *Him* back. Jolene said being with *Him* was her best time.

Corey could still see her: Jolene lying there, broken. Teaser did that.

CHAPTER ELEVEN

TEASER PEEKED OUT FROM behind drawn shades. He was watching the street from Star's apartment, waiting on Aaron and Maisie. A gust of wind lifted a long, red scarf, like a great, crimson wing, gliding down Regent from Broadway. The corners of his mouth angled up, just a little, when he recognized Dave's baby girl. He fingered his torn burn. He knew just what he was going to do with her. And just how he'd do it. Thinking about it made him feel better—better, even, than thinking about the money. When he ran it through his mind, he forgot the hot, smoky grill at the Mex drive-through. Forgot the rat hole on Bentley where he had to live. He even forgot the prison. Some day soon he'd forget during the night, but the nights were still bad.

He still lost himself some nights. Like he used to do inside. *Living dead.* He swallowed, feeling the tightness in his throat. He was afraid of gagging, so he took slow, careful breaths. Dead souls rose at night. He knew that. He remembered all the nights with her dad. Dave never stopped talking. Ever. The Master.

Maisie was almost to the apartment now, hanging onto the arm of her boyfriend. Some boyfriend he turned out to be, letting her watch him, letting her boss him around. Funny how the boss bitch thought she had it all figured. He grinned. Daddy's Girl.

They were almost to the door when he noticed another kid, hanging back, stepping into the entryway of a white, painted-brick building, across the street from Star's. Only the kid didn't go in. He just stayed there, in the shadows. Teaser put what he needed in his jacket pockets, told Star what to do, then he was out the door. He crept down the back stairs and took the alley to Broadway. Teaser turned north on Broadway, so he could come down Star's street. At the corner he pulled on the ski mask. It covered his entire head, except for the holes for his eyes. Yes, the kid was still there, leaning back against the wall, writing something in a notebook. Teaser took a minute, scoped it out, made his plan.

Teaser walked into the entryway, reached into his pocket as if for a key. When the boy looked up, Teaser held his buck knife to the kid's throat, pressing, Little Buck making the thin red line. Teaser turned the boy face against the wall, then he pulled Little Buck slowly across the boy's cheek. He watched the blood, running from the cut. The kid didn't move a muscle when Teaser used a tool to open the door to the hallway. Teaser pulled him in. Without a word, he used a pick to unlock the basement door then ordered the boy down the dark steps into the unfinished basement. There was a large pipe running behind the old furnace. Teaser cut the kid's other cheek—a reminder—then made the boy face the wall, legs spread, palms against the old brick. From his pocket he took the fine wire he liked. He looped two strands of wire over the pipe then tied one strand to each of the boy's hands. He raised him up until the kid stood on his toes.

❖

WILL COULD FEEL THE blood trickling down his cheek. It was seeping from his wrists, too, where the wire was cutting his skin. He felt dizzy and weak, like a baby. The crazy guy had really scared him—made him soil his pants— the way he said he'd be back, the way he put his fingertips to his lips after he touched the blood. The guy wanted to kill him, he was sure of that. And there was nothing he could do but wait. Wait for the guy. Wait for his mom.

He wondered if his mom would understand. Understand how he got in this trouble. Why he got in it. In a way, it was her fault. She'd understand that, he thought, but that wouldn't change the way she was.

Will felt the blood on his neck. The pain in his toes was getting worse. When he pulled on his wrists to ease the pain, the thin wire tightened, and his wrists hurt so much he thought he'd pass out. He bit down hard on the gag in his mouth, then closed his eyes, tears mixing with the blood on his cheeks. For a long time he drifted in and out of consciousness. When he was awake, he thought about his mom—how it was with her, when he was little and they were on her boat, and later, on the run from Nick Season. He wasn't sure why he kept remembering that, except it was like a dream, a happy dream where he and his mom were working together, looking out for each other. It was just the two of them then, and they were like one person. She often knew what he felt before he did. In his mind, he whispered her name, then Will drifted back to some far off place.

When he woke again, he was remembering the end of their last boat trip, after Abe found them. They were going back to face Nick, and it was scary, really hard. The last thing she told him was how they'd be okay; how the two of them had gotten pretty good at hard things.

❖

STAR WAS POURING FROM a bottle of red wine when Teaser opened the apartment door. There was blood on his khaki army jacket, irregular black spots running down his left sleeve. He hung the jacket on a peg, out of sight. Underneath, he wore jeans and an old, navy-blue sweater with a hole at the elbow. Teaser took off his sweater and T-shirt. He sat in the corner, running his tongue over his front teeth and looking out the window.

Maisie noticed the muscles in Jimmy's neck. They made little ripples, as he turned his head side to side. *Why*, she wondered, *does he always wear that blue watch cap over his head?* She'd never seen him without it.

"What's with him?" Aaron asked Star.

"Jimmy needs time to himself. Then he takes care of everything." Star raised her glass of red wine, turned to Maisie. "To your dad," she toasted.

Aaron and Maisie raised their glasses.

"Your idea worked great," Maisie told Star. "I mean I don't go into the rehab program until Monday."

"Okay. Cool," Star said. She stroked Maisie's hair, touched her back.

Aaron turned to Jimmy, who was still staring out the window. "Maisie has a question for her dad." He waited. "Jimmy, she needs to talk with you."

Jimmy ignored him.

Aaron stepped forward. "Yo, Jimmy—"

Maisie put a restraining hand on his arm. "Let me," she whispered.

Maisie sat on the floor in front of Jimmy. She ran her finger along his cheekbone. She was feeling good, on a roll. "Jimmy, I need to know something. Something that will tell me for sure if he's really my dad."

Jimmy stared at her.

"I trust you Jimmy, you know that. Still, my dad wants to be sure of things—like I won't tell Verlaine—right?"

Jimmy looked into her eyes, but he said nothing.

"I do, too. I just want to know one thing." Maisie hesitated. She saw how to do this. "Trust goes two ways, Jimmy," she said, softly.

His face was expressionless, like a mask.

She extended her hand, palm down. "Do it."

Jimmy lit a wooden match off the floor.

"Hey," Aaron was on his feet. "Are you crazy?"

"It's okay, Aar." Maisie gestured at Jimmy. "Do it."

Jimmy took her wrist. Maisie covered her mouth with her free hand while Jimmy slowly raised the burning match under her extended palm. Aaron winced at her stifled screams. Tears ran down Maisie's cheeks.

Jimmy shook the match out, then released her palm. There was an oval-shaped burn where the flame had almost touched her palm. She put her palm to her mouth, trying to ease the pain. Maisie was still crying.

Aaron stared, flushed. "What's wrong with you?" he asked, a whisper.

"Stop it, Aaron," Maisie sobbed. "I had to. Can't you see?"

"I see a burn, that's what I see."

"He needs to trust me, too, okay?"

"I don't get it."

"Aaron, you're just a boy." Star traced the Z on the side of his head.

"And what are you, my mom or something?"

"Please stop." Maisie looked at him, drying her eyes.

Aaron stepped back. "Okay Maise, just ask your question. Okay?"

"I will. And now he can answer." She looked at Jimmy. "Right?"

Jimmy took a wet wash cloth from Star, applied it to Maisie's burn. "What would you like Jimmy to ask your father?"

"One time, he took me away. He helped me. He saved my life. Ask him about that—where we were, what he did."

He opened the apartment door. "Wait here," he said, then he closed the door behind him.

Maisie let out a breath. She'd done it, and she felt proud.

❖

JASON WEISS, COREY'S WELL-CONNECTED lawyer, took a sip of his Bombay Gin martini. He was sitting with Corey in front of the fireplace at the Fireside Lounge in the Sorrento Hotel. The large circular lounge had small groupings of antique sofas and chairs, and, best of all, it was paneled floor to ceiling with mahogany.

"When that beautiful face gets so serious, I worry," Jason said.

"This is politics...I don't understand politics..." Saying it, she felt sad, worn out. "And then there's Jesse..." Corey made a cross with her forefingers, raised it in front of her. She sighed, lowering her fingers; her cross wasn't working. Corey returned Jason's rueful smile then pressed on, "Lou Ballard says Jesse blackballed Lieutenant Norse. Is that true?"

"Yes, as you know, Nick Season used her. He humiliated her beyond what she could bear. When she saw who he was, and what she'd done, Jesse simply burned with shame and rage. From that moment on, she made it her mission to be sure that his cronies were, shall we say, noted." He made a face, sorry; Jesse was, well, Jesse. "Since then, Nick's history, his 'tainted' connections, come up every time Lieutenant Norse is reviewed for promotion. He's going nowhere. Jesse's friend, the mayor, sees to that."

Corey let it sink in. Classic Jesse. She'd taken her sweet time—hell, she'd nursed her revenge. Corey turned away, glum.

Jason sat back, ordered another round.

Eventually, she turned back. "Was Norse dirty?"

"Hard to know. Let's just say he always understood a favor." Jason rubbed his ear lobe between thumb and forefinger. "Corey, Jim Norse is no Nick Season. He's something else entirely. Jim's—*how do I put it?*—an ambitious, a rapacious, horse trader. There's a story about his divorce. He gave up one weekend a month with their children for the summer house."

Corey watched him; he wasn't kidding.

"A man like that, we'll find a way to work with him." Jason gently touched her arm, raised his palm—*let it go*—then he lifted his martini glass. "To you," he toasted, clicking glasses with hers. "Don't let this worry you yet."

Corey kissed his cheek. Jason made her feel safe. "Thank you."

❖

Teaser crossed the street, turned toward Broadway. He tried to feel the wind, blowing against his face. He was on his way over to the basement—killing time—

wanting to see if the kid could feel anything. Watch him. He stopped. There was this scraggly-looking one-armed beggar in the alley behind some garbage cans, and he was yelling at him.

"Where's the boy?" the one-armed piece-of-white-trash asked.

Teaser was wondering if he'd heard right, when the piece-a-shit asked it again. What the fuck was he doing here? Following the kid? Teaser was a careful person. More careful than anyone he knew. And this was like an alarm, throwing a switch somewhere in Teaser's brain.

He wondered if it was a dream when the one-armed man broke a beer bottle and came at him.

❖

THE BOTTLE OF WINE was empty, and they were working on a second bottle. Aaron was high, feeling better. Maisie had a band-aid on her burn, and she turned her hand over every few minutes to adjust it.

Star was looking out the window, wrapping then unwrapping a piece of yarn around her thumb. She smiled when she saw Teaser, cutting across the street. He was moving fast, purposefully, in that way that only he could do it.

A minute later Jimmy came through the door.

"Did you see him?" Maisie asked. "Did you talk with him?"

Jimmy kept his coat on, went to the window, then he turned back. "Yes."

Maisie gave her best smile, hopeful. "What do you do? Call him up?"

"Be patient, little one," Jimmy said. "Star will tell." He pointed at her, then Jimmy went to the kitchen sink, rinsed his hands.

"When Jimmy wants to contact your father, he calls a number and leaves a message," Star explained, still working the yarn on her thumb. "Dave gets paged, then he leaves a message for Jimmy at the same number. Ten minutes later, Jimmy calls the number back, enters the pass code, and picks up his message."

"And?"

Jimmy came closer. When he stood directly in front of her, Jimmy held Maisie's face in his long delicate fingers. "As a little girl, you and your father went camping in Big Sur. You were walking on boulders beside the river when you were bitten by a rattlesnake. You almost died. He carried you out of the wilderness. He ran three miles to the road."

Maisie put her arms around Jimmy's neck. "Oh thank God!" She turned. "Aaron, it's really him: my dad. You see?" She felt great waves of feeling—relief, affirmation, purpose—gently washing through her body.

"Look, I'm sorry, Jimmy, it's just, I dunno, I wanted to be sure," Aaron explained.

"There's more."

"More what?"

"Your father's message."

"What?"

"We leave now. Right away."

❖

Corey called Abe, then Abe called Tom Gleason, the counselor, when Will didn't come home after school. The calling continued long enough to establish that Aaron and Maisie had checked in with their respective families. They were going to a party later in the evening, and they had permission to go out to dinner first. No one knew where they were eating. Abe asked Toby if he was sure they were going to this party. Toby firmly told him that he'd had his fill of Logan-Stein cynicism and second guessing, particularly about his son. Abe hung up on him. He was that worried.

Lou was at the house fifteen minutes after Corey's call. It was 7:30 p.m., and Will knew to call or be home by 5:00. "What do we know?" Lou asked before he was in the door.

Corey was pacing, in some sort of zone.

"Will was at school," Abe explained. "A friend saw him walking toward the Blue City Cafe, a place where the kids hang out—"

"I had Franklin—you know the guy who sells Real Change near the Blue City—watching out for Will," Corey added. "I've been to the Blue City. I can't find him."

"I think we just found your friend Franklin a block and a half east of Broadway, in that alley behind Regent."

"Oh God, oh my God." Corey was sure she'd come undone—unable to move, unable to breathe. All this as she raced out the door to Lou's car. Abe and Lou were right behind her.

❖

TEASER WATCHED THE POLICE from behind the blinds. They'd found the dead beggar. Interesting. When the one-armed asshole broke the beer bottle, just like that, Little Buck turned that mangy piece-a-shit to jello-fucking-pudding. Teaser had to move then, really fast, because some lady was standing at the window. He cracked a little smile. He was good at staying cool under pressure. It was like living dead.

He pulled the body behind the cans, ranting about homeless drunken trash. The lady hadn't seen what happened, and maybe she'd let it go. Teaser stepped down the stairwell to the basement, cool as ice. When he came back up, the lady was gone. He walked away slow, acting like it was no big deal. At the corner he turned north, away from Star's. He went two more blocks before swinging back, on Twelfth. He looked up at Star's apartment, where Daddy's Girl and her rutty Chinaboy were waiting patiently.

At the apartment everything came together just so— Star took them straight to the ferry, and Teaser stayed back, waiting to see. Star called, they made the 5:25. Teaser waited. He was good at waiting. It was like being in jail, waiting for Dave to stop. Dave was some kind of martial arts expert. That's what kept Dave alive. That and the shank he stuck in Teaser's thigh the first time Teaser tried to back him off.

Teaser thought about cutting Dave's throat while he was sleeping. But even if he could kill him—a big if—Teaser knew he'd take the fall, and then he'd be inside, *unprotected*, forever.

The sirens interrupted Teaser's train of thought. Cars were coming down Broadway, then turning into the alley behind the painted brick building. He couldn't see the cars, but he saw the lights—white and blue—bouncing between the buildings. He raised his binoculars. Now there were two cars, maybe three. The ambulance came next. Red and white. Then another car. It was a black sedan, and no lights were flashing. Two men and a woman got out. Something about the woman. Where had he seen her? He had to get a better look. Teaser left the window, went down the back stairs. When he reached the entrance to the alley, he hung back, watching the woman. When she turned, he edged closer, stooping behind a fence.

❖

COREY TOOK ONE LOOK at the stab wounds in Franklin's chest and she assumed the worst. Franklin was following Will, and somehow, he'd interrupted the killer's business with her son. What if Franklin had tried to get past this

killer to help Will? Unless the killer had taken his body—
dead or alive—Will was nearby. Corey stepped away from
Franklin, away from the people. She imagined broken
glass in her gut. Felt it.

She looked at Abe, lowering her guard for just an
instant. She knew that he, too, was at the gates of Hell.

Abe touched the small of her back then stepped away.
She withdrew into herself, grateful that Abe knew to let her
be. She was shedding her skin, trying to think like Franklin.
Trying to be Franklin. Imagining him walking down this
alley. Why was he in the alley? Had Will gone down the
alley? What if Will had gone down the street, gone into
one of the apartments? Be Franklin. Right. No one would
buzz a one-armed, shabby-looking homeless man into their
building. Was Franklin looking for another way in?

She ran between two buildings to the street. Focused.
Scanning. On Regent, there was a locksmith, a used
bookstore, a hairdresser, three or four run down houses,
and several apartment buildings. The first was gated. She
checked the lock before hurrying on. The second was a
dilapidated wooden house, converted to tiny apartment
units. She went up the stairs, through the open door.
The entry was dark. She took the stairs two at a time,
stopping at the landing. There were two units on this
floor. She pounded on the door. No answer. On the
next floor an elderly woman called through her locked
door that she hadn't heard anyone today. Back in the
entry, the door to the basement opened easily. Corey ran
down the basement stairs, turned on the light. Nothing.

The next building was dirty pink stucco, a shoddy, three-story eyesore. A sign said apartments were available. Inside, she saw an open door. A woman was baking, and the sweet smells of apple pie floated into the lobby. Corey knocked on the open door. "Hey, you see a boy come through here today?" she yelled. "It's important."

The woman poked her head out the kitchen door, thought this over. "The real estate jerk's been in and out all day." She stepped out further. "You want some pie? He pays me to bake 'em, cover up the stink in the lobby."

Corey was already gone.

The fourth building was a white brick four-story with four units on each floor. The building had a buzzer system, she rang three buzzers, said she was with the police, and someone buzzed her in. She looked around the lobby. There was a stairway going up. Behind the stairway, a door led down to the basement. Where would he be going? To one of the apartments? She started up the stairs. At the landing, she heard a dog barking. Through the window, she saw the yard where the little dog was tethered. He was near the basement window.

Corey raced down the stairs, tried the basement door. It was locked. She kicked it open. By now, one of the tenants was yelling for the police. The basement was dark and damp. The darkness and the stale, foul air made her claustrophobic. She made her way down the steps, hanging onto a hand rail. "Will," she screamed into the dark. "Will, please. Can you hear me?"

A policeman came down the steps behind her, gun drawn. "Lady, against the wall," he ordered.

"I'm with Sergeant Lou Ballard," Corey snapped. "I need your flashlight."

"Lemme see some ID."

"My son's life's at stake. Please turn on the flashlight." It came out raw.

The policeman turned on the light. Corey grabbed it, ran the light along the wall, stopping at the window, then continuing on behind the fiurnace. Will was hanging by his wrists. Still. His face was streaked with blood. Lines of blood ran down from his wrists, disappearing under his jacket.

She lifted him, tears streaming down her cheeks. Corey held him in her arms, laying her head on his chest. She lifted her head. "He's alive," she whispered. "Cut him down."

❖

TEASER WAITED AT THE fence, working hard at watching. Wondering where he'd seen this woman. Several minutes later she came out. The boy was on a stretcher, tubes running from his arms. The lady was next to the boy, holding his hand. The boy was lucky. He wasn't in the plan. He knew Maisie, and he was near Star's apartment, so for now, Teaser had to let him live. The boy didn't matter anymore. And the one-armed beggar didn't count. He didn't know anything or anyone. It was the lady that worried him.

Teaser studied her as carefully as he could. She brushed by a cop that wanted to ask her questions, shooting him a dead on don't-fuck-with-me look. She'd been inside, he could see that. And then he saw the scar on her neck and he knew—this was the bitch who did Luther. Blew his kneecap off like she was lighting a cigarette. Damn. Coincidences didn't happen to careful people. He made his way back to Broadway then circled back to his car, a used, royal-blue Mustang. They'd be watching Star now, every move. Scar bitch had painted a bull's-eye on Star's back. Fucked up a fine-tuned plan. Even the apartment was off limits now. They couldn't make their move today. No. No. No—the spotlight was too bright and it was shining on Star. Okay. There was an opportunity here to do what he did best—turn a liability to an asset. A sow's ear to a silk purse. Like he did with Dave. Like he'd do with her.

It came to him, turning off Pine, just how to do it. It came easy, like all of his best ideas. It was just there, in his mind, when he needed it. Teaser picked up his cell phone. He could feel the hairs rise on his neck.

CHAPTER TWELVE

SERGEANT BALLARD WENT WITH Abe to Toby Paulsen's house on Queen Anne Hill. Toby was wearing his Amherst bathrobe when he opened the metal door.

"Do you know where Aaron is?"

"I do, yes. What's the problem?"

"Will was attacked today," Abe explained. "Another man was killed. We can't reach Verlaine or Amber Daniels, they're presenting at some kind of retreat. We left an urgent message."

"Will?"

"He'll be okay." Abe turned away.

"Thank God." Toby closed his eyes, grave. "What happened?" he asked, taking Abe's arm, leading them in.

He listened carefully while Sergeant Ballard went over what they knew about Will and about Franklin.

"I'm sorry. This is horrible," Toby said, when Lou was finished. He put a hand on Abe's shoulder. "Is there anything I can do? Does Will need anything?"

"We found him in time. This freak had him hanging by his wrists. Tied to a pipe with wire. Will lost some blood. He's still very weak." Abe wiped little beads of sweat from his brow with a crumpled kleenex. "Apparently, whoever did this didn't intend to kill him. Or, if that was his intention, Franklin may have saved his life. We're still in shock."

"I'll do anything I can to help Will. Anything." Toby frowned, pensive. "But what does this have to do with Aaron, or Maisie Daniels?"

"Nothing, I hope," Lou replied. "Will was following them when he was attacked. We think they were going to this woman named 'Star's' apartment. Will was found in the basement of a building on Regent. Franklin was murdered in the alley behind that building. Will identified the building Aaron and Maisie went into. We're pretty sure we found Star's apartment inside. It's empty now. We want to find Aaron and Maisie as soon as possible. We tried the party where they're supposed to be, but they didn't show up."

"Why didn't you call me?" Toby shook his head. "Why would you send police officers to pick up Aaron and Maisie at an Olympic school party?"

Lou adjusted his tie. "Who were we supposed to send, limo drivers?"

Toby didn't laugh. "Sergeant, how do you dissect a butterfly? With a sledge hammer?"

"For christsake, Toby." Abe ran a hand through his hair. "Lay off that righteous—"

"Damnit," Toby interrupted Abe. "You people don't get it. My son is fine. Aaron called not ten minutes ago. He said they decided to skip the party. Maisie's got an upset stomach. He's bringing her here. They'll be back in an hour."

"What if you're wrong?" Abe stepped closer. "It only has to happen once." He turned and left.

Lou snorted, pleased. "We'll be back."

❖

WILL WAS RESTING IN a private room at the hospital. Corey hadn't left his side since she'd found him in the basement on Regent Street. He was hooked up to all kinds of tubes and wires. The cuts on his face weren't deep, and Corey thought the twin bandages looked like war paint.

Corey had pulled her chair right beside Billy's—Will's—bed. He was sleeping. After they checked him out, they'd given him a sedative, and a pain killer. While he slept, she held his hand. She was still so afraid, so upset and angry. The doctors said he'd be fine, physically. Emotionally, they couldn't say. She was glad the doctors had stayed out of that.

Will was waking up. Corey was still holding his hand. She pulled herself together. "Hey, Will." She watched him barely manage a smile. "Can I call you Billy for a while?"

"Sure," he said, slowly. He was still foggy.

It was quiet then, until Corey said, "You know, Storm won. In L.A. You want to see New York Liberty on Tuesday?"

"Yeah...sure."

She lifted his hand. "You okay?"

"Uh-huh...I think so." He squeezed her hand. "Thanks, Mom. Thanks for finding me...it was getting pretty hard."

She let her tears flow, finally. Billy held her hand in both of his while she cried. The tears ran down her cheeks. She wondered if she'd ever stop crying; she knew she wasn't in charge of this. There was a knock at the door. Corey took a towel and wiped her eyes. When her crying finally slowed, Will nodded okay, and Corey let in a police officer. He handed her a manilla envelope. She'd been waiting for this, a picture of "Teaser" White. She studied the photo, still wiping away her tears. Teaser's face was sensitive, she thought.

She took a slow breath. "Can I ask some questions, Billy?"

"I guess. Sure."

"I want you to tell me what the guy looked like. Anything at all. Just go over everything, even if you said it already. I want you to picture him in your mind."

Billy closed his eyes. "Army jacket, green, camo-colored. Some kind of blue stocking cap with holes for his eyes. It came down to his neck. Let me see, uh, jeans. Gloves, black ones. Old hiking boots. And this sharp knife with a bone handle. At least I think it was bone." He shrugged. "That's all I remember."

"Keep him in your mind." Corey took out the picture. "Could this be the man?"

Billy looked at the photo. "I can't tell."

"Take your time."

He tried again. "He seemed smaller than that." He hesitated, studying the picture carefully. "Un-unh, I don't think it's him."

❖

As AARON WAS DRIVING his father's Volvo off the ferry onto Bainbridge Island, Star's cell phone had rung. It was Teaser. While Aaron carefully stayed in line, Star mostly listened, saying only "okay" or "got it." He was going over the plan, hitting the high points, light speed, knowing she could do it. When Teaser was done talking, Star said, "Okay, Jimmy," then, "Okay. No problem." During this, Aaron turned left at the light onto Winslow Way. After she turned off the phone, Star gave Aaron instructions, "Turn around at the Thriftway and drive back on the ferry."

Star decided Aaron must have thought it was some kind of test or something because he just did it. But it wasn't, and his father's Volvo ended up on the main deck, near the back. Before the ferry left, she had him call home, told him what to say.

Thirty-five minutes later the *Wenatchee* was approaching Seattle. They'd made a round trip. On the ferry ride back to Seattle, Star had explained that the meeting was off. Cancelled. She'd quickly gone over what "Jimmy" had said, then told them that they'd discuss it later. Aaron was still in the driver's seat, confused. Maisie sat beside him, stewing. In back, Star was reading a movie magazine, trying to figure how to play this just so. Teaser had said she had to make them sweat. She scratched her arm, where she had a rash that came on while they were waiting in the ferry line, and went over Teaser's instructions again. She knew he was counting on her to do this slick as spit. Teaser knew how smart she could be when she focused her energy on a project.

"I want to talk with Jimmy," Maisie announced, fingering the band aid on her burned palm.

"You can't," Star said, plainly irritated. "We've been over that already."

"Then go over it again," Maisie said. "I still don't get it."

"It's off. Period."

"Why?"

"Honey, right about now the last thing I need is a spoiled little rich girl who can't hear the word *no*."

"Jesus—"

"Star," Aaron interrupted. "You could lighten up, okay? I mean you can see why Maisie's upset. Why don't you go through it one more time? Just tell us what happened. It would help if we understood."

"Yeah. Please," Maisie implored. "Hey, I'm sorry. I'm just really bummed. I mean you can't imagine how up I was for this."

Star let them wait. She liked the way this was going, silky.

"The last time. Right?"

"Right. Absolutely."

"Okay." She leaned toward the front seat. "Here's the deal. Your father was watching my apartment. He saw your friend, Will, following you. He searched him, checked his wallet, then left him tied in the basement of an apartment building across the street—"

"Is Will okay?" Maisie interrupted.

"He scared him, but he didn't mess him up."

"You're sure it was Will?" Aaron asked, confused.

Star shot him a look, *are you a damn fool or what?* "William Logan-Stein?"

"Will," Aaron said. "Uh-huh."

"Now that's bad, but on his way out, Dave found this dead guy, some kind of vagrant. The guy had been stabbed to death. I mean right there, in the alley." Star paused, letting the bossy little fuck chew on that. "Your dad didn't see anyone, and he had no idea what happened. Anyway, he kind of freaked. He called Jimmy and said not today, it wasn't safe. He said he thought he could trust you, but now he wasn't sure." Star raised both hands. "He said it was off until he figured out what was going down. You fucked up. End of story."

"Fuck. Fuck..." Maisie was crying. "We had nothing to do with this. Nothing. I swear it."

Star let her cry, then offered, "Your dad's afraid someone was trying to set him up."

"Who? Verlaine?"

"Maybe."

"He doesn't know anything. I swear. And Will probably wanted to get stoned or something. I bet he was just waiting there, working up the nerve to knock. He doesn't know anything either." Maisie wiped her eyes on the sleeve of her shirt. "And I don't have any idea about the dead guy. Not a clue. That had to be some kind of fluke deal."

"If that's true, *if*, you don't need to worry. Jimmy will help."

"What can we do?" Maisie asked.

Star let that one hang a minute. "Dave's going to be watching this, like a test. Go home. Tell your parents you didn't feel well or something. You're going to have to play dumb. Are you up to that?" She looked first at Aaron.

"Yeah. Sure."

"That's not a problem. Un-unh," Maisie confirmed. "When can we see Jimmy?"

"I'll work on that. You have to stay away from my place for awhile. I'll get you a message at the Blue City." Star frowned, serious. "Your parents, and the police, are going to ask you all kinds of questions. They'll be all over you, I mean in the worst way. Remember, Dave's out there, waiting and watching. If you say anything about your dad, or about Jimmy—it's over. You'll never see your dad again." She glared at Maisie. "He's a careful man, and he's spooked, I can tell you that." She waited, a long beat. "Your only hope is that Jimmy can cool him out."

"Tell my dad we won't say a word. I promise that. Tell Jimmy, too. And we'll talk with Will, tell him to leave us alone."

"Be careful. If they even get close to Jimmy, your dad will disappear. All it takes is one nosy cop and—*poof*—he's gone."

"I promise. We can handle this," Maisie said. "What do I do?"

"Honey, you can't even know what happened."

"Okay. Right. How about this? We're totally surprised. When they ask questions, we just tell everyone that the three of us have something special going. Great sex, you know?"

"Uh-huh," Star said. "How does it work?"

"We just say that whatever happened to Will didn't have anything to do with us. We were getting it on. That will make them change the subject. And there were no drugs. I'll take their damn test. Will was just at the wrong place at the wrong time."

"Okay. Good. It protects your dad."

"Yeah, it's cool," Aaron said. "And Will knows it's true."

"Are you cool, Aaron?" Maisie asked.

"So-so. I'm pissed at Will. I mean he really messed it up. If he hadn't been following, your dad never would have found the other guy. Jeez, that guy could have been there since last night, even longer."

"If you think you're pissed, imagine how I feel," Maisie said. "Jesus, I didn't get to see my dad and now I've got to go into that fucking drug program." She looked at Star. "Will I be okay?"

"I'll come see you, help you out with any problems."
Star straightened a lock of Maisie's hair, thinking she
was playing this smooth as a Jimi Hendrix riff. She could
picture Teaser—so proud of her. "Okay?"

Maisie took her hand. "Okay."

❖

COREY ARRIVED AT TOBY Paulsen's soon after Aaron and
Maisie. Maisie's parents, Verlaine and Amber, Abe and
Lou Ballard were also there, seated around the dining
room table. Lou was methodically questioning Aaron
and Maisie. Abe signaled Corey, and they met in the
hall. He looked haggard. "How's Will?" he asked.

"He's okay. A little groggy, but okay. Thank God."
She put her hand on his neck. "He sends his love. Lou's
got a man watching him. I told him you'd be by later."

"Good." He pulled her close, held her. "I was
scared," Abe whispered. "I start sweating when I think
about it." He closed his eyes, opened them.

"Uh-huh. Uh-huh," she repeated, softly. She held
him for a long while, feeling herself slowly unwind.
When she was ready, she stepped back. "Abe, I thought
it was Teaser. I don't know why, maybe it's the wire, the
way he was hanging there. It reminded me of Jolene,
wired to the bedposts. I mean I know Billy's—Will's—
wallet's gone, and he wasn't hurt... Anyway, it wasn't
rational. Just my gut..."

"Did Will see a picture?"

"Yeah. He says he didn't think it was him."

"I don't get it."

"I don't either. I'm guessing Teaser's, somehow, a step ahead of everyone." She took his hand, feeling another wave of anxiety, what could have been, coming on. When it passed she felt deficient, achingly aware that she hadn't done well protecting her son. She turned to see Aaron and Maisie. She didn't like Maisie's coy little smile. "What's going on here?" she asked, trying to move on.

Abe led her into the dining room. "They say they were at Star's for sex. Afterwards, they rode the ferry. No kidding. That's their story. I don't believe it. Lou's taking them through it, step by step."

Corey nodded at everyone, then she and Abe sat down at the long pine table. She was worn-down, too. Not ready, yet, to deal with this.

"Lay off, Verlaine," Maisie was saying. "If it's safe sex, I can *do the dirty deed*," she made her *what-a-scuz* face at him, "with anyone I want. Remember?"

"Someone was killed," Lou said, softly. "He was following Will—your good friend Will—who was hung by wires from a pipe. He could have been killed too."

"Look, I don't know any Franklin. And Jesus, I can't believe what happened to Will, but we were making love at the time." Maisie ran a hand through her short hair, smiling just a little, as if she were remembering the sex. "And by the way, Star was there, I sure-as-hell know that."

"Has Star introduced you to anyone else?" Lou asked.

"Not yet," Aaron said.

"Has she talked to people on the phone?"

"She doesn't take calls when we're getting it on."

"Maisie," Abe's big face was as wrinkled as his ancient tweed jacket. "I'd like to help—"

"Shrinks don't help, they mess around in other people's private business." She sighed. "Stay out of mine, okay?"

"I can't. I'm Will's father—"

"Stepfather, isn't it?"

"Maisie, you've proven you can be nasty, but it doesn't become you, nor does it change what I have to say. I think you're both in danger, I'm not sure how or why. You need to tell Sergeant Ballard anything and everything you know. I think lives are at stake."

Maisie groaned.

"Look, what happened to Will is very scary," Aaron said. "And maybe what Maisie and I were doing was bad. But that doesn't mean that man Franklin died for it. Or Will was mugged for it."

"I agree. Why are we assuming that these things are connected?" Toby asked. "If—"

"I'm sorry," Corey interrupted, impatient. "They are connected."

"How can you be so sure?" Toby asked. "Your paranoia—and that's what it is—turns the sad facts of urban life into some kind of diabolical conspiracy. What happened was horrendous, but we have no evidence that it was connected to these young people."

"Unless they're lying," Lou interjected, before Corey could take Toby's head off.

Corey turned to the Daniels. She'd seen enough. Aaron and Maisie were lying. Skillfully. She was afraid it was something they were learning to like. An acquired taste, like eating snails. It would be awful if that happened. She focused on Amber. "What if their beliefs led them into something they didn't understand? What if they thought they were doing the right thing by lying? Can you imagine that?"

"Well…" Amber paused, considering this.

Lou's cellphone rang. "Ballard," he said. He listened, then punched off. "The ferry bit checked out. A cashier at the cafeteria on the *Wenatchee* ID'ed their photos. She even described a girl with a gold ring in her eyebrow and a long, red scarf."

Maisie raised her scarf. Amber nodded, relieved.

"Are you surprised?" Toby asked.

"Yeah, I am," Lou said.

"Nice," Maisie muttered.

"Sergeant, it's possible we got in over our heads with Star," Aaron offered. "But she didn't do anything to Will, or to Mr. Franklin. If you like, we'll stay away from her for awhile."

"I want to talk with her," Lou said. "If she doesn't come back to her place, can you set that up?"

"I'll try," Maisie said. "If I hear from her."

It was quiet for a minute. The only sound was Abe tinkering with his pipe. Corey picked at her thumbnail, restless.

Abe looked up. "I'm afraid Maisie and Aaron aren't telling us everything. I believe that they're exercising extremely bad judgement that could put them, and Will, in danger. I don't think either of them should be without adult supervision at all times."

"Why don't you keep them home for a couple of days?" Lou suggested.

Toby tapped his fingertips on the table while he considered this. "If you think it's advisable."

"I do."

"Fine." Verlaine nodded.

"We're grounded?" Maisie asked, incredulous. "We haven't done anything."

"It's a precaution," Toby said.

"Against what?" Aaron countered. "It's not fair."

"Grounded? I haven't been grounded since I was thirteen." Maisie looked at Verlaine. "This is crazy."

"That's enough," Verlaine said.

"It's just a few days, and it's the holiday," Amber added.

"You're not telling us everything," Abe said. "It's not a game, Maisie."

Maisie turned away, giving up. Aaron took her hand.

Corey and Abe stood. "Toby, Verlaine, Amber." Corey looked at each of them in turn, amazed at their naivete. She didn't have the energy to even try reaching them. Corey turned her gaze to Aaron, then Maisie. "If you're lying, you're risking your lives. For God's sake Maisie, is it worth it?"

Maisie glanced back. "Abe, is she always so gloomy?" she asked. "I mean Corey, don't you ever fool around?"

CHAPTER THIRTEEN

THANKSGIVING DINNER WAS A topic that the Logan-Steins and Jesse had learned to avoid. Soon after Abe and Corey married, Jesse insisted they celebrate the holiday at her house. She promised it would be a small, family affair. Several weeks later she let slip that she'd included just a few close friends. That first Thanksgiving, seventeen people showed up, most of whom Abe and Corey had never met. This year, Corey, Abe and Billy were celebrating Thanksgiving at home. Jesse was welcome, though when they invited her, she explained that she was hosting her own intimate Thanksgiving dinner.

Abe and Corey arrived at Jesse's at 9:00 a.m. Thanksgiving morning. Corey ignored the winding driveway, the covered parking. She still parked on the street, in case she wanted to leave in a hurry. At the big fir door she was always uneasy.

"Are you staying for dinner?" Jesse greeted them at the door. "Where's Billy?"

"Mom, we need to talk," Abe said.

"Is Billy okay? You said he'd be fine," Jesse persisted.

How, Corey wondered, *did she make it sound like—I know something's wrong, and why did you keep it from me?*

"It's not about Billy," Abe explained. "He is fine."

Abe took his mother's elbow and steered her to the sun room, where he sat her on the camel back loveseat. He and Corey sat across from her on the matching sofa. "We want to talk about the mayor's task force on neighborhoods," he said. "The one you chair."

"Oh... Why?"

Corey imagined she saw Jesse's antennae come out—long, green stems—between the "oh" and the "why."

"You're focusing press attention on Luther Emerson's murder."

"So?"

"The police want to close the case, get you off their backs."

"Good. They can make an arrest."

Abe leaned forward, focused. "Corey and I are the suspects."

"Agh," Jesse stood. Corey thought she saw waves of steam rolling off her mother-in-law. "Corey?" Jesse eventually asked.

"No, Jesse, I didn't murder anyone." Corey tried to stay civil. She went over their history with Luther, detailing what they'd done the night he was killed. "But this is complicated," she explained, "Lieutenant Norse has it in for you. He believes you blackballed him—"

"Perhaps you've misunderstood." Jesse's smile was saccharine and dismissive.

"I doubt it."

Jesse cranked up her megawatt smile. "We can handle this. You didn't kill him," she said. "Norse is a realist. I'll talk with Jason."

Corey looked up at Jesse. "I already did," she said. "He's going to lay the groundwork with Lieutenant Norse. But so long as I look good for it—"

Jesse turned to Abe, interrupting, "She did shoot this Luther."

"You did fuck Nick Season," Corey wanted to say to the back of her mother-in-law's head. She bit her tongue instead and looked out the window, resigned. She was thinking Jesse was expert at making her feel—*What was it?*— not quite good enough? Yeah. No one else could do that.

Corey watched a cloud and listened to Abe. He was going over how Jesse's press conference made it impossible for the police to ignore what they'd done, then he reiterated how Norse was looking for payback. When Abe finished, Corey turned back.

"Okay. Fine," Jesse was saying. "I'll back the group off Luther Emerson. But Abe, you and your wife can't go around shooting people just because you don't like the way they treat their children—"

"I shot him," Corey interrupted, fed up, "because he went after my husband—that's your son—with a skinning knife." Corey held her mother-in-law's eyes. "Jesse, you may be God's own gift to city hall, but you never seem to get it when we need you."

Jesse shot Abe a look. When would his wife stop having these lapses? "If you'd called when Billy—"

"See you later, mom," Abe interrupted. "Happy Thanksgiving."

❖

"WHY CAN'T YOU LEAVE me the fuck alone?" Maisie asked Abe, wondering why he'd become such a total pain. A shrink that dropped by your house? Yuck.

"I'm worried." He watched her across the table in the Daniels' garden room.

"We've been through this already."

"Toby Paulsen called." When she didn't react, Abe added, "He'd like to help."

"Jesus, is there anyone who doesn't know you're my shrink?" Maisie's knee was working. "Who told him? You?"

"Your dad talked to him about the drug program. He mentioned me. He should have asked you first."

"Well he didn't." And he never would.

"I'm sorry. But he's frightened."

"Two things scare Verlaine—sitting at a bad table and missing the perfect time to exercise his stock options... and, oh yeah—saying 'nigger' by mistake."

"Okay, you're angry at him. I get it. How about this? I'll work with your dad—"

"Stepdad."

"Right, stepdad. I'll try and back him off a little."

"And what's my end of this deal, I blow Verlaine?"

"Maisie, work with me."

"I tried that...and got dumped in the junkie bin."

"I'm sorry you feel that way."

"Yeah, sure."

Abe gave her a moment then changed the subject. "Would you help me understand what you and Aaron are doing with Star?"

"We're both doing the same woman. Okay? Is that some kind of a crime?"

"No, it's not. But it may be more dangerous than you know."

"It's safe sex, remember."

"Cut me a little slack, huh? I'm not Verlaine." He raised his big hands, an "I surrender" gesture, trying, at least, to make her smile, make some connection.

She sighed, and started tapping her thumb on the kitchen table. She didn't have time for this. She had things to do. Like getting ready for her dad.

"I want to know if you've ever seen Star around this man." Abe showed her the picture of Teaser.

She looked at the photo, carefully. "Un-unh," she said, looking closer still, frowning. "Who is this guy?"

Abe watched her. He leaned in, looking puzzled. "People call him Teaser White. He's a convicted felon, just out of prison. He may be a murderer. If you ever see him, or if Star mentions him, tell me or Sergeant Ballard immediately."

"If Teaser," she made a wry face, "comes over, you'll be the first to hear." Maisie was looking at him now. "Now why don't you just back off? Okay? I've had enough of this third-degree deal."

Abe didn't respond. His face was lined, thoughtful. "Suppose, Maisie, that you made a mistake about Star. Suppose that she wasn't just interested in sex or in partying. Suppose she had an ulterior motive..."

Maisie kept tapping, wondering why he never, ever, stopped talking. Maybe that's why Will was always with his family. He had to talk about everything.

"Now suppose you were so angry at Verlaine, at most of the adults you know, that you couldn't see it."

Shit. Suppose you have no idea whatsoever just what's going down here. Or what I'm going for. Or how important it is. "Or suppose that I was ganged up on by a bunch of sanctimonious PC hypocrites who can't stand the idea that I actually live my own life."

"Who?"

"All of the grown ups at school talk the talk. Verlaine, Aaron's parents, my teachers, my advisors, all of them get real earnest and tell us about every kind of equality, about treating people fairly even if they're different, about doing the right thing even if it's hard, about a person's right to control their own life. And by the way, I intend to get into every Ivy I apply to. So why is it that when I try sex with a street-savvy, really cool woman, everyone gets totally bummed out? Everyone! The PC hypocrites, the dot com millionaires, the ironic hipsters...even you!"

"You know I'm not like that."

"I hoped you weren't but I was wrong."

"What do you want me to do?"

"Cancel the rehab." And disappear. Poof. Out of here.

"I can't do that. You have to give up the drugs."

"Like my mom?"

Abe didn't say anything.

"She called that lady shrink, cut back her meds. You got her off," Maisie smirked at the double meaning, "without your pathetic little rehab."

"Your mom's a grown woman, and prescription drugs are not illegal. And you're too smart to think that."

"It's nice to have your trust."

"Maisie, I'm not your stepdad, I'm not your teacher nor your advisor. My only goal is to keep you safe and well—"

"Then just fuck off. Okay?" She turned back at the kitchen door. "And don't talk about me with my mom."

❖

THANKSGIVING IS RIGHT, TEASER thought, watching the leaves blow by the gates of the Western Corrections Center. He was waiting in his royal blue Mustang, thinking how he could turn trouble to opportunity. Here was this prison-trash-bitch making Star, making the connection to Luther. Maybe even putting him with Luther. The spotlight was on. But he didn't numb up. No. He just changed the order of things. Which made it more interesting. And when Aaron and Maisie came home, the light dimmed. So now he could do the last part—even if he had to do it first. And Maisie and her itchy Chinaboy could come last. No problem.

He started feeling the little things, thinking about Maisie last night. Daddy's Girl. He poked at his burn. Yeah, there was a tingling. Sort of a buzz. He ran his tongue between his teeth. He could feel the scar, a little ridge snaking across his tongue. It was time, he realized. Time to use his name. He'd already picked the name. Picked it, tried it, and saved it. Loki. He said it out loud, once, then again, savoring the sound of it. He'd found Loki, hunted him down in his research on the dark gods, the demons, and the vampires. Loki was handsome, engaging, and unpredictable. He had great cunning and strategies for every eventuality. He had domain over fire and was a master magician. Loki was an evil, shape-shifting demon who could be, and do, so many things. He could be a woman or a giant or a falcon or a vampire. A shrewd, careful, fine-looking vampire. Perfect.

He flashed his lights. There Dave was, right on time. He was carrying a bag with his things, coming toward the car. Teaser wanted to laugh. The man's shaved head was too small for his body. It looked like a golf ball because Dave was so built up, like a linebacker. Five years on the free weights. Five years pumping iron, practicing weird martial arts, and talking nonstop, like a woman. Teaser felt a wave of nausea, then he thought about Maisie and collected himself. Dave stood by the far door of the Mustang, waiting. Teaser leaned across the seat, opened the unlocked door for Dave.

"What's that shit you're wearing?" Dave asked.

Teaser should have known. He came all this way to pick him up and Dave was going to treat him like a dog turd.

"You hear me? You look like some fucking street scum. Do I have to buy your clothes?"

"Sorry, Dave," Teaser said. "I didn't think to dress up."

"We're outside now. You're part of my plan now." Dave leaned over, put his hand on the back of Teaser's neck. "You want to please me outside, pussy?"

Teaser bit the inside of his cheek. He hated when Dave called him that. "You know I do, Dave." Teaser started the car. "Do you want to drive?"

"You drive. Is everything ready?"

"We found a place on Bainbridge Island. Very quiet, very private. And I fixed up the basement, like you wanted."

"Good. That's good."

"Thank you, Dave."

❖

"How about we go fishing? The Yakima?" Will asked Abe as they left the hospital. Will went slowly, step by careful step. Walking was harder than he remembered.

"It'll be cold," Abe reminded him.

"We can fish nymphs. You know, below the Thorpe Bridge..."

Abe put an arm around his stepson. "Okay. Let's do it."

They walked a little further before Will said, "I'm sorry, you know," He made a sweeping gesture with his hand, "for every—"

"No, no," Abe softly interrupted. "I'm the one who should be apologizing."

"Uh, what did you do?"

"You did what you said you'd do: tried to get Star's address. And you did it with our permission. You wanted us out of it, sure, but we knew that." Abe slowed. "You didn't go in her apartment. You didn't do anything we asked you not to do." He turned to face Will. "We didn't stop you. We should have kept you out of it. Period. Even if you didn't like it."

Will thought this over. His dad was old-fashioned, but he was right there. Huh. He turned away, saw his mom's truck. The old black vehicle made him feel good. He wasn't sure why. He looked back at Abe. He'd learned from his dad to say just where he was—not to worry it too much. "Thanks," he said, summing it up.

Corey pulled up, and in ten minutes they were in their living room. Thanksgiving smells had made their way out from the kitchen and settled comfortably in the nooks and crannies of the old house. Corey lit a fire in the big river-rock fireplace. The table was set with Corey's grandmother's china, colorful cloth napkins, and two festive flower arrangements. Will gave his mom a thumbs up as she drifted toward the source of the smells.

"I saw Maisie this morning," Abe told Will, who was watching the fire. "She seems," he paused, "suddenly angry, and impatient. Help me out here. Do you know why?"

"Are you her shrink?"

"I can't answer that."

"Yeah, he is," Corey yelled from the kitchen. "It's common knowledge now. Abe, for godsakes, you can tell your own son."

"You can tell him, I can't. Sorry, Will."

"It's okay. Anyway, she's usually pissed off about something. Mostly at Verlaine."

"Our last session, I couldn't reach her. That's why I need your help. I'm convinced Maisie and Aaron are in danger, and I have to ask you some questions that you may not want to answer."

Will frowned. "Are you guessing, or are you sure?"

"Pretty sure, yes."

"This stays between us?"

"Yes." Abe fussed with his pipe, tried to light it.

Will watched his dad jerk back as a match burnt his fingertips. He smiled, wondering how it was that Abe was so good at complicated things when he couldn't light his own pipe. "Okay, let's go."

Abe finally blew out a steady stream of smoke, satisfied. "Does Maisie often lie?"

"To adults, sometimes. Especially to Verlaine. She pretty much comes and goes as she pleases—Verlaine's honor system." Will made a face, *get real*. "Maisie calls it the get-out-of-jail-free deal." Will relaxed a little when Abe's eyes twinkled at that. "She lies when she doesn't want them to know what she's doing."

"And Aaron?"

"I guess, but it's not like ordinary lying." Will hesitated, thinking this through. When he tried to get something just right, it made him feel like Abe. "Aaron makes rules, like his dad. In some situations lying isn't against his rules."

"I don't get it."

"He says lying is when you say one thing and do something else. He thinks grown-ups do this all the time without knowing it—like saying every person is unique and special but giving special status to Ivy Leaguers." Will paused, pensive. "Aaron believes it's okay to lie if you know it and if you're doing it for a good reason. So if he decides something's right to do—like helping Maisie—then he'll lie if he has to, to get there."

"Give me a recent example," Abe said.

"Sexual freedom. The real thing."

"So what did he do?"

"First, he set it up so he stayed at his grandmother's. She's really old, not all there. Most of that week he was at Star's, where he and Maisie and Star could do whatever. At least once they stayed all night. He lied to his grandma—told her he came back late then left early for school. She's in bed at those times, and she can barely hear, so she believes whatever he says."

"Didn't anyone check on him?"

"The thing was, he jiggered the voicemail so it picked up on the first ring. He called in, got the messages."

"And his dad doesn't get it?" Abe leaned in. His brow had furrowed, making little lines run down to the bridge of his nose.

"His dad doesn't want to get it. He just wants Aaron to think like him. To be like him."

"So Aaron takes advantage of him?"

"He's not mean. He tries not to hurt people—that's one of his rules. It's more like he thinks what he does is better—more deliberate, more self-aware—than the way grown ups do things. And he's good at it." Will watched his father listening carefully. He liked that Abe really tried to understand what was what. Will decided to help him out. "The truth is, Aaron can play his dad like a violin. He knows how Toby thinks, how Toby wants him to be. One way or another, Aaron usually gets what he wants." Will raised a palm—an Abe-like, *Yes, it's true* gesture.

"That helps." Abe nodded. "Does Aaron actually know what he wants?"

"Aaron wants sex." Will shrugged, a fact was a fact. "Afterwards, Maisie pretty much decides what he wants."

Corey was in the room now, paying close attention. "Did you show Maisie the picture?" she asked.

"Yeah. She said she didn't know Teaser. I think her reaction was genuine."

"Huh. It's possible she's never seen him." She frowned. "I hope that's true." There was a knock on the door. "That's Lou," Corey explained. "He called to check on Will, and I asked him for dinner."

"Sergeant Ballard?" Will asked.

"He's lonely."

❖

TEASER PUSHED THE MUSTANG down Wyatt Way, swinging left around the head of the Bay, then making the soft right up Bucklin Hill. Dave had talked non-stop on the ferry, checking Teaser out on every detail of his plan. Teaser had to keep thinking about Maisie, and about what he was going to do, or he would have gone for Dave's eyes, and even if Dave didn't kill him, that would have ruined everything. Mercifully, Dave had fallen asleep as they drove off the ferry, and he was still sleeping as the Mustang passed Blakely School. Teaser took a slow breath, looking over at Dave. The guy had full lips, a small nose, and light brown eyebrows you could barely see. It was the big brown eyes, though, and the easy lines that spread out from them when he smiled, that got you in trouble. You thought you could talk to him. That he understood things. When all he was doing was getting what he wanted.

There was a big view down to Rich Passage on the right, before they moved through the trees toward Port Blakely. Teaser took another breath. Outside of Winslow, where the ferry docked, the City of Bainbridge Island was still semirural, and here, where much of the land had been owned by the Port Blakely Mill company, it was still sparsely developed, largely two and a half acre parcels. Teaser didn't like the country. There were too many ways to get fucked up, like insect bites, breaking an ankle in some damn animal hole, or just losing your way. He turned right on Country Club Road. He remembered this corner. Star had told him that this was where three young locals, two teenagers and a twenty-two year old, had been killed in 1989. That stayed with him. Star had a head full of things like that. When she couldn't sleep, or got tired of her music, sometimes she went online. One of her online projects was to research murders of Seattle-area teens.

Dave stirred when they turned right up Fort Ward Hill. Here the firs were so high and thick that sections of the road were dark, though it was still afternoon. Dave woke up when they turned off the road. The dense, lush groundcover made it impossible to see through the trees. It made Teaser uneasy. The winding path was not a county road, and the people who owned this isolated rental cottage hadn't filled the potholes. The Mustang bounced along, twisting and turning through the forest for another quarter mile. The road dead-ended at a clearing. The cottage was centered in the cleared area. It was painted white with blue trim below a black shingle roof. The stone path to the front door wound through a winter garden, and there were fruit trees in back.

"The house looks okay," Dave said, after they opened the front door. Inside, the cottage was clean and sparsely furnished. Dave eyed the kitchen table and chairs. He said they looked "adequate." He nodded toward the cupboards. "You get the supplies?"

"Everything you asked for." Star, in fact, had done the shopping—he gave her little projects, kept her busy—but Dave didn't need to know that.

In the living room, there was a couch, two armchairs, and a coffee table in front of the brick fireplace. "How much?"

"$750 a month."

"Are you shitting me? For this?"

"You've been away over five years. On Bainbridge Island, $750 is nothing."

"The basement?"

Teaser pointed toward the basement door, gesturing for Dave to inspect it.

Dave checked the door, he could see where it had been fortified, and soundproofed. He flicked the light switch, then walked down the steps. The basement was a windowless box. Everything had been cleared out. Soundproofing materials had been crudely nailed to all the walls and to the ceiling. There was a drain in the center of the concrete floor and a cot against each wall. On one wall, a new Polaroid Instant Camera sat on a plywood shelf. An iron ring had been bolted to each of the other three walls. Handcuffs, with a three-foot chain between the shackles, were hanging from each ring.

"We don't need the hardware," Dave said, his voice soft. "That's not in the plan."

"She has a friend."

Dave tensed up, scowling. "What friend?"

"I decided to change the plan, Dave."

Dave turned toward him. "You don't ever decide anything, you dickless fuck. Who's the man?" he snarled, then louder, "Who's The Master?"

"You're the man, Dave." Teaser gripped a jabstick, a syringe pole, he'd hidden under the steps. While The Master stared at him, angrily, he stuck the long needle into Dave's chest, automatically injecting a large dose of a tranquillizer. He'd found it on a site that specialized in tranquilizing wildlife in the field and selected a syringe load that would anesthetize a three hundred pound black bear. "You're The Master, Dave."

Dave squirmed on the floor, then he lashed out, roaring, swinging a strong arm toward Teaser's leg. Teaser stepped back, just watching, mesmerized. Moments later, he wasn't sure how long, Dave went out.

Teaser watched The Master, lying there. And he felt something good.

A half-hour later Teaser was sitting on an overturned bucket, running his tongue over his lower teeth. He was watching Dave wake up, taking it all in. Dave was cuffed to the wall, naked. His golf ball head was moving, just barely.

Teaser saw the growing awareness, the fear, in Dave's face. He wondered if Dave could imagine what he'd planned for him. He tried picturing the look on Dave's face when he first saw Maisie. It made the feeling inside start to swell.

Teaser stood, his eyes hardwired to Dave's face. Slowly, he spread his arms. "I am Loki, Master, welcome to my house," he said.

CHAPTER FOURTEEN

THE LOGAN-STEINS AND LOU Ballard were at the end of their Thanksgiving feast. The lingering smells of stuffing, corn bread, cranberry sauce, sweet potatoes, and now, pumpkin pie, had taken over the dining room. Two empty wine bottles sat beside the turkey carcass on a side bar. Lou was still working on a second helping of pumpkin pie, liberally splashing on the whipped cream.

Billy bounded into the room, plainly excited. "I just got an email from Morgan," he interrupted them. "She wants to come back for Christmas. Can she stay with us?"

"Of course," Abe said as Corey said, "We'll see."

Corey laughed. "OK, sure. Sometimes, I'm an old-fashioned mom."

"Hardly," Abe reassured her.

"Speaking of which..." Lou said, between mouthfuls. "I gotta ask this, Abe. I mean it's years I've wanted to ask you this."

"So ask." Abe looked at Lou, wary. "I don't have to answer."

"What's the deal with your mother? I mean I never even heard about anyone like her."

Corey looked at her plate. Will laughed out loud.

"She's very able," Abe offered, cautious.

"C'mon..."

"Give him a taste," Corey suggested.

"Right. Okay." He sat up straighter, readying himself to slog through the swamp that still sucked him down when he thought about her. "My mother's mother, 'Bootsie' Larsen made her only daughter swim in the freezing cold waters of Puget Sound, off Richmond Beach, every day—May through September—between the ages of five and fifteen. She believed it built character and purged impure thoughts. At sixteen, my mother was a tennis champion, a world class sailor, and valedictorian at Saint Nicholas—Lakeside for girls in those days. She went to Stanford then on to Yale law. At twenty-eight, Jesse was running her own consulting firm, making and breaking big-time politicians."

"Hmm... Mother like yours, smarter than everyone, connected. How is it you turned out, I dunno, the way you did?"

Abe shrugged, his face lively again. "My dad gets the credit, or the blame, for that...he was this quiet doctor, and he was, well, he was just there for me...we used to take walks and talk. He was a good listener and always responsive. He didn't care what other people thought.

He said it was a waste of time to worry about that." Abe stopped talking, done. He stood, stretching his arms, trying to bring back memories of his father. What he remembered was a big, soft-spoken man who got along with all kinds of weird people. Even his mom. He wished he'd told him how much the walks had meant.

Thinking about his dad usually made him feel good. Tonight it left him low, and a little sorry that he and his mother weren't better friends. Corey said he was too hard on himself. That the miracle of Hanukkah, as far as she was concerned, was that he was still trying with his mom. Maybe it was just the holiday.

Corey watched Abe emptying his pockets, looking for something. She handed him a matchbook off the sidebar, put her arm around his shoulders. "Being her daughter-in-law is..."

Corey looked over at Will.

"I don't mind," Will said.

"I dunno—it's like having your period twice a month."

❖

THE BLUE CITY STAYED open on Thanksgiving. In fact, Marge, the owner, served free pastries to those who didn't have a place to go for Thanksgiving dinner. Aaron came in around 4:00 p.m., ordered a mocha with extra whipped cream for himself and a decaf soy latte for his dad. His dad was waiting in the car, circling the block. Aaron had worked it so that Blue City Cafe coffees would be the culmination of their boring Thanksgiving dinner.

When Marge turned her back to draw the coffees, Aaron asked her, as nonchalantly as he could, if there were any messages for Maisie. Marge puttered around behind the counter before coming up with an envelope and handing it to Aaron. Maisie's first name was written in careful script.

"When did this come in?" Aaron asked.

"How do I know? This isn't a post office."

"Yo, Marge, happy Thanksgiving."

She sighed, tried to remember. "It came through the mail slot before I opened this morning," Marge said, pleased to be able to recall the specifics. "And to you, too, Aaron, a happy Thanksgiving." She smiled as she handed him the coffees.

"Thanks." Aaron sprinkled dark chocolate on top of his whipped cream, then took a sip. "See you later," he called over his shoulder, going out the door.

It was cold, windy, as he turned onto Broadway. His dad's Volvo had just passed by, and Toby was circling the block again. Snow flurries were swirling in the dark, virtually empty street. Aaron stepped into the sheltered entry of a Korean restaurant, where he set down the coffees then tore open the envelope. Inside, a piece of paper was carefully folded into thirds. He unfolded it. The message was printed in block letters. It said:

TONIGHT, 7:30 P.M., SEATTLE CENTER, CENTER HOUSE, SOUTH ENTRANCE.

❖

THE DANIELS FAMILY—MAISIE, VERLAINE and Amber—were sitting around the fire, when Aaron and Toby Paulsen arrived. After coming back from the Blue City, Aaron had called Maisie. They orchestrated it so that he would be invited over to her house. When Maisie suggested that Toby come along too, Verlaine agreed.

After holiday greetings were exchanged, Verlaine ushered them into the library. "How's Nora?" he asked Toby.

"She called this morning. Decided to take the bus home, meander through the heartland. She recharged in New York City and now she wants some time alone. Unplugged, she calls it. No computer, no phone, down time for reflection and introspection." Toby paused. "She said New York was great. She loved the museums, the galleries and the plays. And she saw *Carmen* at the Met last night."

"Ah, New York," Amber spread her hands, smiled at Aaron and Maisie.

Aaron smiled back; he thought Amber seemed friendlier.

"You know, it's great to pack into the wilderness, but New York City is the most exciting place I know," Toby said.

"Pericles believed the city is the source of life," Verlaine said.

Maisie turned to Verlaine. "You said New York was full of snobs and too expensive for ordinary people."

Amber laughed. "It's that, too."

"Could you excuse us a minute?" Aaron asked, before Maisie could say anything else. "There's something I need to discuss with Maisie. I'm interested in this stuff though, so don't go too far without us."

"Take your time." Toby smiled.

"No problem," Verlaine said, watching the kids leave, then turning. "Toby," he leaned in, "we're putting together a table at the Market fundraiser."

Aaron and Maisie went directly to her room.

"Let me see it," she said, after closing the door.

Aaron put the envelope on her bed. Maisie read the note. Her mouth pinched up, and her eyes closed in frustration. He knew what was worrying her, and he'd been working on a way to solve the problem.

"We're grounded. How do we get out?" she finally asked. "Have you thought about it?"

"Nothing but." He sat beside her. "I say we keep it simple. Plead for a break—we could suggest that old movie that's screening at school tonight, part of the film club's holiday series—then we take off. Later, we leave a message on my dad's machine: Off to the coast. A done deal. We'll explain after we've connected with your father."

"Yeah. Good. Even the know-it-all stepdad will have to understand that."

"What about Abe?"

"I'm supposed to see him tomorrow afternoon. He'll cool out when I can explain everything."

"Let's do it," Aaron said. Pleased. He knew how important this was for Maisie, and he wanted to make it work. Show her how he felt. He thought it was love. Yeah, if this wasn't love, he didn't know what was.

Maisie leaned over and kissed Aaron. Their kiss lasted a long time, tender and deeply felt.

❖

TEASER MADE THE 5:30 ferry, the *Wenatchee*. He missed the old ferry, the *Walla Walla*, though he never understood why that ferry was named after a town known for its onions, and its prison. He remembered a poster near the ferry's over-sized kitchen. On the poster, the slogan described Walla Walla as "a place so nice they named it twice." Thinking about that made him numb up, so he went outside to check out the night sky.

It was cold on the upper deck, and he could feel the harsh wind, just a little, on the back of his neck. Loki had feelings, he knew that now. He had an idea of it when he was watching Dave, hanging there against the wall, writhing. When he used the coat hanger on him, just to see, he could feel everything, even his heart, pumping too fast. It was so intense that he worried about biting his tongue off, right there in the basement. But he didn't seize up. He wondered what would happen when he started on Maisie.

He was sorry that the clouds were blocking the night sky. Loki liked the stars, he decided. Teaser walked to the railing, looking down at the water. Black night, black water, black wind. Silence was black. And death was black. Teaser knew black. He lived with it. Red was Loki's color.

He felt the wind, but he wasn't cold. It would take time, he reminded himself. For now, it was enough that he could feel anything at night. Still, he wished the feelings didn't come on so hard, then leave so unexpectedly. He knew that would change, soon. Loki thought about Maisie. Daddy's Girl. He felt this tingling feeling on his hands, his neck, and then his groin. He took out the cell phone, called Star.

"Where are you?" she asked, before he could say anything.

"On my way. Not to worry."

"It's set for tonight. You okay, Tease?"

"Call me Loki."

"Loki?"

"Never mind."

"You sure you're okay?"

"Do as I say. I'm ready."

"Don't be mean. What can I do?"

"A baby girl."

"Tonight?" She laughed.

Teaser felt a flash of anger. It was odd, because he never got angry at Star. Ever. Then he realized it was Loki who was angry. Loki wanted girls, baby girls. Baby girls who still had their hot, fresh, baby blood. He wanted one right now—and Loki was just waking up. Teaser felt something new, and strange. It was as if a wave was rising from his groin, washing feeling through his body. He stiffened up, frightened, then it was gone. And Loki was down.

"Say something, Tease. I didn't mean anything bad. You want her tonight? I got my eye on one. We can change our plan."

"You know what to do," he said, softly, then he hung up.

❖

MAISIE AND AARON TOOK Amber's Jeep Cherokee to Seattle Center. Toby and Verlaine had agreed—after some expert pleading—to let them see a revival of *The Graduate* being shown at Olympic by the school's film club. Amber was reluctant, but Verlaine went along with Toby. Toby felt there was nothing to worry about. As he put it, "There's such a thing as being too cautious. They'll certainly be fine at school. They could use a break. And they'll check in."

At 7:20 p.m. they made their way through the old-fashioned carnival, past the booths where you could shoot targets, or throw darts at balloons, or fire a crossbow for stuffed animals. Seattle Center drew a lively crowd at night. Family groups, couples, singles and all kinds of kids. The young people came from all over the city to hang out, size each other up. Occasionally, they'd try the old carny rides, pay for a chance to win stuffed animals or trinkets, or eat the junk food. There was something vaguely seedy about the carnies, looking for marks; and tonight, the kids were a little too loud—on their own, or grouped up, spending their holiday here rather than with their families.

Teaser watched as Aaron and Maisie approached the Center House entry from the South. The House offered fast foods from around the world, a children's museum, performance spaces, retail opportunities, and warm places to sit. It was a place to meet, gather, or simply cruise. Teaser leaned against a shooting arcade. From his spot, he could watch the large doors at the entry, unseen.

Aaron and Maisie stood in front of the doors, unsure what to do. A teenage Korean boy brought Aaron a slip of paper. It had a phone number on it. Maisie went to the pay phone, beside the door. The number answered on the first ring.

"Star?" she asked.

"It's Jimmy, little one," Teaser said. "Are you ready?"

"Oh yes." She breathed a sigh of relief. "Thank you."

"Go to the ferry dock. Park in an indoor lot, downtown. Take the 8:10 to Bainbridge. Walk off to Winslow Way. I'll meet you in the Thriftway parking lot, near the park at the back."

"Great," Maisie said, going really fast. Jesus. She was so pumped she could feel the sweat starting under her arms, at the small of her back. "See you soon."

"Soon," he repeated, melting into the crowd. Invisible.

❖

"I'M SCARED," COREY SAID.

Abe was doing dishes, pensive. He'd been thinking hard about what had changed for Maisie. What had caused her to change. He'd gone over it carefully, and he didn't know. He turned away from the sink. "I'm worried about Maisie," he admitted.

"Are we too jumpy?"

Abe laid the dish towel on the sink, remembering the look on Maisie's face when she told him to fuck off. "I don't think so, no."

Lou shouldered his way through the kitchen door, somehow carrying wine glasses, dessert plates, and salad bowls.

"What about Maisie?" It was Will, right behind him, dumping a load of dishes, then serving himself another piece of pumpkin pie.

"It's like she's on some sort of misguided mission," Corey answered. "What we used to call a death trip." She watched her son take a mouthful. "And her parents are just out there, missing everything."

"That's what they're like." Will finished off the whipped cream.

Abe smiled. He enjoyed Will's appetites, his comfort with them. "Always?" he eventually asked.

Will wiped his mouth. "Maisie says they don't ever see the way things really are. She says Verlaine's more concerned with what a person thinks than what a person is. Like he won't be friends with someone who's for capital punishment. Maisie says it's a way of being."

"Hmm-hmm." Abe's brow furrowed. Will's explanation bothered him. "Is it possible that Maisie could be fooled by someone who promised her something genuinely good? She might ignore who they were—like Verlaine does—because she wanted to believe it."

"The men in this family think too much." Corey was watching Lou, who had taken over the dish washing. "What can we do to help her?"

"She doesn't want our help," Abe said softly, mostly to himself. "She doesn't even know she needs help."

"What about Aaron?"

"Mom," Will put his arms around his mother. "You're wonderful. And you might be right. Okay? But sometimes there's nothing you can do. I mean it, sometimes you have to stay out of it."

"I can't, Will. Let's go see Teaser's CCO."

"His what?" Will asked.

"Community Corrections Officer. These guys supervise people like Teaser."

"Now?" Abe asked.

"Right now. Lou, what's Johnny Raiser's number?"

"Johnny Raiser?" Lou said. "Don't bother him on Thanksgiving unless you got a damn good reason."

"Okay, Lou," Corey interrupted a long silence, "What do you suggest? What can we do?"

Lou looked up from his washing. "I grind my teeth a lot," he offered.

CHAPTER FIFTEEN

THE THRIFTWAY LOT WAS dark, with six or seven cars clustered around the glass entry doors. At 9:00 p.m., Aaron and Maisie walked through the lot, past the post office, toward the back entrance. They stood beside the covered parking area, facing the little park across the street. Teaser, watching, let them wait. He could feel the breeze on his face, feel the concrete wall against his back. Five minutes later he waved them through the covered parking shelter, onto the street where the Mustang was waiting.

"What did you tell your parents?"

"Late movie," Maisie said. "I checked in from the ferry terminal. And Aaron left a message on his dad's machine that we were driving to the ocean afterwards, to see the sunrise. Toby will call Verlaine when he gets home."

"Good. Dave gave me precise instructions. Do exactly as I say." He handed them blindfolds. "Put them on. If you take them off—even once—he won't show himself."

Aaron balked.

"No problem," Maisie said, pointedly, and Aaron put his on, too.

By 9:20 p.m. they were turning off Fort Ward Hill onto the neglected dirt road.

At 9:25 Teaser led them, blindfolded, down the stairs to the basement. The basement light was on. He saw Dave, bloody, bound and gagged, looking at them. Dave, semiconscious and confused, stared at Teaser.

"Where are we, Jimmy?" Maisie asked.

He ran his finger across her cheek, then kissed her lightly on the lips. "Little one, do as I ask."

She nodded, feeling his lips, excited, kissing him back.

"Soon you'll see your father. He's watching now." Teaser stared at Dave. "Daddy's girl," he whispered in Dave's ear.

Dave understood. His face slowly reconfigured until he looked like a man sentenced to burn in Hell. A horrified gagging sound rose from Dave's belly.

Teaser took it all in, every detail.

"What was that?" Aaron asked.

"The dog. He's muzzled now, for you." Teaser was watching Dave. Savoring this. "Dave's a careful man."

"This is spooky," Aaron said.

"Put your hands above your head."

Maisie did as she was told.

"I don't get it," Aaron said.

"It's part of the plan," Teaser said.

"Do it, Aar, please," Maisie said.

Aaron put his hands above his head. Teaser was ready. He backed him up, then cuffed him, chaining

Aaron's wrists to the ring on the wall. He told Aaron that this was how Dave wanted it. Before Aaron could say anything, Teaser covered his mouth with duct tape. Then Teaser tightened the chain until Aaron was on his toes, against the wall.

"What's going on?" Maisie wanted to know.

"Just a minute more, little one," he said. He eased her back against the wall and cuffed her wrists. He looked at her, then Teaser ran his tongue along her lips. "You're about to meet your dad," he whispered. And turning, so Dave could hear. "You're about to meet your dad, and his friend, Loki."

❖

STAR HAD SPENT WEDNESDAY night and most of Thanksgiving day at a girlfriend's apartment in Tacoma. Star and Lisa had looked out for one another in Juvie and become friends. Now, Lisa shared the two-bedroom apartment with her boyfriend, Frank. Teaser paid their rent, and they helped him whenever he asked.

Star went with Lisa to a Belltown bar at 7:00 p.m., where she made it a point to flirt with the bartender. As instructed, she opened the door to her apartment at 9:00. Less than an hour later, the first group of policemen arrived. Teaser had said they were watching the apartment, that they would come within the hour. She smiled. Teaser was right. As usual.

She leaned against the window, waiting. Checking her arms for a rash. Not really itchy, though, because everything was happening. Star watched a policeman, going through her bureau.

She pictured the beach house, thinking about Teaser. Who was Loki, anyway? Just one of his phases, she decided. Teaser could be like that. She'd call him whatever he wanted. Loki? You bet. It was the least she could do.

Since she met him, her life had changed. He had a way of taking charge. Something about the way he was. The way he walked down the street. Like he owned it. He took charge of her, too. With Teaser, she could smooth out and ride the roller coaster. And she always had money, more than she needed, so she didn't have to turn tricks, ever. Best of all, he made sure that she always had things to do, projects. And he'd worked with her, taught her how to get them done...just so.

He took care of her in other ways, too. No one could get her off like Teaser, and she didn't have to go down on him, or anything. She found girls for him, though. Young ones. She had to learn just what he liked. One day she saw him pitch a fit when one of his babies had her period. And she understood. Okay. Plenty of baby girls on the street. No problem. And it was a good arrangement, she thought, because she and Teaser were straight on it. He wasn't like some trick who pretended to be normal, then beat up the girls he picked up. He did little things for her, too. Like looking out for her, and buying her new clothes. The most important thing, though, the thing that made everything else work, was that because of Teaser, she was clean. No junk in over three years. Even when he was inside. She'd come close a couple of times, but the memory of doing the cold turkey, wired to the bed, that kept her off.

The sound of something falling made her look up. She watched the cops going through her stuff and replayed Teaser's instructions. "So long as they're with you," he'd explained, "you're in the clear. In the clear," he'd said again. "They're going to ask you questions. About the dead guy, about the kid, about Maisie and Aaron. You know what to tell them. How to do it...ice out...engine runnin' cool...playin' 'em like a jazz riff... silky smooth."

"No sweat," she'd answered. It was a good project. And after going over it with Teaser, she knew that if she focused, drilled down, she owned it.

Then he added. "Star light, Star bright. Loki will remember."

She'd looked at him, kind of funny. It was just one of his phases, yeah. One time, he opened Baby Holly's vein, and just watched her bleed. Loki? Fine. She'd call him whatever he wanted. She'd do anything he wanted. It always turned out for the best.

❖

TEASER LEFT THEM CHAINED, gagged, and blindfolded, while he started a charcoal fire, outside. When he had the fire going, he came back. Aaron was twitching, so he took off his blindfold, then laid Little Buck against his cheek. Aaron's head snapped back and he was still. Maisie was making gagging sounds. He carefully took the tape off her mouth. Tears were flowing down her cheeks.

"What are you doing?" she sobbed.

"Are you ready to see your father?"

"Why am I like this?"

"You'll understand soon." Teaser kissed a tear from her cheek.

Dave was barely conscious, hanging from the wall opposite Maisie. Teaser slapped his face, waking him up.

Teaser went to Maisie. Slowly, he took her blindfold off. She looked first at Aaron—a line of blood on his face, chained, gagged, and wild-eyed with terror; then at the bloody, newly-scarred man—chained, gagged, and hanging by his wrists, naked. Teaser took Dave's jaw in his hand. He raised his head. "This is Dave," he said, "your father."

She screamed.

Teaser watched, feeling good, getting excited. He decided to go slow. It was everything he'd ever imagined. He felt the wave, rising, then he could feel the shaking in his hands. It was an early warning sign. Go slow, take deep breaths, he told himself. He went over to Dave, who was crying, exactly as he'd pictured it. Teaser felt the wave, swelling again. He took slow breaths. He heard Maisie behind him, sobbing. He turned and put his hands on her face, trying to calm her. She started screaming hysterically, which made him tremble. Feeling Loki's power, he ripped her dress off, then her panties. When she was naked, he said, "I am Loki, little one. Your father was my cellmate. He raped me at night. He made me do unspeakable things. I stopped feeling." He leaned in, putting his cheek to hers. Maisie was shaking. "Do you understand what that means, little one?" he whispered. "I couldn't feel anything." His voice was harsh. "Teaser couldn't feel anything. And Loki was born."

Maisie screamed again, shaking her head wildly, back and forth.

He could feel himself harden, watching her scream. Loki wanted this girl, even though she was too old. Teaser put Loki down. It was harder than ever.

He turned back to Dave, leaned over his twisted body. "It's Loki's turn now, Dave. Loki's turn. Did you think you could use Teaser, humiliate Teaser, and never pay? Did you think you could do that?"

He went upstairs to the sound of Maisie's wails.

❖

ABE WAS RESTLESS. HE called Sam, who reluctantly agreed to drive him to the office, where he'd left Teaser's file. In the Olds, Sam was going on about violent hits in the NFL. "Life-threatening tackles," he patronizingly explained, when Abe didn't respond. He went on to detail how and why violence like this was only acceptable in America. Abe tried to ignore him.

Abe was preoccupied with Teaser. He was carefully going over everything he knew. However he came at it, Abe couldn't get a feel for him. Teaser was still a shadow, a vague dark shape twisting and turning in the night. From where Abe stood, the shape was shifting without rhyme or reason, motive or meaning. In the history Lou had sent him, it said Teaser had been arrested at fifteen, and referred for a psychiatric evaluation. He'd found and faxed Dr. Mark Kramer, the court appointed psychiatrist who had examined Teaser at that time, asking for Kramer's report on Teaser. He hoped the evaluation would be at his office.

It wasn't. Abe mumbled to himself, something coarse about doctors. He hand wrote another, more forceful note, and faxed it off to Dr. Kramer.

Abe opened the file he'd started on Teaser. His real name was Theodore White. He was born in Bakersfield, California. He was accused of assaulting a fourteen-year-old neighbor girl when he was fifteen, but after Kramer's evaluation, it didn't go to trial. There was nothing else in the file until Theodore "Teaser" White was brought up for selling stolen property in L.A., when he was twenty-six. Teaser cut a deal, gave up his fence, and the charge was dropped. He left L.A. soon after. The next entry came from Seattle, six years later, when he was charged with rape of a child in the second degree, for consensual sex with Holly Park, his barely twelve-year-old girlfriend.

From the start, the prosecutor found Holly unreliable. When she ran away, the charge was plea bargained down, and Teaser went to prison for fourteen months.

Okay. Abe sat back. Teaser's father was often in jail, he had a history of violent felony convictions. His mother had been in and out of state mental hospitals. How had Teaser gotten by?

Abe heard the hum of his fax machine. Apparently, Kramer's office was at home, and Abe's more forceful, though still collegial, fax had gotten his attention.

Abe lumbered to the back room. Yes, Kramer had responded. The cover letter explained how he'd given Theodore a battery of tests, then seen him four times. His report followed. Dr. Kramer encouraged Abe to call, saying that he still remembered the case. The boy was so bright, and he'd managed so well in the worst of circumstances. Abe looked out into the night, letting that sink in.

He turned to the report. Apparently, Theodore White began having epileptic seizures when he was four. Kramer suggested that the first seizure may have coincided with a particularly vicious beating Teaser received from his father. Abe settled in, grim.

The report focused on Teaser's so-called assault on the fourteen-year-old. What had happened on the night in question began, in Theodore's words, as his first real "date." He'd asked a neighbor girl he knew from high school to go to a movie. Afterwards, they parked on a secluded street. They were in the back seat, petting heavily, when Theodore had a violent seizure. He bit off her lower lip and half of his own tongue. When the police finally found them, the girl was hysterical, blood all over her face and body. Theodore was unconscious, lying in a pool of his own blood.

Abe closed his eyes, imagining the scene. He saw Teaser waking up, covered in blood and burning with shame. It probably took just an instant for him to put it together, what he'd done. Sex and mayhem. Abe closed his palm over the knuckles of his balled fist, wondering what it was like to be Teaser White.

❖

COREY WAS READING IN bed when the phone rang. "You're welcome, Lou. What's up?" She stopped moving. "Star's at her apartment? I'm on the way."

She was able to reach Abe, who said he'd meet her at Regent Street.

Ten minutes later she was staring at Star, who was leaning against the window of the efficiency apartment. Lou was asking her questions. Another police officer was taking notes. Corey looked her over, sizing her up.

Star wore a loose, white T-shirt, jeans, and an old leather jacket. Her hair was blond. Her face was pretty, and glacial. Her loose fitting clothes didn't hide her fine figure. She had an edge—streetwise, sexy, don't-fuck-with-me. And Star was wound like a coil spring. Corey wondered when she'd done time. At the moment

Star was staring out the window, off somewhere. Corey sensed that she was readying herself. There was no way this experienced woman was interested in Aaron and Masie for sex. No way. She guessed Star was twenty-two.

Lou handed her the file. Star's real name was Sharon Goodwin, and her story was familiar. She was raised in New Haven. Star had run away to be in a band, part of the music scene, at 14. She was picked up for prostitution before she turned 16. Three months later, she got caught buying drugs and went to Juvie. She was 17 when she got out. Star would be 22 on the day before Christmas.

Corey felt an over-sized hand on the small of her back and Abe was there, reading the file over her shoulder. He was focused, oblivious to the police activity around him. Corey waited, restless, eager to catch a break. They were due. When Abe was finished, they walked toward the window. He was gearing up, too; she saw it on his face. Lou introduced them as the parents of the boy who was found wired to a pipe in the basement across the street.

"Her story fits," Lou explained. "They were all here, fooling around. Star rode the ferry with them. She was with a girl friend last night and stayed for the holiday. The friend confirms. They were at a bar earlier this evening, also confirmed. She says she doesn't know Teaser White."

Corey looked her in the eye. Star met her look. "Why are you having sex with these children?" Corey asked, getting right to it.

"Sergeant," Star turned to Lou, indignant. "Straighten this lady out. I don't have to answer that—"

Abe intervened. "If you're not connected to what happened to Will, or to Franklin, we're sorry to bother you. If you know anything about it, please help us now, before anyone else gets hurt."

"Hey, I'm sorry about your boy. And now I'm sorry I ever got near those kids." She bit her fingernail, taking her time about it.

"Why were you with them?" he asked. "They're sixteen."

"Mister, look, I get off on it. It's a thing I do instead of getting wasted." She glanced at Abe, *This is from the heart.* "I mean I don't want to shoot up, so I look for other things to get me off."

"Why these particular kids?" Abe set his jaw, on this like a pit bull.

"No reason. I mean I go to the Blue City sometimes, and I met them and they liked me. That counts for something with me." Star nodded, ever so slightly. *Yes, it's true.*

"Will you see them again?" Abe wanted to know.

Corey stared at her, impatient. She wanted to know, too.

Star looked around the room. She wasn't in any hurry, not at the moment. "I can if I want. You got nothing on me. Like you said, they're sixteen. I didn't do anything wrong."

"I'll make it my business to find something on you," Corey said, aching to bust through this story. "Until you tell me about Teaser White." She said it loudly. Heads turned.

"Who's that?"

"Don't bullshit me," Corey said, intense. "You know who."

"Fuck you." Star shot her a scornful look. "I want my lawyer."

Corey moved even closer, in her face now. "After you tell me about Teaser, I want to know about his eleven-year-old girlfriends, Holly and Jolene."

"What?" Star asked Lou. "Is she crazy?"

"Your pal seduces little girls," Corey said, taking Star's upper arms in her strong hands. She wanted to slam her against the wall. "Do you find them for him?"

Star abruptly pulled free—she was strong, too—pointed at Corey. She was steaming, hot steam rising off dry ice. "Who is this crazy bitch?" she hissed.

"Break it up, ladies." Lou shook his head. Corey and Abe stepped away, through the open door and into the hall.

Corey's face was drawn and tight. She was pulling threads from the sleeve of her blue wool pullover. "She's lying," Corey muttered to Abe.

"Good at it, too," Abe muttered back, making a fist then spreading his fingers. "Very good."

"She's right about one thing. We've got nothing on her. The cutoff age for statutory rape is fifteen." Corey was still picking at her sleeve. She was pretty sure this feeling she had was what the kids called really bummed. "What do we do?"

"Let's go see his CCO, Johnny Raiser," Abe finally suggested. "Ask him to locate Teaser."

"This late?"

"You bet."

They came back in, turned to Lou. Star was on the phone, leaning against the wall, tapping her fingers now, smug, even defiant. She raised her middle finger at Corey.

"She's talking to her lawyer," Lou explained. "You're a pain in the ass," he said to Corey.

Star set the phone down. "He's on his way," she announced, smirking.

"Is he expensive?" Corey asked. "You need a good one."

"Fuck you," Star replied, dismissing her with a brusque, backhanded wave. "And get the hell out of my apartment."

Lou turned to Abe and Corey, "I'll finish up here."

Abe and Corey heard her snap, "What is this good cop, bad cop shit?" as they were leaving.

On the street, Abe stopped. "You okay?" he asked.

"I feel like I haven't slept, you know, jazzed, running on empty." She saw where the sleeve of her sweater was starting to unravel. She took his arm, trying to slow down. When she finally did, she felt low, used up. She wanted to get home, crawl under the covers.

"You tried to get the real story," Abe said. "One of us had to do that," he added, meaning it.

"Do I have to get so worked up about it?"

"Probably not." He hesitated. "You want to back off?"

She leaned against him. "When did that ever work?"

❖

TEASER TURNED THE BRANDING iron sideways. He studied the red-hot snakes, then buried them once more in the charcoal. It was almost ready. He worked hard to go slow, stay calm, hold onto the feelings. He'd had the iron made specially, with Loki's symbol. He'd drawn the symbol in prison. It just came to him one night, like a dream. He drew it, fast—three snakes, balled up together, their heads poised to strike, fangs showing—then he worked on it until he had it just so. Later, he did a simpler version—just the one head, mouth open, fangs bared. He burned that one into his own shaved head using a mirror and a red-hot wire. It took a long time, but it didn't matter. He felt nothing. The day Luther was released, Teaser gave him his drawing to take to a blacksmith, who made the branding iron. The iron was perfect, he knew that already. Dumb-as-dirt Luther thought the iron was part of Dave's plan.

Teaser looked into the black forest that surrounded the house. He couldn't remember the last time he'd felt like this. He took off his watch cap, touched Loki's sign. Loki, he decided, was lucky. Lucky to feel things. Lucky to see things so clearly. And he was Loki more and more now. Maybe Teaser had never felt like this. No, he remembered one time, with his older sister, Polly. It was in Bakersfield, California. Teaser was eleven, and it was the first time she touched him.

He'd shared her bed since his first seizure, when he was four. When he was nine, the seizures stopped for six months, but she kept him in her bed, anyway. He figured out later that it was one of the things his sister did to keep their father away. Which was a big problem when their dad wasn't in jail. Luckily, his father had been in jail seven of his eleven years. When Teaser turned twelve, his father got sent away for ten more years. He was stabbed in the neck that first year. And that took care of Polly's problem.

His father was just a vague memory—a strong man, who used his fists to get what he wanted. His dad would pick him up by a leg and throw him across the room if he didn't do what he ordered. Like fall asleep. One time, his dad wanted him to steal a carton of Camel cigarettes. When he said no, his dad beat him, then hung him by his feet in the basement. His sister found him, hours later. He'd pitched a fit, upside down like that, and she found him looking into a pool of his own blood. His sister protected him from his father. She called him "her teddy" which was sweet. Later on, she called him "Teaser" because he knew how to get her hot. He hated his real name, Theodore, but he liked the name Teaser. It made him feel good, the way she said it. Like he had power over her. So he let it stick.

He checked the branding iron, and just like that, he was Loki, thinking about Maisie, feeling the wave again. That first time, he hadn't known what to expect. His sister had just turned thirteen, and she'd been drinking;

he remembered the smell of whiskey on her breath. He'd felt this sense of anticipation. The kind of anticipation he felt right now. And when he came for the very first time, inside her, it was everything he'd ever imagined. When it was over, she went to sleep.

In the morning, she acted like nothing had happened.

Something had happened though. Teaser turned the branding iron, then put it back in the coals.

❖

COREY AND ABE WERE in her truck, trying to find Johnny Raiser's street on the map, when Lou Ballard banged on the window. Corey rolled it down. "For Christ's sake Corey—"

She leaned out. "She's lying, Lou, and you damn well know it."

"How do you know what I damn well know?"

"Why are you here?" Abe asked, leaning over Corey.

"I got a call from Lieutenant Norse. He knows Corey shot Luther Emerson."

"How did he learn that?" Corey asked, her gut tightening. Just before Lou said it, she knew. "Agh," she whispered. "Jesse."

"Uh-huh. Jesse called him, tried to straighten him out."

Corey fell back in the seat. "Agh," she groaned again, louder. Her mother-in-law was viral. If you made contact, you died, infected by her good intentions. And her brazen disregard for others.

Abe stepped out of the truck, came around to where Lou was standing in the snow. "You're sure she called Norse?"

"He was unhappy about it, too." Lou shrugged. "Norse wants Corey downtown in the morning."

"Is she being charged?"

"He's asking."

"Can you put him off? Jason Weiss," he watched Lou grimace, "her lawyer. He'll call him."

"Weiss? It's her funeral." Lou turned to go.

Corey watched him, already back on Teaser. The only way she knew to deal with Jesse was to ignore her, act like she was dead. Jason would put this off. He had to. She leaned out the window, yelling, "Listen, Lou." Corey reached in her purse. "Show this picture of Teaser to Star, see what she says."

Lou stepped back over, glanced at the photo. "Lousy shot," he said.

"How bad?" Corey asked.

"That's not Teaser White."

❖

"Lou? What the fuck—" Johnny Raiser, Teaser's CCO, was asleep when they called him.

"Where's Teaser White?" Lou yelled.

"He's with a friend for the holiday. What are you waking me up for?"

"The picture being sent out. The picture that people have been using to identify him. It's not Teaser."

"Who the fuck is it?"

"How the fuck do I know?"

Lou looked at the picture, again. "Teaser's young looking. This guy's too old, and he's bigger." He lifted his head, frowning when his beeper went off. "I got incoming... Johnny, could you meet us here? Regent, half a block east of Broadway. You'll see the cars."

Lou dialed, asked for Lieutenant Norse, "Yes, sir, I spoke with her... Jason Weiss will call you, sir...I'm afraid he's her lawyer...mother-in-law, right...she's nothing like Jesse...a bucket of warm spit? I see..." Lou's grin disappeared. He punched off the phone, leaned in the window. "Being your friend is a nightmare."

Corey nodded, elsewhere. She was trying to picture Teaser. The face she saw was protean. It kept changing, mutating effortlessly to suit its purposes. It made her queasy.

❖

THE SNAKES WERE RED, Loki's color. Hot waves of heat rolled off his branding iron. Loki carried the red-hot iron down the stairs, where Maisie was still sobbing. Dave was twisting, shaking his head up and down, making muted, gutteral noises. Loki ripped the duct tape off his mouth. "Please, Teaser—Loki—whoever you are. It's me you want. Let her be." When Teaser didn't respond, Dave raised his voice. "Please...for God's sake, I beg you."

Loki took off his watch cap, baring his sign, then he raised the iron toward Dave. Dave screamed, throwing himself back against the wall. Maisie wailed when Loki turned toward her.

He picked up the Polaroid, then Teaser raised the iron, slowly. The boy lunged at him, kicking wildly. Loki smiled. When the hot iron was inches from her abdomen, Maisie made a heart-breaking sound, and he captured her nakedness, her abject terror. He could feel the wave rising, stronger than before.

Maisie had fallen to her knees, her back pressing against the edge of the cot, her arms above her head. Loki felt a strong surge rising from his loins. He stepped back over to Dave, who was moaning, incoherent. Loki told Dave his plan. Dave cried out, an indelible wail.

Loki stepped closer to Dave, raised the iron, ready, watching, then set it on his abdomen, just so. It was perfect—the way his head arched back, and the wild sounds.

Loki turned and stepped over to Maisie, who was sobbing incoherently, though her eyes were shut tight. "You're next, little one..." he whispered, touching her tear-stained face. And thinking about what Loki would do, step by step, he started shaking, little tremors passing through his body. His left arm tightened, and the branding iron fell, clanking against the concrete floor. His body was alive, his nerve endings were raw, and hot. Loki could feel the wave, a great cleansing wave, washing through him. He felt the wave building, then breaking. Loki had never seized up. He wondered if Loki was strong enough to fight it back. Maybe. He could feel his body start to stiffen, and the shaking got worse. He lay on his side, and, desperate, Teaser balled up Maisie's torn clothing and crammed it between his teeth. The last thought he had before the seizure took over was that he was ashamed.

❖

MAISIE WORKED TO OPEN her eyes. She used all of her strength. Her eyes opened, but she couldn't see anything. Where was she? Where was Aaron? She was screaming now. On the inside. Loud, incessant wails—*inside screams.* Unstoppable. She couldn't see anything at all. And she couldn't hear anything except her own inner screaming. When she tried to breathe, she felt the iron, red-hot, about to brand her abdomen—and the inside screams got louder. She was spinning, spiraling relentlessly downward, sucked into a bottomless pit.

❖

AARON WAS AFRAID THAT Maisie had passed out. She was hanging like a rag doll, silent, her head turned away, chin on her chest. He heard a gagging noise and looked over at Jimmy, who was curled up, shaking really badly now. Maisie's clothes were balled up in his mouth, but his head banged against the floor and some kind of white foam was coming out of his mouth. After maybe a minute, Jimmy went stiff. Aaron prayed that he would die. Then Jimmy's eyes closed, and he loosened up a little. Aaron saw he was sleeping, and he felt the fear coming on again. Palpable. Wave after wave. He thought he would die when the monster woke up. He turned back to check on Maisie. Her body had shifted, and she slowly turned her head his way. When he saw her face, Aaron tried to scream through the duct tape. He'd never seen anything like her eyes. They were off, unfocused. He couldn't get her attention. She was looking right at him, but she couldn't see him. She was in the void, lost in space. He banged his chains against the wall, again and again.

❖

Corey and Abe walked to the corner, where there was an ice cream parlor with a pay phone. Abe was checking on Aaron and Maisie. Corey leaned against a low brick wall. Star had frightened her. Billy had been right about her. Something was off. And getting Teaser's picture wrong had made it worse. She was still reeling from that.

She tried watching the kids hanging out in the parking lot. Most of them were sitting on the low wall, smoking, staring out at the street. A young boy, thirteen maybe, asked her for change while Abe was on the phone. He said he wanted to get some milk. Corey said, "Sorry, no."

"Where are they?" she asked, when Abe came back.

"Aaron and Maisie are 'out for the evening.'"

"Out? No..."

"I said they were supposed to be supervised. Verlaine told me to calm down. I pushed him. They're okay, he insists. Apparently, they've checked in."

"Does he know anything specific?"

"A late movie." Abe shrugged. "He wasn't very forthcoming. Verlaine suggested I take a hot bath and relax. He said that."

"Maisie's right. He's an idiot."

"He and Toby think we're overdoing it."

"Uh-huh," she muttered, reminded, again, how hard it must be for Billy. Even the kids who ran away were strangely like their parents. Her expectations of Billy—their relationship—had to be beyond understanding, inexplicable, to his friends, these people's children. Overdoing it? Jesus. She hoped she was. Mostly, she hoped Aaron and Maisie were still safe.

Abe took her arm.

Corey started walking back toward Star's apartment, trying to get a grip. She was mucking about in the swamp, losing her way. No one was doing anything. The police had no "hard" evidence. The parents, the people in charge, weren't listening. They thought she was crying wolf. Even in the cold air, she was overheating, sweaty. "You know, you're about the only person in this who doesn't think I'm some rabid dog, foaming at the mouth."

Abe watched her, taking his time. "Lou's not taking this picture business lightly. He'll be all over Teaser, if they find him," he eventually offered.

"Teaser's ahead of everyone. They won't find anything to tie him to whatever is going on. Whatever he's doing, it's already happening." With her free hand, Corey was hitting every parking meter they passed.

Abe slowed, then he turned. The lines in his face had softened. "So it's up to us." A statement, and a question.

Corey stopped. Abe could often distill a complicated thing into one decision. "Yes," she said. "It is." And saying it made her feel better, a sea change. She didn't have to convince anyone, anymore, of anything.

"Let's hear Johnny Raiser out, then get on it."

"Thank you, Abe." She took a slow breath. The night air was cool and sweet.

CHAPTER SIXTEEN

TEASER WOKE UP ON the floor. There was a puddle of urine beside him. He'd soiled himself, he realized, and he stood up, wobbly and weak. He felt like sleeping for a day. He looked at his watch. 11:15 p.m. Not too bad. He'd been out for less than an hour. Loki was strong. Stronger than Teaser. Sometimes Teaser didn't wake up for hours afterward.

He was Teaser now, and he was late. He looked at Dave, passed out against the wall. Dave's eyes were red from crying. Teaser looked at the burns on Dave's abdomen. When they healed, they would be perfect. Loki's mark. Teaser turned at a noise. The boy glared at him, still bloody, bound and gagged. Teaser thought he was staring at his stained pants, so he picked up the branding iron, and swung it against the side of Aaron's head, laying it right on that ugly red Z in his hair. Aaron's head jerked back, cracking against the wall. From now on, the little fuck would watch where he looked. Maisie was unconscious. She'd passed out, her

chin on her chest, her back against the cot, her hands
above her head. He didn't need her now. He taped her
mouth, then Dave's. He wrapped a blanket around her
neck, covering her shoulders and her chest. Loki needed
them later.

He checked the Polaroid. Yes, the picture was just
right. Loki had done a good job. Upstairs, he cleaned
himself, took a shower, then changed his pants. Teaser
felt better when he called his voicemail. Okay, the Man
had called. Johnny Raiser, the Fat Fuck Man. Fine. It was
almost time. He'd call him back, making sure to stay real
polite. "How can I help you, sir?" he would ask Johnny.
Of course he wouldn't have to say anything else. The Fat
Fuck Man was dumb. So long as he thought he was in
charge, he wouldn't even ask hard questions. Okay. He'd
see Johnny in the morning. He'd drive back through
Tacoma, confirm his alibi. After, he'd see that Maisie's
picture was delivered. He'd still have time if he moved
quickly. On the way, he'd check in with Star. She'd be
okay. Star was always cool under pressure. She'd learned
to use her nervous energy to stay cool. He'd helped her
with that. He'd taught her how to shut down on the
outside, then laser focus her energy from deep inside.
It was a game they played together, they called it *riffin'*.
And now she was really good at it—so long as she had a
plan, he could rely on Star.

❖

JOHNNY RAISER WORE AN old trench coat over a torn
sweatshirt and blue jeans. He looked tired and irritated
as he squeezed his bulk out of a ratty old Chevy Malibu.
Johnny had been a parole officer in Albany, New York.
He retired to the Northwest to fish. When he'd caught
enough salmon, he went back to work as a CCO. Abe
introduced him to Corey.

"Have you found him?" Lou interrupted the
introductions.

"Jesus, Lou, he's staying with a friend. I got his
voicemail. He's got my cell phone number, and he
knows to call."

"He worries me, Johnny," Abe said. "I talked with—"

"Did Abe get you going on this?" Raiser asked Lou,
interrupting. "Did he start with his horrors of prison?
Abe calls me—"

"Corey's worse." Lou raised a hand before either of
them could jump in.

"So what are you so hot about?" Johnny asked.

"This picture deal. I don't like it," Lou replied.

"Someone screwed up. Mistakes happen. The guy's
done everything just like he's supposed to. In spite of,"
Johnny tapped Abe's shoulder, "Dr. Doom and Gloom's
'something went wrong in prison' theory. 'Teaser' White
checks in, goes to work, pays his bills, does what he's
told. Hell, I'm sure we'll hear from him."

As if on cue, Johnny's cell phone rang. "That'll be
Teaser," he said.

"Can you bring him in?" Lou asked.

Johnny raised his cell phone. "I need to see you... Just listen. Where are you? Go home, now...uh-huh. Stay there. We'll find you."

"Are you sure that's him?" Corey asked. If it was, Teaser was leading Johnny around by his nose. Johnny was okay, but he was no match for Teaser. Even worse, Johnny didn't know that.

"Lady, you think he's got a robot talks in his voice? Knows what to answer?"

"I think Teaser's dangerous. And you're foolishly underestimating this man if you think just because he checks in, or calls you back, he's okay."

"Who put the hair up her ass?"

"You did, Johnny," Abe explained.

"Hey, fuck you and your half-baked—"

"Settle down, Johnny, relax," Lou said. "We'll see Teaser. How long will it take him to get back to Bentley?"

"Couple hours, max. He's driving from Tacoma."

"Okay. 6:30, tomorrow a.m. His place."

"We're coming," Corey announced.

"Corey, if I see you, I'm arresting you." Lou turned to face them both. "I'm not fucking around on this."

❖

COREY AND ABE WENT to a favorite downtown bar, a room with fir paneling and high, beamed ceilings. They were steered to a corner booth. Corey ordered single malt scotch for Abe, Wild Turkey for herself.

She closed her eyes, pressed the bridge of her nose with thumb and forefinger. "I'm not sure where to start."

Abe knew what she meant. There was a sequence, a momentum to events that was hard to organize. Bits and pieces pulled from different places. One little thing could often tie it together, give them a picture, some kind of gestalt. He didn't know where to start either. "Let's go back. Why were we so worried?"

Their drinks came. She raised her glass, a silent toast. He clicked glasses with her.

"Maisie and Star." She tilted her head. "That's what got me going. Maisie's rich and angry. Star was an addict. I'm guessing she turned tricks, and we know she's done time. Something's going down."

"Okay. Say Star found Maisie. But Maisie went along. And kept going. That's what I still can't figure. I don't see what Maisie gets from Star."

"Sex?"

"There's that, certainly. But there's got to be more. I've spent hours with Maisie, and she's very smart. What is it that would make a smart girl hook up with Star, trust her, follow her lead, then lie about it to her parents, her doctor, even the police?" Abe spun the glass peanut bowl, glanced at a stain on the tabletop.

Corey thought about his question. "Maybe it has to do with Teaser, not Star," she suggested. "Teaser and Star are connected."

"Yeah. I think so, too. Why do we think that?"

"Because they are." She caught herself. "Sorry."

Abe waited. Corey had this sense—like perfect pitch—for what was real. More than anyone, she could cut through the denial and deception that shrouded Aaron and Maisie, Teaser and Star. She was zeroing in on something, he'd seen her do it before. She'd circle slowly, and then, inexplicably to him, she'd be on it, like a hawk on a vole. Sometimes, it was over quickly. Others, it took days. He watched her eating peanuts, one at a time.

She leaned forward. "Okay. Star hits on Aaron and Maisie, right before Teaser gets out. Teaser's released and things start to happen. Luther, who protected Teaser inside, is killed. Teaser's picture isn't of him. Will gets hung by his hands, like Jolene. Franklin is murdered. Aaron and Maisie start covering up something."

"Okay, but we need more, something hard," Abe said, spinning the bowl again. Corey caught it as it fell, set it out of his reach. He didn't notice. "We have to actually tie Teaser to Star, any connection at all."

"Say I start digging around in Star's past," she suggested. "At least Lou got us her real name."

"I'll talk to the people at Western. Try and sort out what happened to Teaser in prison."

"Luther, too."

"Uh-huh. Yeah. I've been saving this." Abe took Teaser's file from his worn leather briefcase, set it on the table. "This is what I went back for tonight. Read Teaser's history, then look at the fax."

Corey read through the history, quickly. Then again. "Nice family," she muttered, then she read the fax. "Oh no. Jesus."

"Right," he said, remembering his own horror when he first read it.

"The kid's living alone, abused and abandoned, then he bites this girl's lip off, not to mention his own tongue, on his first date. Can you imagine?"

"He was trying to do something right. The girl was even his own age."

"She was the last one, you can bet on that." Corey grimaced. "Dad's an animal. Mom's a mental case. It's a miracle Teaser can walk and talk."

"Dr. Kramer says he was particularly bright and resourceful. That's what allowed him to keep it together as long as he did."

"This is what you went to school for, doctor." She rubbed her eyes, tired. "Help me out here."

Doctor? He almost smiled, remembering how, at her evaluation, she'd called him Abraham and said she didn't care for psycho mumbo jumbo. He sipped his whiskey. "Okay," he said. "We know terrible things happened to Teaser when he was young. He found a way to manage parts of it. He's sick, he wants young girls. He punishes them if they cross him, like Jolene. But he's not killing anyone..."

"Then something happens in prison."

"I think so, yes. Perhaps he's brutalized, again. So horribly that literally he stops feeling things—like the self-inflicted wounds."

It was quiet. He watched her trace the scar on her neck.

"I hate this," Corey finally said, giving up. "I can't get inside his head."

Abe nodded understanding. "Here's a guy who stops feeling in prison. Says he doesn't feel anything. His motivation, I'd guess, is to start feeling again. Even hurting himself doesn't bring back the feeling. He's numb. Dead. So he has nothing to lose. I'd bet that's when Teaser focused on what made him stop feeling things. And why. And then, most importantly, what could he do to feel again?"

He saw the first signs of recognition.

"Maybe he thinks hurting people will make him feel something?"

"Yeah. And if he's chosen Maisie, there's a reason."

"Why Maisie?" she asked.

He tapped the tabletop, not liking where this was going. "He wants to hurt someone who hurt him."

"Could Maisie have hurt him?"

"Did she even know him before he went to prison?" Abe shook his head. "I don't see it."

"I don't either." Corey looked at him. "I'm sorry. I'm too tired. And I'm skittish. I can't even focus."

"I'm supposed to talk with Kramer in the morning. I don't know what else to do."

"I don't either. I'll pray we have time."

He made a grumbling sound. "Let's go home," Abe finally said. He wished he had a better idea. He didn't like coming up short. Abe stood, reaching over for the peanuts.

Corey missed the bowl as it spun by. As it sailed off the table, Abe was there, catching it in his palm.

❖

"YOU DID GOOD," TEASER said from a pay phone. It was almost 1:00 a.m. He was still Teaser, and he was feeling things, little by little. Every now and then he pinched his arm, making sure it wasn't some kind of dream. It was like the fit had washed Loki out of his system, but left a little of the feeling behind.

"I miss you already, Tease." Star said. She was at the pay phone at the Broadway QFC.

"I have a present for you. Something special."

"You think of everything, baby. I want to see you."

"Soon, Star Light, soon. You okay?"

"They messed up my stuff. But I'm okay. I was on my game. How long do I have to wait?"

"Carry the cell phone. Sometime tomorrow, I'll call you. Hang up. You go to the pay phone on Madison. I'll call you there, every thirty minutes."

"No sweat."

"The police follow you?"

"Yeah, I think so."

"Buy milk, cookies and ice cream, then go home."

"They know about the picture."

"That's cool. That's in the plan."

"They know about Jolene," she said.

"Who knows?" Teaser numbed up, just a little.

"Some woman. Some real bitch woman."

"Maybe five foot seven? Dark hair? Scar on her neck?"

"Yeah. I remember the scar. They called her Corey. That skanky bitch was hard to play."

"I know that one. Not to worry. That one's mine." He pinched his arm. He was still okay. He could sense Loki though. Coming on.

"You still there, baby?" Star asked.

"I was thinking. Thinking about our beach. Our great, big, white house. I was feeling the sand between my toes."

"I love you baby. Make it over soon. Okay?"

"Real soon. Call the lawyer number I gave you. Tell him I'm going to need him in the morning. Not to worry. Teaser's in charge. Not to worry. Teaser's taking care of Star."

❖

TEASER WAS SLEEPING WHEN Lou Ballard and Johnny Raiser came into his room at 6:30 a.m. "What time is it?" Teaser asked.

"Get up, asshole," Johnny snarled. "I think you've been fucking with me." He showed him the picture. "Is this you, Teaser?"

"No man, that's not me." You fat dumb fuck.

"You sure it's not you? It's supposed to be you."

"Don't play with me, boss."

"The picture of you in the computer, it's supposed to be you."

"Man, no way that's me. That's Dave."

"Who?"

"Dave Dickson, the man shared my cell." Teaser wanted to smile. The guy made it so easy.

"Why did his picture come from downtown instead of yours?"

"I don't know anything about that, sir." He thought the sir was a nice touch.

"How could shit like this happen?" Johnny asked Lou.

Lou ignored him. "Is Dave still inside?" he asked Teaser.

"I dunno," Teaser said. "His time was just about up."

Johnny called a number, asked two questions, turned. "He got out yesterday."

"Get everything they have on him," Lou barked.

Johnny conveyed the order, and punched off his cell phone. He turned to Teaser. "Tell me about Dave," he said.

"Dave did five, maybe six years. When I got there, he was like the Man inside. Had the run of the place."

"Kissed a lot of ass?"

"They liked him."

"Did he have the run of you?"

Teaser didn't say anything. He looked down, working hard, not letting the fat fuck get to him.

Lou turned to Teaser, stepped closer, right in his face. "Do you know Sharon Goodwin?" he asked. "Calls herself Star?"

Teaser rubbed his eyes, apparently tired. "No sir."

"I think you do. And you know Luther Emerson."

"I don't know any Star. But you know I know Luther. The man was killed right behind this place, and you know that, too."

Lou backed away, adjusted his tie. He turned to Johnny. "My office, say thirty minutes?" When Johnny nodded yes, Lou was out the door.

Teaser could sense Loki settling down.

❖

Corey began making calls at 7:15 a.m. She checked shelters, youth centers, churches, food banks—everywhere—looking for some trace of Sharon "Star" Goodwin. Andy Norton, on staff at a U-district youth center, had remembered a girl with a star tattoo. Andy was a friend and they helped each other when they could. He agreed to look for Sharon in his old files. Corey said she'd come by later. Since then, she'd made twelve calls, and stopped at two shelters. So far, no one knew of a Sharon Goodwin.

At 9:20, Corey was at the youth center, looking for Andy Norton. She was at loose ends, frazzled and more and more apprehensive.

The center was in an old wooden house near the U. Colorful posters brightened up the walls. On the first floor, there was a medical room, a classroom, a drug and alcohol counseling room, a sitting area with a small kichen, and several small case managers' offices. The place felt safe, and cheerful.

She found Andy in the kitchen, pacing a small circle near the water cooler. Andy was tall, solid. His head was shaved, he favored Hawaiian shirts, and he had three small silver earrings in his right ear.

She took the offered mug of coffee.

"I found the file. Sharon Goodwin came by four years ago, when she was seventeen. About that time an older man, a Mr. White, stopped in, asking for her. We arranged a meeting. The file just ends there. She never came back."

"Teaser White." There it was. The connection. Shit.

"Teaser?"

"I don't know what it means," Corey said, riding out a wave of anxiety. "The guy's mental." She shifted gears, in a hurry now. "Do you have the names of Star's parents?" she asked.

"Douglas and Sally Goodwin. When she didn't return, I called them in New Haven. Mom wouldn't talk with us. I spoke with dad. He said his daughter, Sharon, was dead."

"Nice." Corey's beeper went off. She looked at the number, asked Andy if she could use the phone. She dialed, listened to Abe, took the file and ran from the office.

❖

COREY WAS AT THE youth center, and Abe was on the phone with a therapist at the Western Corrections Center, when Amber found an envelope in the foyer. It was 9:25 a.m., about an hour after Sergeant Ballard let

Teaser go. In the envelope there was a Polaroid shot of
Maisie, chained, naked, terrified beyond words. Amber
read the bold scrawl on the back. "$2,000,000. Today.
Instructions to follow." She fainted.

Verlaine heard her fall. He came down the stairs and
saw his wife sprawled on the floor. At first he thought
she'd had a heart attack, and he was trying to remember
how to do CPR. Then her eyes opened, and she pointed
at the envelope.

When Verlaine saw the photo, he said, "Oh my God."
When he read the ransom demand, he said it again, and
then again. Amber looked at him, staring at the note,
then she walked to the phone and called Abe Stein.

❖

BY THE TIME ABE called Lou Ballard, Teaser was long
gone. Teaser's lawyer, Dick Manter, had been waiting
for Teaser when he arrived at Lou's office. Manter made
a career out of defending unpopular cases, particularly
drug dealers and child molesters. He was a master of the
technicality, a non-stop talker, and Lou Ballard hated
him. There was nothing to hold Teaser for, and Lou let
him walk before his normally high blood pressure shot
through the roof.

When Abe told him about the ransom note, Lou
threw a wad of gum into the wastebasket and picked up
a jelly doughnut, which he ate in two bites. Over the
phone, Abe could hear him swallowing. He was working

on his second doughnut before he told Abe to find Corey and to meet him at Maisie's house.

Corey and Abe were seated at Amber and Verlaine Daniels' dining room table by 10:00 a.m. Toby was there, too. Lou brought three other officers with him. Johnny Raiser was standing by. It was a tense gathering. The parents looked, and felt, helpless. And foolish. Amber's eyes were red. Toby kept shaking his head and rubbing the backs of his hands. The three officers were setting up shop in the kitchen. They wanted to be ready if a call came.

Lou summarized what they knew, then he threw the real photo of "Teaser" on the table. No one recognized him. Teaser was good-looking, even in a prison photo. His face was gentler than Corey had expected. When Corey asked a question, the parents leaned in, listening carefully.

As an afterthought, Lou set the other photo beside it. Amber started screaming.

Verlaine took her in his arms. "We'll get her back, hon," he whispered. "We'll get her back."

Amber kept screaming, pointing at the photo. She screamed, incoherent, sobbing something into Verlaine's shoulder.

Lou said, "Dave Dickson, Teaser's cellmate." He turned to Amber.

Corey pried her from Verlaine, held her firmly at arm's length. "What are you saying?" Corey asked, slowly. When Amber didn't stop screaming, Corey slapped her face.

"That's Dave," Amber barely managed, between gasps. "Maisie's father."

Verlaine closed his eyes tight, rubbed his temples. Amber started crying again.

Corey turned. Abe's face was grave. When he met her gaze, she knew he had it put together, too.

❖

LOU WENT OVER WHAT they knew about Dave Dickson. He'd done almost six years before his earned release. It was his second conviction for dealing drugs. He was a well-behaved inmate. Dave knew computers—he was an expert at programming—and he'd helped them with glitches in the new set-up in the prison. Teaser had been his cellmate for about a year. Dave had been released just the day before. He never showed up at the address he'd given. No one knew where he was.

"Is Dickson the mind behind all of this?" Verlaine asked. "Maisie was asking about him, just before Thanksgiving."

Lou ignored the question. "Do you have $2,000,000?" he asked.

Verlaine flushed. "Do I have to answer that?"

"You don't have to answer anything. But I need to know if they're being realistic about the ransom, or if it's just some fantasy number."

"Realistic," Verlaine replied.

"Why would he kidnap his own daughter?" Toby asked.

"Would he hurt her?" Corey asked Amber, ignoring Toby.

"He loved her. Even when he got crazy." She took a breath, tried to collect herself. "I can't imagine he would hurt her." She turned away, covered her face. Verlaine tried to comfort her.

"Why did he take Aaron?" Toby asked.

"I don't think Dave's behind this," Abe said, quietly. "Look at this picture. Maisie's terrified. I can see Dave going after the money, but I don't see him doing this," Abe pointed at the picture, "to his own daughter. Moreover, Luther Emerson was killed before Dave was released. So was Franklin. Will was wired to that pipe while Dave was still in jail. This feels like Teaser White. Star lured them in. Teaser set them up, waited for Dave to get out, then took them. What's so difficult, is that we can't prove any of it."

"And unless we can, Teaser stays on the street," Lou muttered.

"Maybe he's working for Dave," Verlaine offered.

"Un-unh," Corey said. "It's possible they were in this together, but Teaser took over. And that's bad news." She didn't want them to know how bad.

"How can you be so sure?" Verlaine asked.

"Stop it, Verlaine," Toby snapped. "Corey and Abe, I'm sorry. Oh dear God I am so sorry." Toby paused, looking away. His shoulders sagged. "It's too little too late, but I was wrong. And patronizing. There's no excuse. I'll listen. And for what it's worth, I'll follow your advice."

Corey looked at Toby, surprised. "Thank you," she said. Abe nodded in agreement. Corey turned to Lou. "Can you hold him?" she asked.

"I have men looking for him. We can follow him if we find him. But we can't hold him unless, and until, we have something more." Lou looked around the table. "Here's what we're going to do. Verlaine, can you raise the money today?"

"Yes. If I have to, I can go on margin. Borrow it."

"Call your broker. Now...okay, the FBI is on the way..."

Corey winced. "C'mon, Lou. Can't you—"

"No I can't. They're the experts on this kind of deal."

Abe turned away. She knew he was imagining Teaser, what he was capable of. Corey got his attention, tilted her head toward the kitchen.

"I know Roy Stinson, the guy running the team, and he's okay," Lou went on. "So we wait for them. And we wait for the specifics on the ransom. In the meantime, my guys will be on Teaser."

In the kitchen Corey took a slow breath, watching Abe. He was bracing for something. So was she. "Teaser's got Dave," she said.

"I think so, too," Abe replied. "This morning, I spoke with one of the psychologists at the prison. She said that Teaser wouldn't talk with her. She said what she knew about him, she knew from a guard. The guard believed that Teaser was Dave's punk in prison."

She pursed her lips. This kept getting worse. "I didn't want to say this in front of her parents, but it's Dave he wants to hurt, isn't it?"

"I think so, yes."

"And he's going to use Maisie to hurt him." Her voice was tentative. This was the worst of her fears.

She watched him, going over it again. "I'm afraid so," he finally said.

Corey's mind was racing, though her stomach was churning, taking orders from some part of her brain she couldn't control. "I'll stay on Star. I don't think we have much time. Teaser's not going back to his apartment. He's started, and I don't know how long he'll be able to keep a grip on himself." She wasn't sure where that came from, but she knew it was true. Teaser had stayed ahead of everyone, in charge. That kind of perfect control couldn't last once he let himself go. She sensed that Billy was still alive because Teaser, too, had some idea of what would happen if he eased up, even a little, on the controls.

"What's wrong?" Abe had read the look on her face.

She took his arm. When things got really bad, Abe would somehow hook up to the world. He'd resist the usual distractions until the problem was solved. She was still fighting off horrible images, working to get her bearings. Eventually she said, "I'm okay," kissed the side of his face and stepped away.

"I'll talk with the guard at Western. And I'm going to talk with Kramer. I'll carry my pager. You can reach me anytime."

The doorbell rang. Verlaine opened it to let in the FBI. The agent in charge of handling the family was a woman in a blue pants suit. She took Verlaine, Amber, and Toby into the living room where she explained that she could help them manage their feelings during this crisis.

Abe and Corey left through the kitchen door.

CHAPTER SEVENTEEN

STAR WAS WAITING IN the condo when Teaser called. She was listening to Scream Queen, a group she liked, rockin' on *Tomb Raider* and working hard at waiting.

"Did the watch dogs follow you?"

"I lost them on Broadway, like you said."

"Go over it again."

"I had the car in the underground garage, parked where you wanted it. I went in Urban Outfitters, picked out a fucking peach-colored sweater. At the counter I gave them the credit card and went to the ladies. Then I ducked out through the mall, down to the garage. The police creeps are still searching every damn shop on the street."

"You go the long way?"

"I ditched the car at Safeco Field. I cut through the parking lot, doubled back, then picked up the girl." She looked toward a child, sleeping on the couch. "We came around the back way, and went through the coffee shop before going in the alley. No one was behind us when we went in. I waited, checked it out."

"I'll be there in five." He hung up.

She knew exactly where the phone booth was, so she was ready with her binoculars when he came down First Ave. toward the square. There he was, the khaki army jacket, the blue watch cap. She loved to watch him, the way he walked, like a wild animal; the way his eyes saw everything; the way they found you, then bored into you, like you were the only person in the world. He looked good, better then she'd ever seen him. Something about the way he moved, the way he owned the street.

❖

Teaser's little condo was on the sixth floor of a high rise, just off Pioneer Square. He'd bought it five years ago, after breaking into a Capitol Hill drug dealer's house and scoring, big-time. The way he saw it, real estate was a good investment. He held title to his hideaway as Frank Redstone. This was his secret place, his safe place, and it was part of his plan.

On the couch, against the wall, a prepubescent girl slept in a heroin-induced stupor. Her head rested in Star's lap. Star looked up when Teaser came in.

"She's eleven," Star volunteered. "I've had my eye on her." And anticipating his question, "She's still a baby."

Teaser smiled, ran his finger along the girl's flat chest.

"She doesn't even know where she is." Star looked at him, as he ran his fingers along the sleeping girl's neck. "You okay, Tease?"

Teaser took her chin in his hand. His grip was strong.
"Call me Loki."

"I'm sorry, baby. What did I do?"

"Loki."

"Loki. Yeah. Loki. Loki's cool."

Loki went to the window, looking down on Pioneer
Square. Snow flurries were blowing across the square, swirling
white dots, riding the wind. It was getting colder, he could
tell by the way people were walking. He tore at the burn on
his hand. It hurt. Terribly. Finally. Loki felt everything.

He turned to watch Star walking toward the
bathroom, then he turned to the baby, still asleep on
the couch. Loki felt the surge. This was perfect. He
needed this now. A baby would satisfy Teaser. Turn off
his damn brain. And a baby would help Loki be ready,
ready for everything. Everything was going to happen
tonight. And Loki knew just what he needed to keep
from seizing up when it did. He knew what he'd do with
the baby now. And he knew what he'd do with Maisie
later. Just thinking about it got him hard. He looked at
Star, simmering, before Teaser put him down.

"You better go," Teaser said to Star.

"You going to take care of me first, Loki?" She was
unbuttoning her blouse. Star bared her breasts, fingered
one of her large brown nipples.

Loki felt the wave rising. Star was a full-grown
woman, and seeing her bare breast made his back turn
sweaty. Loki reached back. He wanted to slap her to her
knees. Teaser stopped him, just barely. And then Teaser
was back, in and out though.

Slowly, carefully, Teaser put Loki down. It was hard.
He had to work on this. How to be Loki, then Teaser.
When Teaser wanted.

"You have to go now, baby," Teaser explained. "I'm sorry."

"Yeah? You tell that asshole Loki, then, that I don't
want him around. I want Teaser back."

Teaser took a beat, silent. He could feel Loki. Red-hot
in his gut. Loki wanted to use her, and then he wanted
to cut out her heart, the pump for her fouled, baby-
making blood. Why did Loki want Star? And why did he
want to hurt her? Star was the only person Teaser loved.
He tried to reason with Loki, explain about Star. Loki
backed off. But Teaser knew he wasn't convinced. Loki
didn't understand the rules. He didn't even care about
them. He'd have to work this out. Loki was important.
Loki lit up the darkness. He could feel things, powerful
things, without dying. Yes, little by little, Loki had
brought Teaser's feelings back. He'd left a little more
behind every time he took over. And after tonight, he
would feel on his own, Teaser was sure of that.

"Okay. Teaser's back. Okay?" He touched her cheek.
"He's back." He put his arms around her. "Teaser's going
to make you happy. Teaser always takes care of Star light,
Star bright."

He took a package from his jacket pocket. It was
carefully wrapped. He'd chosen shiny black wrapping
paper and a yellow ribbon. "I have something for you."

Star opened it, took out the silver necklace, then held
it to the light. "It's so fine baby." She let out a little gasp of
pleasure. "It's so beautiful." She put it around her neck.

Teaser pinched his arm. No feeling at all.

❖

"Mr. Goodwin, my name is Corey Logan, I'm calling about your daughter, Sharon...I'm sorry, but she's still your daughter...Mr. Goodwin, she may be in trouble... she does exist—"

Corey looked at the phone. "Shit," she said.

Her next call was to the public defender who had handled Sharon's case. She was out of town, climbing some mountain. The receptionist explained that it was her first vacation in two and a half years.

Corey paced, her face drawn and tired. She was thinking about Aaron and Maisie. She looked out of her window toward Bainbridge Island. Snowflakes were dancing by, blown upward in sudden gusts, little white specks defying gravity. She watched a freighter, grey against the dishwater sky, making its way toward the huge orange tentacles that would unload the containers stacked on its decks.

Corey wrapped her arms tightly around herself.

❖

Loki watched the baby bleed.

It was almost time to forget the past. First he had to finish with Dave. Square things, as Dave liked to put it. Loki was pretty sure he could do that without seizing up.

Yes, he could do that now. Loki made a sound, deep in his throat. He could feel himself rising—steam coming off molten lava, smoke rising from a raging fire—drifting upward, toward the moon.

❖

ABE MET JACK ROSS, the guard from Western Corrections Center, near the courthouse, downtown. The psychologist he'd spoken with at Western had said Jack Ross knew about Teaser and Dave. They met in front of the courthouse because Jack knew just how to get there.

Jack had initially refused to meet with Abe. Abe had called Lou, explained his problem. Lou said, "Uh-huh," then he asked, "What time?"

They sat in a booth at a coffee shop Abe liked. Jack was big, with blond hair and blue eyes. He wore leather cowboy boots and looked like a lumberjack from Sweden. The occasional sparkle in his blue eyes was the only suggestion that there might be more here than a large shank of lamb. "Thanks for coming," Abe said.

"You got a good friend. What's the deal?"

"I need to know about Teaser White, Dave Dickson, and Luther Emerson. People say you know how things work inside."

"Those three, jeez..." He let it trail off.

"Start at the beginning."

"The beginning, right." Jack looked away. "I'd have to say, from day one, Teaser had an attitude. Like he didn't belong inside. Like he was better than that. Now, that didn't go down too well. He was gang raped that first week. Messed up pretty bad." Jack shrugged. "It freaked him out."

Abe shook his head. "I understand. What happened then?"

"He made a deal with Dave to protect him. Luther was Dave's helper inside. They shared him 'til Luther left. Then he belonged to Dave."

"Belonged?"

"His punk. Dave was the boss, his Master. You know?"

"I think so. Did he do this voluntarily?"

"Yeah. Sure. The alternatives were worse."

Right. "What was he like?"

"A psycho. The guy kept to himself. Never talked. He kept getting hurt, though. Weird things—a nail in his arm, toenails pulled off, finger smashed in a machine—then that damn burn on his head. At first I thought Dave was torturing him. But Teaser said he was doing it to himself. Tests, he called them. Said he could do whatever he wanted to himself. The thing was, he didn't seem to mind. He said he couldn't feel anything. Said he was living dead."

"Yes, I read about that in his file...didn't you try and stop it, get him away from Dave?"

"Mister, that's none of my business."

Just what, Abe wondered, *was his business?* Abe let it go. Guys like Jack had to survive in prison, too. "I see. Right. What about Dave?"

"Model prisoner. Smart. One of those guys the other inmates listen to. Sort of an organizer. Fixes things, gets what he wants. I'd go to him if I needed help with a problem inside. I could usually strike some sort of deal."

"Tell me more." Abe wondered if Dave may have been positioned to get the photos changed.

"He was a computer nut. He helped the higher ups when they had problems with the new computer system. He wrangled a laptop, hooked into every damn thing he could. Always on some research project."

"How could Dave's picture get in Teaser's computer file?"

"Dave could figure a way to do that. He'd pay the right person if he had to."

"How would that work?"

"Every prisoner has a bracelet with their photo on it. When they're released, the photo is checked against the file photo. As soon as Teaser left, Dave or his guy could change his photo in the computer. His guy could do the same for Dave." He shrugged. "Done slick, no one would know right off."

"Dave could do that?"

"Yeah, sure. It might cost. But Dave was connected." Jack shook his head. "Confuse the hell out of people, huh?"

Abe ignored him, preoccupied. This had clearly started as Dave's plan. He guessed Dave had planned to switch the photos so it would be harder to identify him. Abe wondered when Teaser had taken charge. Clearly, Teaser was an expert at manipulation. He'd conned Aaron and Maisie, deftly misled Johnny Raiser, his CCO. Why not Dave? "Could Teaser manipulate Dave? Could he have been behind whatever Dave was doing?"

"No way. Not while he was inside. Teaser was Dave's pussy—excuse my French—his gal-boy, his sex slave."

❖

ABE WAS OUT OF breath when he came through the office door. He'd lost track of time, talking with the guard.

In the office Corey was sitting on his old desk, trying the Goodwins again. "Mrs. Goodwin?" she asked in a muffled voice when Sally Goodwin came on the line. "Mrs. Goodwin, you don't know me. But I desperately need your help…I'm trying to save the lives of two children who've been kidnapped. Your daughter's also in danger…I know you disowned her—" the line went dead. "Fuck," she said to the phone. She turned. "Is the call set?"

"Kramer should be waiting."

A minute later, Dr. Mark Kramer was on the speakerphone. Abe cut short the pleasantries. "We're dealing with a kidnapping," he explained. "We think Teaser's got two kids."

"Who's Teaser?"

"Theodore White. Sorry. Is he capable of that?"

"I don't know." Dr. Kramer hesitated. "At fifteen, he was certainly extremely able. Theodore kept himself together in the face of the most difficult circumstances." He rustled through some papers. They heard him sigh.

Corey tried to picture Teaser at fifteen. She couldn't. She kept seeing Billy, who was fifteen when she came out of prison.

Kramer went on, "As you know, his childhood was horrific—sadistic father, psychotic mother, horrible seizures, so on and so forth. His sister abandoned them, leaving her baby. On his first date, well, you know what happened. In spite of all of this, he was still functioning. When I saw him, Theodore was trying to make sense out of the world. He wanted to talk with me about his ideas."

"Like what?" Abe asked, facing the speakerphone.

Corey sat on the desk, near the speaker. She was listening carefully. She needed to understand Teaser, get inside his skin.

"He had a theory, something about cycles of birth and death. He said that having a seizure was like dying and being born again. He thought sometimes you were alive and sometimes you were dead. He wondered if that's why certain feelings came and went. I still remember how bright he was and how thoughtful."

"How many times did you see him?" Abe asked.

"Four or five. I did the evaluation, then he came back once or twice, just to talk."

"How serious were his problems?"

"He was very angry—at his parents, his sister, about his history—but he was working hard to manage it. He was figuring things out, developing rules and strategies. I'd say he was disturbed, but he wasn't dangerous, if that's what you're asking."

"It is," Abe said.

"He hadn't hurt anyone, intentionally. And that wasn't on his mind. No, he had other preoccupations."

"Such as?"

"Although he never came out and said it, he was confused about women. He was uncomfortable around girls his own age, or older."

"How did it come up?" Abe asked.

"He talked a lot about teenage girls. About how they changed. He was preoccupied with their physiology. He asked me about puberty, ovulation, and menstrual cycles. No one had ever explained those things to him. He wanted to know why girls had to bleed before they could have babies. When I tried to answer his questions, it upset him. He told me that he hated girls who bring children into the world and don't care for them—like his sister, and his mother. He hated his sister for leaving her baby with him."

Corey got that. A baby was an unimaginable responsibility for a disturbed teenage boy. Still, she didn't have a feel for Teaser. It was hard for her to imagine his reactions, harder still to get near his feelings, or to think like him. She looked over at Abe, who was pacing, troubled.

"What happened?" Abe asked Kramer.

"His mother gave—or sold—the baby to an agency. What no one knew was that Theodore had been taking care of the baby for most of the summer. His mother had moved in with her boyfriend and left the baby in his care."

"The adult Teaser likes eleven-year-old girls," Corey eventually offered. "He seduces them and keeps them."

"I'm sorry, I didn't realize...does he hurt them?"

"Not unless they cross him..." she paused. Something was working its way around the edges of her mind, just outside her grasp. She shook her head at Abe, frustrated. "So far as we know," she finished.

"I see."

"His problems got worse in prison. Teaser was gang raped, then raped repeatedly over a year long period by two different men." Abe turned to Corey. "I confirmed that with a guard, this morning."

Corey shook her head. Prison stories like this still upset her.

"Dear God," Kramer muttered. "What happened?"

"I think he stopped feeling things. And plotted revenge against Dave Dickson, his cellmate and the primary perpetrator. It's Dave's daughter, and her boyfriend, who were kidnapped. We think he killed the other rapist soon after he got out of jail."

"Stopped feeling things?"

"Literally, he'd burn himself, or put a nail through his arm. He told the guard he was living dead. I think he's hoping to bring his dead self back to life."

"Agh..." They heard Kramer take a slow breath. "He is dangerous then. I'm sorry."

"What do you know about the baby?" she asked.

"Not much. His sister had the child out of wedlock. The family pretended the baby was the children's younger sister. Theodore resented that."

"What agency took the baby?"

"I don't know."

"Can you tell me who to call? How to find out?"

"I'll call you right back."

"One more question. How old would that baby be today?" Corey asked.

"I saw him—what?—eighteen years ago. She was two or three, so she'd be twenty or twenty-one."

"Thanks." Abe killed the speakerphone, turned to Corey.

Corey was looking at the floor. She turned her head. "It's Star."

Abe nodded, just barely. "His niece."

Corey's face revealed her mind, working on that. She looked up, tentative. "His niece...and his daughter."

❖

TEASER WAS AT THE pay phone when Star called. He was watching the snowflakes melt against the phone booth. Loki was gone, resting, getting ready for tonight. Teaser picked it up after the first ring. "Everything fine?" he asked.

"I love the necklace, baby. Thank you, again."

"I want you to be happy, Star light, Star bright. Our future begins tonight. Everything begins tonight. I want you to stay in your apartment, where the police watchers can see you. I want you to stay there until tomorrow. Do you have what you need?"

"I've got my music, some magazines, a new game and some chocolates. I rented some movies, too, Tease. I got aliens and I got action. I thought that would keep my mind busy."

"Good. I'll meet you tomorrow, at the apartment in Tacoma. You take a taxi from the stadium, like we worked out. I'll drive around. If I'm not there, wait at the apartment, wait for me to call the beeper. I'll leave the number in our code. You call me at the number I leave. Okay?"

"Got it. No sweat. Make it end soon. I want to be at the beach."

"Soon. Very soon…" Teaser hung up.

Teaser had a voice disguiser in a metal case that weighed about ten ounces. It had fourteen settings and allowed him to change his voice from adult to child, or male to female, with great ranges of bass and timber. He chose to be a child with a high voice. When the voice scrambler was ready, Teaser called Verlaine's house. Verlaine, and the FBI, picked up on the first ring. What predictable assholes. Teaser spoke into the scrambler. "Go to the downtown post office. P.O. Box 6961. You have two hours."

Teaser hung up, and walked on the 3:00 ferry. It was really snowing now, large flakes melting on the deck.

❖

"It makes sense," Abe said, watching Corey. She was at the window, studying the snowflakes. Unfettered by other people's ideas about how to think, she'd found her way. Teaser's daughter. Right there. Plain as the nose on your face. No one else had thought to look. "Perfect sense."

She turned. "Listening to Kramer, I finally got a feeling for Teaser, at least Teaser as a boy. Why would that boy—with his family history—take care of his sister's baby? No way. I think he took care of the baby because it was his. That baby was his first, maybe his only, connection to a person."

"Okay. He tracks her down, discovers she's had problems, and takes her in. He helps her clean up, cares for her."

Corey thought about it. "Does he tell her he's her father?"

"Never. He's ashamed, mortified by what happened."

"Mortified?"

"Humiliated beyond his capacity to understand. He couldn't even think about it. Having a baby with his sister? The idea was unbearable." Abe tapped his oak desk, working on this. "Then, when he tries sex with a girl his own age, it ends with both of them blood-soaked and disfigured. Another unbearable humiliation. I'd bet he can't stand to be around sexually mature women. The only exception could be his own daughter."

"Nice." Corey rubbed her neck. "So he takes care of her. I don't even want to know how. And she finds him little girls. She was a hooker, so she's seen some cruel, kinky guys. It probably seems to her like a pretty good deal."

"I think so, uh-huh. And Star's likely very smart—after all, she has his genes—so they connect around that, too." A picture was forming. Abe could see how Teaser's unconscious mind had worked hard to recreate this semblance of family. He must have created strict rules, especially for sex, that would protect his family from himself, from his carefully controlled rage. Then the real world messed up everything. "Things are going fine, until one of his little girls, Holly, gets pregnant, then she turns him in."

"He must have freaked out."

"It's his nightmare. And then in prison, the humiliation started again, only it was even worse. He suffered regular, repeated humiliations. He could anticipate the pain, the shame. It made him shut down—stop feeling." Abe stood, pensive. "With no feeling, he became some kind of remorseless, vengeful beast."

"Loki..." She hesitated. "But listening to Kramer, I felt something for him. And what he must have gone through in prison. The nights..." Corey's eyes shifted back out the window. "When he came out, Star was the only thing he had."

"Uh-huh. When he came out, he couldn't even feel his own body."

She watched the snow, swirling outside.

Abe saw her finger traveling along her scar. He sensed she was weighing the same risks he was. When she turned back, her face was set.

"Star's our way at him," she said.

There it was. He didn't have a better idea, either. "Lou will go crazy."

"Lou can't know."

The phone rang. It was Kramer again. "The little girl was taken by a fly-by-night agency here in Bakersfield. She was placed with a family in New Haven named Goodwin. I'll fax the paperwork."

"Adopted." Corey groaned. "I should have thought of that."

"One more thing doctor," Abe said. "Is it possible that Teaser was the little girl's father?"

"I considered that, the way he talked about the baby. He may have had some sexual contact with his sister. He was having seizures at night, and he shared her bed until he was eleven or twelve. But at the time, he denied it, convincingly. I should have mentioned that, though. I'm sorry. Yes, it's a possibility, however remote."

Corey shot Abe a look.

"Thank you, doctor," Abe said.

"Godspeed. Save those children." He hung up.

"Kramer's okay," Corey said. "But like most shrinks, he needs a regular whack on the head with a two-by-four."

"Every couple hours," Abe muttered. He made a grumbling noise, then he was serious again. "We better work out our timing."

"Are we thinking the same thing?"

"I'm afraid we are," Abe said. He came around and sat beside her on the front edge of his desk. The lines in his face deepened. He was considering consequences, and it was sobering. Some of the possible outcomes were grim.

"You see any other way?" Corey took his arm. She was tensing up, too.

"No." He didn't even have to think about it. "There's no time. Maisie and Aaron are out of time."

Corey took a minute, leaned against his shoulder, then she stood. "You got that old Polaroid?"

He pointed toward his closet.

Corey found the camera. "Let's do it."

❖

Lou Ballard sat in when the FBI agents returned from
the post office. In the P.O. Box, they'd found an envelope
with a key, and another picture of Maisie. In this shot,
she seemed virtually catatonic. The picture showed her
from the waist up, naked, her hands chained above
her head. Instructions were printed on the back. The
instructions specified that the money be packed into a
large duffle bag, then Verlaine Daniels was to get on the
7:20 ferry to Bainbridge, walk off to the Bainbridge Post
Office, Box 8942, where further instructions would be
waiting. The key to the P.O. box was in the envelope. If
anyone followed, if there was any police or FBI presence,
or if Verlaine was wired, the children would die.

In the living room, Toby Paulsen and Amber and
Verlaine Daniels huddled together in front of the
fireplace. Toby had been trying to contact his wife, Nora,
but she was on the road, unplugged and unreachable.
He didn't even know where she was. Fresh snow covered
the Daniels' front lawn, like a layer of vanilla icing. They
didn't notice.

Lou Ballard came in, carrying a cell phone. "It's
Corey Logan for you, Toby."

Toby took the phone. "Toby Paulsen."

"Would you like to help?"

"Anything."

"Lou told me the FBI heard from Teaser. That it's on. I want to make the drop."

"He wants Verlaine."

"He gets me."

"What if the FBI refuse?"

"It's your kids, you have to find a way to call the shots."

Toby was quiet, uncertain.

"They'll want one of their guys to come along. Or wire me or something. It has to be me. Alone. No wire."

Toby hesitated. "Are you sure about this?" he finally asked.

"There's no time for this now, Toby," she explained, gently.

He took a breath. "I'm sorry." He looked at Verlaine and Amber. "Okay. Tell me what to do."

"You and Verlaine and Amber insist it be me, on my own terms. Say it over and over. They'll bully you, scare you, then tell you horror stories. Legally, they're in charge. So you have to play hardball. Refuse to put up the money. Tell 'em you'll go to the press. Get Lou Ballard to help. Whatever works. Just hang in. It'll be a battle, but Lord knows, you can handle them if anyone can."

"I'll do it." He paused. "Can you tell me what's going on?"

"There's hope, Toby. That's all I can tell you."

"Thank you," Toby said. "Thank you, Corey."

CHAPTER EIGHTEEN

TEASER WAS ON THE ferry deck, letting the snow flakes fall on his face. From Teddy, to Teaser, to Loki. Finally Loki. He remembered being Teaser with his sister, Polly. Then she got big and had her baby. And he wasn't anything anymore. She stopped paying attention to him when she learned the baby was coming. At first he wasn't sure why. Later he put it together because she never said who the father was. He figured that out. And he was ashamed. After the new baby, he got his own bed. He was twelve, and he hated the baby. Polly was only thirteen, which made it even worse. They told everyone that the runt was their little sister. But people knew. He hated Polly more than the baby. He would torment her until she cried. Sometimes he would poke her with a coat hanger. He learned to heat up the end from toasting marshmallows. One time he touched the red hot tip to her breast. It made him feel good, except she moved away the next week, and he never saw her again. He helped take care of the little baby though, until his mother took it.

After the baby was gone, he was pretty much on his own. His mother came by maybe once a month with groceries. It was odd at first. Then he got used to it. He missed the baby. He wasn't sure why. Then there was the girl he liked. The last thing he remembered was touching her breasts while she guided his hard penis into her spot. He thought her lip would grow back or at least get sewn on, like his tongue, but it never did. He couldn't go back to school after that. That's when he decided to be invisible.

He went to another school until the charges were dropped. The court made him see a psychiatrist. Which was okay, because it helped him understand certain things. Like how his sister had tricked him. The doctor was nice and he knew a lot, but he wasn't as smart as he was. When everyone had forgotten him, he lied about his age, got work on a freighter and disappeared. Before he left, he went to say goodbye to his mother, but he couldn't find her.

He spent six years on ships, mostly in Asia. It was a good way to be alone. There were no women on a ship. And there were places where he could find young girls at almost every port. He needed them more and more often.

At sea he learned to be an electrician. He wanted to prepare for the future, whatever that was. The guy who taught him said he had a feel for it. The truth was, it came easy, like most everything else.

In his free time he worked to know, and control, his feelings. He got so when he saw a calendar picture of a naked woman, he didn't feel anything. The one thing he couldn't understand was why it made him so angry when someone bossed him around, or criticized him. And there was no way around that on a ship at sea. After he burned one of his bosses with a hot wire, he jumped ship in L.A.

L.A. was okay, and he rented a bungalow in Hollywood. Most of the time he thought about money and how to get it. He didn't need a lot, but he didn't want to worry about it either. He had some definite ideas about the value of his time, too.

So he did research and considered his options. After months the best choice worked its way to the top, more or less by itself. He decided to become a thief.

He was a perfectionist. He chose his spots carefully. Planned every detail so there were no surprises. The key to it was that, as an electrician, he understood the alarm systems. Usually he could figure out ways to disarm them.

Those were good times. He learned to move jewels, even computer parts. He began to understand his capacities.

The L.A. girls were the icing on the cake. He liked to find the runaways: on the street, at the shelters, or in the free food places. He tried different ages, but eleven was usually best. They liked going with him, because he was so good to them. He always took care of the girl. Unless she backstabbed him, like Jolene, who stole his money to buy drugs and had to pay for that. In L.A. he never had a problem. They were always happy, until they had to leave.

Then, out of nowhere, the bad times were back. He began having seizures for no reason he could figure. He'd spend days lying in bed, not wanting to go out. The more he thought about it, the less he understood. Things were perfect, but he was seizing up again, big time. The fits came mostly at night, when he was alone. But he even had seizures in daylight. They lasted for a long time, and he wouldn't wake up for hours after. He always woke up in his own mess. He was out of control— like a woman who couldn't keep from bleeding.

That's when he started thinking about his own little girl. He'd lie in bed after a fit, wondering where she was, what she'd become. Little by little, he realized he wanted to find his baby daughter. She was his daughter. He needed to find her. He wasn't sure why, but he had to...so he did.

It took two years. No one seemed to know anything. It was like she'd died. But he kept hoping and searching. When he finally located her, she was in Seattle. His baby girl was an ex-con, a junkie, and a whore. It was his fault, too. All of it. He knew that.

He took her in. Made her give up drugs. Cared for her. She was his girl, so she was smart. She just didn't know that. So he worked with her, taught her how to channel her energy, how to focus her unusual mind. In time, she was really good at it. She'd already paid a price, though. When Star wasn't with him, her mind overheated—she couldn't sleep or wait. The damage was done before he found her. He looked up at the sky, felt the snowflakes on his face—when they got to the beach, he'd have his feelings back, and his little girl would be able to sleep at night.

After the cold turkey was a good time for them. Teaching her, caring for her. He gave her everything she wanted. Everything. Except the one thing. He couldn't do that. When he thought about her going with men for money, it filled him with shame. The sex act was a curse in their family. It led to tragedy. And Star had already had enough tragedy in her life.

Still, he'd learned the hard way that sex could never be ignored. He knew a women's needs were complicated and important. He knew that much from his lying bitch sister. And she was a lying bitch—she told him if he didn't make her come, she couldn't have her period. And she'd fill up with blood and have a baby.

So he learned to take care of Star. She taught him how to help her come with his fingers. He made himself do it since it was only for her, and there would never be a baby. After a while, he liked pleasing her. Liked it in a way that was different, and unexpected. She said he made her *ride the wave*, and that made him smile. When he told her how he only went with younger girls, she accepted the way he was. The fact that she didn't have to please him was fine by her. She liked finding girls for him. It was a game they played together.

Then Holly ruined everything. He didn't know she was too old. How could he know that? Holly turned twelve, and she didn't even know it. And how could he

let her go? How could he ever have done that? He shook
his head. Loki would have known what to do. But Loki
wasn't there. And Teaser was sent to prison. He couldn't
remember most of what happened to him there. Except
his body died. And then some other part of Teaser died,
an inside part. And Loki was born. Teaser ran his tongue
over his front teeth, felt his scar. And then Loki found
a way to turn all the prison dying times to great good
fortune. A way to bring Teaser back to life. Finally. Rusty
wire to nerves and veins. Stone to bone, clay to flesh,
slag to blood.

❖

THE LIGHT WAS ON in Star's apartment. It was only 4:00,
but it was already getting dark. The unplowed snow was
icing up, making it hard to drive the steeper streets on
the Hill. Corey was in the little passageway between Star's
apartment building and the larger, older building next
door. The older building, once a prestigious address, had
been badly neglected. She'd entered the older building
unnoticed then found a side door. From her hiding
place she could watch the watchers, two men in a car
out front. She'd already ID'ed the watchers in back. The
men in the car were eating sandwiches, laughing about
something. They wouldn't be so relaxed, she figured,
unless Star was in.

Corey signaled to Abe, who was hanging back in the
shadows of the side door. She pointed out the car, then

she faded back. Abe came toward her, tilting his head toward a basement window. The window was near the back with a three foot well in front of it. Corey stepped down into the little well and looked through the dirty window. After wrapping her hand in her jacket, she broke the glass. They cleared out the glass, opened the window, then she lowered herself to the basement floor only four feet below. Abe followed. Corey turned on her flashlight. It lit up the blackened furnace. She found the stairway, and then they were on the ground floor, hurrying up the stairs. When she got to Star's door, she knocked.

"Who's there?" a voice asked.

"Police," Abe answered. Corey could hear music in the background.

"I want to see some ID."

"Sure." Abe took out his wallet. "Leave the chain on, crack the door."

When the door opened, Abe held up his wallet then flew into the door with his shoulder. The chain ripped off the doorframe, and he was inside. Star was already in her kitchen alcove, going for a carving knife. Corey was right behind Abe. She pulled her gun from the small of her back, pointed it at Star's face. "Leave it be, hon. We've got a lot to do, and we've got no time."

Star met Corey's eyes. "You stupid fuck. Are you crazy? I scream and the cops are all over you."

Abe closed the door, turned up the music.

Corey kept the gun on Star, in her face.

"You skanky bitch," Star hissed.

Corey grabbed a handful of Star's hair, pulling downward as she pressed the tip of the gun barrel under her nose. Star twisted and drove her balled fist into Corey's side. Corey smashed the gun—hard—against the side of her face. Star staggered, and Abe pinned her arms from behind.

A minute later Star's hands were tied behind her. She was wearing Corey's coat, and Corey's scarf was around her hair and face. There was a bruise and a cut with traces of blood on her right cheekbone. Her mouth was taped shut, under the scarf. Corey held another short rope that was tied to Star's ankle. Abe led her down the stairs, holding her arm firmly. Corey held the gun to her side.

From the lobby, they led her down the basement steps. Together, they took Star out the broken window, through the side door of the adjacent building, out the front door and then one more block west to Broadway. Corey's pick-up was at the corner, in the ice cream parlor parking lot. Abe put Star between them in the front seat.

They drove to Ballard, to the marina where Corey kept the *Jenny Ann II*. Corey took a minute alone, readying herself to do what had to be done. She didn't want to do it; she knew that much. Readying herself wasn't as hard as she'd expected. She thought about Aaron and Maisie.

Corey powered the boat into the Sound. It was snowing, cold and dark. Ten minutes out, at a shelf she knew, Corey dropped her anchor. They took Star to the covered aft deck, where Corey stripped her naked, cuffed her to a railing, then ran a hose on her. The freezing cold water was enough to make Star tell her life story. What she knew of it. Then Corey put the gun barrel in Star's mouth. When Star gagged, terrified, Abe took the picture. He made sure Corey was in it.

❖

"NO, THAT'S NOT GOING to happen," The FBI guy, Roy Stinson, was saying. Roy was tall, polished, and surprisingly calm, given the circumstances. It was after 5:30, and Toby, Verlaine and Amber were insisting Corey make the drop. Under pressure, they'd stubbornly held their ground.

"You're not listening," Toby insisted.

"No, Mr. Paulsen, you're not listening. We have a man we can disguise to look like Verlaine—"

"We've made up our minds," Toby persisted. "We've talked with an attorney, and we'll go to court if we must... Mr. Stinson...Roy...we'd appreciate your cooperation."

"I'm sorry. Our man is your best shot, and it's your only option."

"We give the money to Corey," Amber declared. "No one else."

Amber took Verlaine's arm. He nodded agreement.

"For God's sake," Roy was shaking his head at their foolishness. "It's your children's lives that are at risk—"

"That's enough." Toby stood. "You're posturing, and it isn't helping. If we lose our children because of our mistake, we'll have to live with that. If we lose them because of your mistake, because you overruled our considered judgment, we'll never be able to live with that."

Roy grunted.

Toby took a breath. "Please respect our judgment. Corey's our choice. They're our children. It's that simple."

Roy turned to Lou. "Can you reason with these people?"

"Corey Logan's a pistol. I'd say you got lucky."

Roy lost his calm. "What the hell is this?"

"Forget the rules," Lou said. "These are smart people talking about their children. You're off the hook, I'm your witness. They'll sign any release you have. Just give 'em what they need. Help them, Roy. It's their show."

Roy glowered at Lou. The doorbell rang.

"She's here now," Amber said.

Toby let her in.

Corey put a hand on Toby's shoulder then smiled at Verlaine. She took Amber's outstretched hand. The parents seemed to be doing better. Having some purpose had made them less anxious, more hopeful. Corey offered a silent prayer that their hopes weren't misplaced.

Lou whispered in her ear, "I went to bat for you. Don't piss him off." He paused. "And you fucking well better get this right."

"Lady, talk some sense into these people," Roy said.

"I'm your best chance," Corey said. "I know how Teaser thinks." She locked onto Roy's eyes. "Teaser knows who I am. He'll deal with me, and I'll deal with you. You can cast a wide net. Then, when I've got the kids, you take over."

"You ever done anything like this?"

"Yes, sir," Corey lied, looked at Lou.

Lou didn't miss a beat. "We've worked together. She gets the job done," he confirmed.

"I don't get it." Roy stepped back. "You all want this? You're serious?" He looked at each of them. "You want this responsibility?"

"We do. Yes," Toby reiterated. He looked at Verlaine. Verlaine nodded.

"Absolutely," Amber said.

"We've got no time," Corey interjected, trying to close the deal.

Lou shot her a look.

"It's the only choice we'll live with," Toby said. "Please help us."

Roy stared at the parents, one by one.

❖

COREY WALKED OUT OF the ferry terminal just after 7:55, as if she'd taken the 7:20 ferry She was carrying a large blue duffle bag. The snow made Eagle Harbor look like a picture on a Christmas card. The trees, the dock, the buoys, the ferry terminal, even the sailboats moored in the harbor, were covered with a soft layer of white.

Teaser watched the scarred prison bitch walking into the Thriftway parking lot. She carried a blue duffle over her shoulder. He could feel Loki, waking up, considering this turn of events. Liking the possibilities—the money and the she-bitch. Teaser didn't like it though. No, he didn't like it at all. Why was she here? His orders were clear. Why were they disobeying him?

He watched her cut across the Thriftway parking lot then enter the post office. She left a line of footprints in the snow. The snow would help him, give him more time later, he knew that. He watched her open the P.O. box and take out the cell phone. He was in the office, the one near the post office, the one he rented for the plan. He watched her, wary. She'd have something to tell him, he was sure of that. But she had the money, and he had the brains. He'd find a way to turn this little twist to his advantage. Floss to gold. Then Loki would cut her throat, empty her fouled blood. Loki was impatient, he wanted to get on with it.

Teaser dialed the cell phone. "I asked for Verlaine," he whispered. "For disobedience, I could cut Maisie's breasts—"

"Shut-up, Teaser," Corey interrupted.

"Who's Teaser?"

"Don't fuck with me." And then, slowly, clearly, "I have Star."

Teaser was silent. How could the scar-bitch have Star? Why?

"Listen very carefully. If anything happens to either of those children, I'll kill her."

Teaser could feel Loki, rising in his chest. He took a calming breath.

"I know what you're thinking," she went on. "The police, the FBI, they're not in this. I'm not wired. They're not following. They don't know I have Star. They won't know if she loses an eye, or if she drowns."

Loki made a noise. Teaser held him back.

"This is Corey Logan. I think you know who I am."

Teaser held Loki down, took charge. "I know who you are."

"Good. Because Teaser, you almost killed my son. You killed my friend, Franklin. This is between you and me."

"You and me. I see." He paused. Star was in danger. Go slow. Careful. Don't let her know what you're thinking. "I like that." Loki liked it, too. "If you have the money," Teaser added.

"I do. And I'll pay. But believe me, if we don't get the children back, you'll never see Star again."

"So?"

"Don't play games with me. She's your daughter."

Loki scratched his nails against the wall. How could the foul-blooded she-bitch know that?

"That's right, you twisted miscreant, I said your daughter..."

Loki wanted to rip out her throat, right there in the post office. Teaser held him off, barely. "What do you want?"

"I'll trade you Star and the money for Maisie and Aaron. Get the children. Bring them to the park at Fort Ward. Park at the upper parking—it's marked to the right as you come down Fort Ward Hill. Take the foot path from the Upper Parking, south and then east, past the restrooms, then down to the shore. If you see the barracks, you've gone too far. It's a low tide at 10:00 tonight. Be there. You got that?" She waited. "I'll leave you something in the playground behind the Thriftway. Taped under the slide. Look at it carefully before you make your decision. I don't care about the money. All I care about is Aaron and Maisie. Look under the slide. There will be a photo and a map showing the meeting place. My phone number's in the envelope. Call me when you've decided." She punched off the phone.

Teaser watched her leave. He saw her stop at the snow-covered slide, tape an envelope to the bottom. He sat there, in the dark, running his tongue between his teeth. She thought she was in charge now. What a stupid slit.

Ten minutes later he had the envelope. He'd paid a teenage boy to be his helper. No one bothered the boy when he took the envelope then made a wide loop to come back to him. Teaser met him in the parking structure, took the envelope, then sent him home. Teaser opened the envelope, took out the picture. He could feel everything. The blood, pounding in his head and chest. The sweat, making his back wet and cold. The pain, when he slashed Little Buck across his forearm. Punishing Teaser.

Loki was trying to take over. Loki knew how to handle Corey Logan. Teaser felt his forearm, felt the blood, oozing down the back of his hand, warm on his flesh. He had to stay in charge until Star was safe. Then Loki could do everything. It was going to be hard. Loki was boiling hot now, in his blood, coursing through his veins. He stared at the picture. Star was naked, cold, and afraid. She had a black eye and there was a wound below it, on her right cheek. He was sure the gun barrel hurt her throat.

❖

THE JENNY ANN II was waiting at the public dock in Eagle Harbor where Corey had tied it off earlier. A wooden ladder went down from the enclosed cabin and the covered deck. Below, there was a kitchen area, a small teak table and four bunks. Star was bound and gagged, tied down to a lower bunk. Abe paced up and down the dock, rubbing his gloved hands together against the cold, working hard to keep from worrying. He'd slipped in the snow, stepping off the boat, and his leg was still wet.

Abe retraced his path through the snow. He was worried. He couldn't help it. Whatever he tried to think about, somehow, it came back around to Corey and Will, his family. Right now they were in harm's way: From Teaser, for messing up his plans; and from the police and the FBI, for about every other thing they'd done. This was going to be difficult, however it went. Corey would know what to do with Teaser, how to do it. He had to know what to do because of what she did. He let out a breath when he saw Corey running toward him. The dock was slippery, but she kept her balance.

She took his arm, nodded she was okay, then Abe followed her to the boat, carefully stepping down onto the deck.

"He knows. He's going to call back. I'd say he's pretty bad off," she explained.

"The kids?"

"I think they're alive. Yeah...have you heard from Lou?"

"Every ten minutes. He's not going to be able to hold off the feds, if it doesn't go just so."

"I'll call him. Give me your phone, I want to keep my line open."

She dialed. "Lou...yeah, I'm in touch...so far so good...keep them out of it...tell them the switch is going down at 10:00 at Fay Bainbridge State Park. It's on the North end...right...thanks."

"You lied," Abe said.

"Uh-huh."

He nodded agreement. No back up. That was the deal. And once it started, there was no way to know what the Feds would do. Abe lay a hand between her shoulder blades. He'd had time to think, and there were things to talk about. "Lou's unhappy about something."

"I misled the FBI guy earlier. Told him I'd done this before." She shrugged. "I didn't see another way."

"Can't be helped." He felt the pressure, too. No time, no choices, and they couldn't fail. "One thing..."

"Go on."

"More than the money, he wants to hurt Dave, bring the feelings back. He'll want to get to Dave through

Maisie. If Dave's not at the meeting place, I don't think he'll kill her."

"I don't think he'll kill anyone until he gets Star back," Corey said.

"Probably."

"And if he gets her back?" she asked.

"He'll hide, make sure Star's safe."

"And then?"

"I think he'll try to kill us all." He'd thought about this. Her face changed as this sunk in. Plainly, it cut to bone.

Abe was already past it, working on finding an edge, something for later. "Let's talk with Star," he said.

"How much do we tell her?"

"More than she can bear."

❖

STAR WAS IN A fetal position on the lower bunk. Abe took off her gag, unsure how much to tell her, or how to handle it.

"Untie me, man. I'm getting fucking hives." She spit it out, angry.

Abe could see where her arms were red. It was, he guessed, the price she paid for her glacial exterior.

"I'll free your hands if you sit quietly and hear me out." He helped her sit up. "We're going to tell you a story, Star. We don't know the ending yet. It may depend on you."

Corey untied her hands but left her feet bound.

Abe considered where to begin. Corey would help, but this was up to him. "There's no easy way to do this," he said. "So just listen carefully. Teaser was raped repeatedly in prison. Brutalized. The man who hurt him was Maisie's father, Dave. He intends to hurt Maisie to get back at Dave."

Star didn't say anything.

"We're hoping to save Maisie and Aaron. That's all we care about. You can have the money."

"And if you get away from the police, you can disappear," Corey added.

"But if Maisie and Aaron die..." Abe let that register. "You will spend the rest of your life in jail, or worse."

"Fuck you, ass wipe," Star hissed at Abe. "I hope Teaser kills you and your bitch, real slow and nasty."

"Do you hope that?" Abe asked, unsure if she could even hear what he had to say.

"Forget what I hope. If you hurt me, he'll torture you then kill you." She scratched her arm, shrugged. "I know that." When no one responded, she started over. "Look, I don't know why you kidnapped me. But I can tell you this, Teaser's not a killer. He's a thinker." She paused. "Unless you hurt me."

"You think Teaser's some sort of prince, don't you?" Corey asked.

"Teaser and me, we're good together. He treats me right. He's the only one ever did that."

"Why do you think he does that?" Abe asked, seeing a way at this.

"'Cause he loves me."

"Okay, I believe that," Abe said. "But why? Why did he find you in the first place? Why did he take care of you? I mean you were seventeen." He glanced at Corey.

"He likes eleven-year-old girls," Corey added, saying it just the way he'd hoped.

"Fuck you, bitch. I don't have to answer that. That's cold."

"Let me tell you why he found you," Abe said, softly. He took his time going through a file then sat beside her. "You were born in Bakersfield, California. I can document that. Then you were adopted by the Goodwins, a family in New Haven. Teaser's from Bakersfield. He helped take care of you until you were two and a half." Abe opened the file. He went on slowly, "Teaser's name is Theodore White. Your real name is Sharon White." He showed her several faxed documents confirming that Sharon White had become Sharon Goodwin. He let that sink in, then said, "Star, he's your father. Teaser's your father."

She snorted—almost a laugh—then she spit at him. "You lying cocksucker."

He wiped the phlegm off his jacket, calmly. "It's not a lie."

She spit again. Corey held her hands. Abe put the gag back on. So much for that. He watched her—eyes shut to slits, snarling behind the gag. He'd have to wear her down, hope to find a weak spot.

"He took care of you until his mother gave you up for adoption," Abe went on. "When she sent you away, he was just fifteen. You were only three, but he'd made a connection with you. You were the only family connection, maybe the only human connection, he ever had. At some point, he wanted you back. That's why he found you. That's why he takes care of you." He slowed down. "I'll take the gag off if you'll stop spitting."

She opened her eyes, just a little, then nodded. Her expression, though, was plainly defiant.

He untied the cloth. He saw where hives were starting to show on her arm.

"You're still a god damn liar," she snapped, ice-cold. "No way."

"I don't expect you to believe us," Corey said. "But don't be stupid. Think about it. Check it out."

"You're messing with me. Tricking me."

"If what we're saying is true, will you help us?" Abe asked.

"Why should I help you?"

"Because he wants to kill Aaron and Maisie." He watched her carefully, wondering if she was even considering this. Apparently not.

"He's not killing anyone."

"Star, Teaser's become very dangerous," Corey said. "He was disturbed before prison. But what happened inside pushed him into the really scary stuff. He says he stopped feeling things. Teaser drove nails into his arms, crushed his finger in a machine. That's major-league-psycho time." She leaned in. "And if he starts killing people, you're going down. Rock bottom. Inside. Hard time, forever, over and out."

Star was shaking her head, no. "Teaser's not crazy. He's just playing you. Teaser's a thinker...fast and smart... light speed...what he's doing, he's tyin' you up in knots." She rubbed her arm against the wall.

Abe kept on, picking up on Corey's notion. "Star, he's a very sick, very dangerous man," he said, softly. "I bet he can cut himself—or burn himself—without feeling it." He waited, watching her shift on the bunk. Yeah, she heard that. "If you help us, perhaps we can help him."

Star was wedging herself into the corner. "You're fucking with my head. Teaser's not a killer."

"Will you help us stop him?" Corey asked. "Star, I can still keep you out of it."

Her hives were spreading up her arms. Star was twisting and turning, rubbing them against the wall, the bed. And she was shaking her head, no.

The portable rang.

❖

TEASER WAS IN THE basement, watching Dave. The Master didn't look so hot at the moment. He hung off the wall like a branded, bloody side of beef. The only movement was in his eyes; they darted back and forth, crazed. Drool ran down from under his gag.

Loki was still red-hot. Angry at the scar bitch. She was fucking up the plan, making him wait. Teaser understood why he was so mad.

Teaser grinned at Dave, then he went over what he was going to do. It had come to him on the way back, driving up the hill in the snow. He had snow tires, because he'd planned ahead.

When he was ready, he dialed the number.

"We were just talking with your daughter," Corey said after picking it up.

Teaser listened. Waiting for Loki to back off. Knowing how he wanted to play it. "I'll speak with her."

"Not yet, Teaser. I want to hear Maisie and Aaron first."

He was ready for this. Teaser put the phone to Aaron's ear. In his other hand, he held Little Buck. It made the thin red line on Maisie's bare breast. She didn't seem to care. Maisie was semi-conscious, in and out. She was looking toward her father. She squinted, seeing something, then her eyes glazed over and her head tilted back.

"We're o...o...okay," Aaron stammered. It came out a hoarse whisper. "Help us," he pleaded.

Teaser took the phone away. "Where's Star?"

Corey handed Star the phone. "Ask him," she challenged.

"You there, baby?" Teaser asked.

"I'm okay. They didn't hurt me." She looked at Corey, defiant. "They say you're my daddy. Is that a crock of shit, or what?"

"Star Light Star bright, don't let them confuse you. Corey Logan is evil. Loki is going to take care of her." And Teaser could feel Loki, clutching the phone, wanting to kill Corey.

"Loki would be good for that."

"Put her back on the phone."

"I want to speak with Maisie now," Corey said. And when he didn't respond, "Who's Loki?"

"Loki?" It was a low whisper, then Teaser was back. "We meet at Fort Ward Park, where you said. At the shore. 10:00." He hung up.

Teaser took a slow breath, turning to Dave, watching him. After a beat, he threw cold water on Dave's head, getting his attention. He loosened Dave's chains so he could lower his arms to his sides, then Teaser bound his hands behind his back with wire. He tied a short wire around Dave's neck, like a leash, then, with his gun drawn, he unchained him and helped Dave up the stairs. Outside, he marched him to the car, where he bound Dave's feet and set him on the floor behind the front seat. Teaser went to the trunk where he had the chloroform. He poured it onto a cloth, then applied it to Dave's face. When he was out, Teaser covered Dave's mouth with duct tape. He returned to the trunk for the old blanket that he wrapped around him.

Teaser went back down to the basement. Maisie was comatose again. Her body hung askew. And her eyes wouldn't focus. Teaser fastened a fifty-foot length of wire around her neck with a slip knot. The way he did it, if he pulled, the wire would tighten. He tried it, and her head jerked up. Teaser smiled and pulled the wire tight again—Daddy's girl was waking up now. He made her stand, facing the wall. He unchained her, dressed her, put her coat on hurriedly, then Teaser bound her hands behind her back and taped her mouth shut. Next, Teaser taped Aaron's hands behind him. He fastened a similar wire to Aaron's neck. When he was satisfied, he wrapped each of their arms tightly to their bodies with duct tape.

When Maisie tumbled forward onto the cot, Teaser grabbed her by her hair, pulling hard. That got her up again. He didn't have time to worry about her. It was all he could do to keep Loki in check. Loki didn't care about Star. He wanted to have Maisie, then peel her flesh, drink her blood. Teaser threatened Loki. He told him that if anything happened to Star, he'd go back to sleep, forever. Loki stayed down after that.

Teaser and Loki put the children in the trunk.

CHAPTER NINETEEN

COREY HEARD THE CHOPPERS, swinging north toward Fay Bainbridge State Park. She made a face, sorry, as she guided the *Jenny Ann II* through the channel between the salmon pens, taking in every detail as she approached Fort Ward State Park. Fort Ward was at the other end of the island, maybe twelve miles southwest of Fay Bainbridge. Snow-covered trees came down to the water's edge. She watched the shoreline until she found the clearing that appeared at low tide. It created a small rocky beach where she occasionally stopped to picnic in the summer. It was a good place to make the switch. The entire area would be deserted on a snowy November night, and though it was hidden from the road, the clearing was easily accessible from land and water. The snow was coming down steadily. A full moon occasionally broke through the clouds and snow. The wind was blowing hard from the southeast, pushing whitecaps through the Sound. The spot she'd chosen was on the west shore, sheltered from the wind and snow. Seeing it in the moonlight, she felt the muscles in her neck tighten. Little beads of sweat dampened her upper lip.

Star was below, sea-sick. The hives on her arms looked like little red berries. They rose from a nasty red rash that had spread to her neck. She told Abe that her stomach had cramped up, that it was "his fucking fault." Abe took her up, leaned her over the rail. He took her arm and went with her to join Corey in the enclosed cabin. He waited until she'd anchored at the boat launch, beyond the meeting place. Then he turned to Star. "Who's Loki?"

Star turned away.

Corey grabbed her arm. "Who's Loki?" she asked.

Star spit in Corey's face.

Corey slapped her face. They were out of time. And she was feeling the pressure.

Star held her burning cheek, seething. Abe sat her down on a little bench that folded down from the wheelhouse wall. He tied her wrists together. "Who's Loki?" he asked.

Corey took a fistful of Star's hair, pulled it. "I'll smack your head back against the wall," she said, meaning it. She needed something more from Star. She didn't know what. She wasn't sure how—or how far she'd go—to get it. She tightened her grip, pulling harder.

"Shit," Star winced. Her face flushed red. "Okay. Shit. Okay."

"Who's Loki?" Abe asked again.

"Teaser calls himself Loki sometimes. That's all."

Corey released her hair. "Since when?"

"Just lately. It's some kind of game."

"Tell us about Loki."

With her bound hands, she managed to use a finger to scratch her neck. "See what you did to me? Shit, I'm burning up."

"Loki," Abe repeated.

Star looked at Corey, weighing something.

Abe brought her a glass of water.

She drank half of the glass of water, one long pull, took a slow breath.

Loki?" Corey softly asked.

Star snorted. "Loki's an asshole, like you, if that's what you mean."

Corey ignored her smirk. "How?"

"Loki doesn't like me."

"How do you know?"

"It's private, okay?"

"No." Corey took her hair again firmly, pulling it hard.

Star gasped. "Bitch," she hissed. "Nasty fucking bitch—"

Corey banged Star's head against the wooden wheelhouse wall. She was tired of being called a bitch. Corey readied to smack her head back again. "How do you know?"

"Okay! Stop!" Star cried out, "...okay?" Corey let go of her hair. Star took a slow breath, then again. "Loki wants to hurt me."

"Why do you think that?"

She looked at Corey, red faced. "You learn about dangerous tricks. He's got the look..."

Abe had been right—Star was smart, like her dad. Corey thought about what she just said before asking, "Does Teaser make love to you?"

"What? That's none of your damn business."

"I don't think he does."

"Why? Because you think he's my daddy?" Star grimaced.

"Partly. It's complicated," Abe frowned.

"Just answer the question," Corey persisted. "Don't make me crack your skull."

"...He goes with younger girls."

"Do you want to know why?"

"Fuck you."

Corey smashed Star's face with the back of her hand, tearing her lip at the corner of her mouth and opening the wound on her cheek. Star covered her mouth, crying out. Her face went white as blood ran through her fingers, down her chin. She slid to the floor.

"This isn't a game," Corey said. "And I'm tired of your smart-ass mouth. Now listen to what he says. Every word." Corey looked at Star's bloody face. She was okay about it. A torn lip was better than a cracked head.

Abe turned to Star, who was huddled against the wall, trying to stop the bleeding with her sleeve. "I want you to understand exactly what you're dealing with," Abe said. "Teaser's father beat him. His mother was mentally ill. He started having epileptic seizures when he was four. His sister took him into her bed." Gently, Abe helped her back up on the bench. "He slept with his sister until he was twelve, and she became pregnant. His sister abandoned their baby after it was born." Abe sat beside her. "You were their baby—Teaser's and his sister's."

Star sat, pressing her sleeve to her bloody cheek and mouth. "Please fix me up."

"Do you understand what I'm telling you?" Abe asked.

"Fix my face, then leave me the fuck alone."

❖

TEASER ARRIVED AT THE upper parking area for Fort Ward Park almost an hour before the meeting time. The roads were not plowed, and he had to drive carefully through the fresh snow. He almost lost control of the car on a patch of black ice when he made the right turn into the upper parking. It was good that he'd put on chains before coming down Fort Ward Hill.

Loki was down, resting, getting ready for later. It gave Teaser a moment to think.

His plan was simple. He'd work the switch, get Star back. Get the money. He'd let them have the kids. Then he'd disappear.

And turn Loki loose.

Loki would have the night he was born for. A bloodletting that would leave him sated, and finally, forever, fulfilled. Loki would begin with scar-bitches' boy, her seed. Then he'd take Corey Logan's blood. Then he'd be ready for Maisie. Again.

He needed Maisie to finish Dave's lesson. Loki had worked on Dave's lesson, every night, for almost a year. Dave would watch Loki take the life from Maisie's living body and pour it into Teaser's dead one. And before he was done, Dave would die, inside and out, to bring Teaser back to life.

He knew that when Loki was finally satisfied, Teaser would feel again. Everything. He knew this in the way a salmon knows where it was born. He knew Teaser would be alive. Completely alive. And Loki would be dead. Burnt out like a shooting star.

❖

COREY ROWED ABE TO the boat ramp, north of the meeting place. The driving snow covered his footprints, and he disappeared into the trees, toward the artillery positions built at the turn of the century. He knew the place. They'd taken Billy to picnic there. He'd have to find his way in the moonlight. Corey returned to the *Jenny Ann II*. She tied off the dinghy then went below. Still on edge. She was trying to think like Teaser, imagine how he'd play this. She couldn't.

Star was lying on the bunk, tied down. Her rash had spread across her chest. Corey untied her, sat her up, retied her. She took one of her cards—it had her name and number, that's all—and put it in Star's jacket pocket.

"Fuck you," Star hissed. Star's hands were tied in front of her now. Her cheek and the corner of her mouth were crudely bandaged. She managed to raise her middle finger.

"Hard time, forever," Corey whispered back, as she carefully retied Star's gag.

Corey went up to the wheelhouse. She sat then turned her binoculars toward the meeting place, almost half a mile south. Her view of the clearing was obscured by several snow-covered firs at the water's edge. The snow was still coming down, and in that protected spot, it seemed lighter, gentler. At the meeting place the trees were white and still. There was hardly any wind at all. Corey settled in to wait.

She watched the snow, letting her mind go its own way. She sat very still, remembering the night on the original *Jenny Ann* when she'd told Abe and Billy all about Nick Season—every damn thing. Here she was, this hard case, rely-on-no-one ex-con spilling her guts to her young son and a shrink who couldn't drive. She'd been very frightened. But these two guys, they'd been right there.

A ferry heaved through Rich Passage. Its rolling wake rocked the *Jenny Ann II*. Corey looked toward shore. Teaser was out there right now. And he had Aaron and Maisie. Who'd been there for them?

Just imagining what they were going through made her nauseous and cold. She turned up the collar of the foul weather jacket she kept on board, then she wrapped her arms around herself. Aaron and Maisie. Aaron was Billy's first friend at Olympic. By the tenth grade, the kids had already grouped up. Billy was one of three new students in his class. For the first few months, no one even talked to him. Billy ate lunch by himself. He wandered around alone most of the day, sulking. One day Aaron invited him to a rock concert at the pier. She never got how that happened. When she asked Billy, he said, "I dunno. Because he's okay." That was that.

Last year, Billy had a date with Maisie. He was almost sixteen. It was the first time he was remotely interested in a girl since Morgan, his first love, had moved to New York City. Billy asked her out. No. They didn't call it that anymore. Still, that's what it was, a date. Billy spent most of an hour getting ready. She wouldn't have known except for the gel in his hair, and the way he smelled, aftershave layered on top of deodorant. They went to The Broadway Alley. They hung out, drank lattes. She'd picked them up, driven them home. She could tell Maisie wasn't sure what to make of Billy. It turned out Maisie wasn't interested. But she let him down gently, without even knowing quite what she was doing, and she and Billy became friends.

Today Billy had taken Corey aside, loaned her his lucky buffalo head nickel. It was a 1926 S he'd found when he was five. Billy once told her it got him through the foster homes, where he'd lived when she was in prison. He didn't know what they were doing, he said, but he thought it might help, whatever it was.

She stood, thinking about Aaron and Maisie, looking at the sea. Corey turned back toward Fort Ward. Abe was out there now. And two children's lives were at stake. She replayed her plan. It was just after 9:00. She'd arrive at precisely 10:00 p.m., as agreed. She fingered the nickel in her pocket. Ready.

❖

TEASER PULLED THE CHILDREN from the trunk, along with a handgun, a flashlight, and two lengths of two-by-fours prepared for the occasion. He carried the two-by-fours in his backpack as he marched Aaron and Maisie toward the meeting place. With one hand, he directed the beam of the flashlight on the path in front of them. With the other, he held the wires and his gun. He had to help Maisie, who had trouble standing up. When he twisted the gun barrel in her ear, she learned to walk again. Teaser liked the snow crunching under his feet. The children moved slowly—cold, lifeless, though the air was warming. He prodded them along with his gun, poking Aaron in the kidney with the barrel. Aaron stumbled, and Teaser drove the gun into his kidney again. Thirty feet further, Maisie slipped in the snow and fell. The beam from the flashlight showed where the wire had cut a thin red line on her neck. Teaser let the wire go as Loki rose, stronger than ever. Loki wanted to pull it tight. They walked on in the snowy darkness.

Teaser had some—no, most—of the feeling back already. He could even feel the little things, like the snow on his hand. Still, he could numb up for no apparent reason. Like now, he lost the feeling whenever he looked at, even thought about, the picture of Star. That's when Loki rose. And Loki was getting harder to handle. Teaser had to threaten him to get his attention.

In prison Loki was dormant. He couldn't hurt Dave, or Teaser would pay, one way or another, forever. So Teaser kept Loki down, and he waited. Every night he listened to Dave's plan, his plan to kidnap Maisie and ransom her back to Verlaine. He worked it so Dave would think he was going along with his plan. He let Dave use Luther—a vicious, stupid animal—as the outside man. Let Dave change the photos, everything. What Dave didn't know was that Teaser had taken Dave's plan and turned it on Dave.

He'd picked Dave up from prison, as Dave had wanted. He'd taken Maisie, lured her—his way—to a safe hidden place. And he would ransom her, yes, as Dave had intended. But Dave was in Teaser's plan now. And Dave would see that Teaser's plan was about more than money. Teaser's plan was about birth and death.

The plan was working. But then Corey Logan changed everything. And Loki got too strong. Loki wasn't dormant now. No. He was like a ball of fire living inside him. When he let him wake up, Teaser felt everything, like his skin was raw.

The longer Loki burned, the harder he was to keep down. Keeping Loki dormant was draining Teaser's feelings. That's what he'd figured out. That's why he had to turn Loki loose. Tonight. Let Loki burn himself out. Before it was too late.

Teaser saw the restrooms and turned in toward the water. The children did as they were told. Loki was hot, like lava. He kept shining the light on the blood on Maisie's neck. They passed a snow-covered outdoor grill set in the ground and followed a path to the shore. He took in the clearing, shining his light on a tree that would serve his purposes. He had time. In the distance Teaser saw an old wooden boat, maybe a quarter mile north, bobbing up and down in the cold, black waves. Smart, he thought.

❖

ABE PASSED AN OLD artillery position, a massive concrete base with pedestals for gun emplacements. He tried to imagine eight-inch guns firing at ships traveling through Rich Passage. Abe wondered if this fort had ever been useful. He guessed not. In the snow it looked like an ornate, oversized cake.

Past the fort he cut through the trees toward the small clearing. He remembered the rocky beach, chosen, he was sure, because it was protected on three sides by the forest. Among the trees the snowfall was lighter, and the wind had died down. At the shore he carefully made his way, tree to tree, toward the meeting place.

Abe could just see the seaside edge of the meeting place. In the little clearing the wind had stopped blowing, and the snowfall had subsided. The rocky shore was soft and white until it met the black line of the sea. The tide had just turned, and the saltwater was melting the snow. Abe hid behind a tree and looked toward the water, waiting. He could see the *Jenny Ann II*, anchored now, not two hundred yards from the clearing. He could see a flashlight beam, moving at the meeting place. At 9:50, he saw a little white dinghy behind the old boat. In the moonlight, he saw it cutting through the black water, coming slowly toward shore. Star sat stiffly in the stern. Corey was pulling—long, sure strokes. He watched her, halfway to the clearing. He was sweating now, even though it was cold. There was nothing he knew to do about that. Abe carefully made his way closer.

He knelt in the snow, peering around a fir. The moon broke through the clouds and lit up the clearing. There, at the meeting place, Abe saw Maisie and Aaron. Teaser stood behind them, a length of white rope running from his hand to a tree beside him. The rope was tied to his wrist. As if on cue, Teaser turned the flashlight beam on the children. Something was wrong. The tilt of the children's heads. They were looking up toward the sky. Their hands were behind their backs, and their arms were bound tight to their sides by some sort of tape. Abe leaned forward until he could see their feet. The children were on their tip toes, standing precariously on pieces of wood. He hurriedly followed the extreme tilt of their heads until he saw a branch, two to three feet higher. The branch was bent down, taut like a drawn bow. It took him just seconds to put it together. Abe guessed that Teaser had wired Maisie's and Aaron's necks to the branch. In the moonlight, he could see where another wire was fastened to the branch, pulled tight with two small pulleys, like a halyard. It ran beside Teaser to the trunk of a fir, where it was tied off. The wire held the branch down. The rope was attached to the wire, at the tree. If Teaser pulled the rope, the wire would come free from the tree trunk, and the branch would snap up, like a sprung trap. If Teaser pulled the rope, the children would hang.

❖

COREY LANDED THE DINGHY then pulled Star out, her gun to the woman's head, her powerful flashlight beam shining on the clearing ahead of them. She knew they had a problem as soon as she saw the children. If Teaser released the wire, Aaron and Maisie could die. Okay. One step at a time. Work the switch. Abe was out there somewhere, armed. Once the kids were safe, he'd decide what to do about Teaser.

She saw Teaser, the rope in one hand, a gun in the other. His face was expressionless. "I've got your daughter, Teaser," Corey yelled. "Or is it Loki?"

Teaser made a noise, something she couldn't place, then he stepped forward. "The money," he ordered.

Corey stepped back, behind Star, keeping her gun on Star while she lifted the blue duffle bag out of the little dinghy.

"Bring the money and Star," Teaser said, taking charge, not wasting a word. "You can check them." He tilted his head toward Aaron and Maisie. "If I pull the rope, or fall, they hang. Make one mistake, and I'll kill them. You're a surprise, Corey Logan. I don't like surprises."

"You're not killing anyone, Loki, Teaser, whatever the hell you call a sister-fucking—" Corey stopped herself, worried by the expression on his face.

Star made a little noise.

Corey watched the rope tighten. Jesus.

❖

LOKI ALMOST HUNG AARON and Maisie. Teaser summoned all his strength, forced him down, let the rope fall slack. He felt the fire though, in his chest. "Soon," he whispered to Loki. "Soon."

Teaser smiled. "Lies, Star light, my Star bright." And after a beat, "What have they done to your face?" And angry, before she could respond, "Set the money by the trees, behind me. Cut Star loose. Do it now."

"Throw down the rope."

"At the same moment you free Star."

"Is she your daughter or Loki's daughter?"

Teaser grinned. Loki was down, certain that his moment was coming. Teaser just had to get Star now, that's all that mattered. "Do as I say."

Corey made a semi-circle with Star, wanting to put Teaser between her and Abe. She set the blue duffle behind Teaser, at the edge of the clearing. Then she walked to Aaron and Maisie. They were bound and gagged, and their necks were pulled tight by the wire. Maisie was in shock, and the side of Aaron's head was badly cut. But they were alive. She walked behind Star until she was facing Teaser, ten feet to the side of the children. She held the gun to the back of Star's head. She'd free Star the moment he threw down the rope. "Whenever you're ready," Corey said.

Teaser opened the duffle, checked the money. Then he raised a small black box and ran it up and down the length of the duffle, checking for tracking devices.

Teaser turned. "Cut her loose. When she takes a step toward me, I'll throw down the rope."

"No. At the count of three, the rope goes down, then I let her loose."

"Untie her hands, then I throw down the rope. You free them while we disappear."

Corey untied Star's hands.

Teaser stepped behind the children. Slowly, he untied the rope from his wrist and threw it to the ground. When Star walked forward, he pulled the piano wire, still tied to his hand, and the children flew into the air, hung.

Corey screamed. She dropped her flashlight and ran to Maisie, wrapping her arms around the girl's flailing legs, holding her up.

Aaron was swinging from the tree branch, unable to breathe, his neck twisted.

Abe ran full out for Aaron.

The last time she saw Abe move so fast, they were up the Inside Passage and Billy was covered with wasps. Still, it seemed like forever before Abe grabbed Aaron's legs, pushing him up.

Teaser was gone, running with Star for the car. He'd slung the duffle over his shoulder. He pictured Corey and the big guy—did she imagine he'd forget about him?—holding the wired children in the air, struggling to keep them from hanging, unsure how to cut them down. Even Loki was satisfied, knowing that he'd pulled the wire, made a fool of the she-bitch. Knowing that tonight, he'd rise, and take them—the ones he'd been waiting for—take them to the moon.

❖

"Hurry, babe," Abe said. He was afraid of slipping. He had Aaron's legs in one arm, Maisie's in the other.

Corey was working frantically, using all of her strength, to pull the branch back down. She wasn't strong enough. How had Teaser done it? "Hang on," she yelled as she ran to the dinghy. Corey pulled the little boat up on the snow. When she had it beside Abe, she turned the boat over. She took a knife from her pants pocket and stepped up onto the bottom of the boat. Corey balanced herself then took the wire above Maisie's head. Using a punching tool on her knife, she worked on the wire until the slip knot was loose, then she opened it wide enough to free Maisie's head. "Okay. She's okay," Corey said, hurriedly.

Abe let Maisie fall to the snow. Maisie lay there, a fetal ball, barely breathing. Abe adjusted his feet, using both hands to hold Aaron while Corey removed the wire from around Aaron's neck. Then Abe let Aaron gently down to the ground. Abe turned, wiped his face and neck. "Agh," Abe growled.

"He's so damn smart," Corey muttered. She looked at the children, lying in the snow. Corey closed her eyes. Not this time, Teaser. Un-unh.

Abe helped Aaron sit up, took the tape off his mouth. As Abe freed his arms, Aaron started gasping. A moment later, he was crying out. Loud, incoherent cries.

Corey was on the snowy ground. Maisie's head was in her lap. She'd removed the tape from Maisie's mouth and arms, but Maisie hadn't said a word. She stared at the night sky, eyes unfocused, while Corey wiped her forehead. She recognized the look in Maisie's eyes. She'd seen it on a claustrophobic prisoner after she was locked down in a small, windowless cell—solitary confinement—for eleven days. Corey undid Maisie's coat, checked for injuries. Physically, she was okay. Corey thought she could imagine what Maisie must have been through, though. What she'd seen. Not just the terror, but the helplessness, the humiliation. She buttoned Maisie's coat, held her, wondering how this ever could have happened. She guessed Maisie was hoping to reconnect with her real dad, and she didn't tell her parents. Teaser had surely sworn her to secrecy, but she didn't talk to her parents anyway. She didn't talk to adults about things that mattered. Somewhere along the way, she'd given up trying. Corey felt heartsick and suddenly very cold. "You're okay now, honey," she whispered. "You're safe." Maisie was in shock, unreachable. Corey lifted her, held her close. "You're okay," she whispered again, hoping against hope that it was true.

"Let's get 'em to a hospital," Abe said, as he dialed his cell phone. His call was answered instantly.

"Lou, we got 'em, and they're alive," he said. "In shock, battered but intact...I'll explain later. Teaser got the money, and he's driving up Fort Ward Hill right now...put your FBI pal on it...this part is his show... Send a chopper to Fort Ward Park. We need to get these kids to the hospital." Abe waited while Lou barked out some orders, then Lou was back on. "Yeah, it wasn't at Fay Bainbridge...we were mistaken...Teaser's deal was no back up...I don't care about the money...for christsake Lou, Aaron and Maisie are alive...that was our whole damn deal...save it. I appreciate your position, and your help... Okay...Teaser's very clever. He rigged the switch so the kids damn near hung from a tree branch while he got away...he did something with wire...I think he'll slip past the FBI...because he's figured everything else...Roy's not my problem...right...meet me at Harborview..." Abe punched off as a helicopter swung down. The searchlight lit up the snowflakes until it bathed the four of them in its hot bright light. They made a large, four-headed ball, huddled together to keep warm in the fresh snow.

CHAPTER TWENTY

THE BOAT WAS ALWAYS in Dave's plan. Luther had bought it, rented a boat house on South Beach, then stored it. Teaser made sure it was always ready. So if he had to use it unexpectedly, like right now, it would be right there, on line. And it was a sweet little thing. It moved like the wind, it had a small cuddy cabin to keep out of the weather, and it slept two, which was all he needed. Teaser parked the car in the empty garage, then he closed the garage door behind him. He looked out a small window down South Beach Drive. Several cars had been along this road. The snow was covering everything, and it was impossible to distinguish his tracks. Teaser asked Star to watch out the window for cars on the road, then, from the far side of the car, he put Dave on a trolley and wheeled him to the waiting boat. Master Dave was wrapped in the thin old blanket that Teaser had fastened around him, head to toe, with duct tape. He was still unconscious. Teaser tied him down to the bunk in the cabin. Later, when Star asked what he'd been doing, Teaser told her he was stowing supplies. And then they were off, heading toward Seattle. He'd leave the boat at a slip he'd rented at an Elliot Bay marina, walking distance from downtown, then he'd take Star to the condo. They'd wait there, safe, until Loki rose and finally erupted.

Teaser was sweating in the cold Sound breeze. He knew it was Loki, getting ready. He ignored Loki while he tended to Star, who was shivering. She still had a rash on her arms and neck, though her hives were mostly gone. Although she said nothing, he could tell she was upset. With one hand, he kept the boat on course. With the other, he carefully helped her into a warm jacket. "Are you okay?"

"Yeah. I guess. But I'm confused, Teaser, they really messed up my mind."

"At the condo, I'll explain." He'd thought about what to tell her. How to do it. She could never, ever, know. And Loki had to stay the hell out of it.

When she took his arm, squeezing, Loki made beads of sweat run down his back.

❖

Toby Paulsen and Verlaine and Amber Daniels were waiting for their children when the helicopter landed on the hospital helipad. Amber rushed to embrace Maisie, who hung limp in her arms and gazed at the stars. Amber carried her inside to a bench, where she held her until the doctors wheeled her away.

Aaron sat in the corner talking with his father, who held his son's hands.

Lou took Abe and Corey to a hospital room that had been made available for police business. At the door Corey took Abe's arm.

"God damnit," were the first words out of Lou's mouth. "Did you do what I think you did?"

"I dunno," Corey said, "what do you think we did?"

"I think you fucking kidnapped Star 'Sharon' whatever-the-hell her name is and traded her for those kids."

"Yeah, we did that," she said, her flat tone hiding how pleased she was about it.

"And Teaser got away, with the girl and the money."

"So far as we know."

"Roy is going to boil you in oil. And then some."

"We're not telling Roy," she replied, matter of fact.

"I see." Lou grunted, displeased.

"Maisie and Aaron are safe," Abe said, simply. "That's what we had to do."

"We saw Teaser," Corey added, her face turning hard. "He's like Hannibal Lector, maybe smarter. There's no way some FBI team was going to get those kids back." She shook her head. She knew what she knew. "Un-unh."

Lou watched them. Silent. And after a moment, "You broke enough laws to spend the rest of your lives in jail."

"The way I see it, we did what the children's parents wanted," Abe offered. "And we didn't kidnap anyone, Lou. I think Star agreed to help us get the kids back."

"Bullshit."

"I don't think Star's lawyer, or a jury, would see it that way," she added, hoping that was so. Corey took a slow breath. She felt pretty good. Aaron and Maisie were safe. She wasn't about to let Lou, or the FBI, ruin that.

"You don't have to know anything," Abe said, slowly pacing a circle. "Just keep Roy off our backs. We'll help bring in Teaser."

Abe kept pacing. She frowned. Abe was ahead of everyone, and losing patience.

Lou was glowering. "How are you going to do that?"

"I don't know yet."

"'Don't know yet' doesn't cut it," Lou snapped.

Corey sighed. "He got away didn't he?" she asked.

"Right. The FBI can't even find his car."

"Where's the FBI guy?"

"Out front, handling some reporter. Toby leaked it. Just the tip of the iceberg. Told Roy he'd tell the whole story. Give him all the credit if he let you walk. Roy wanted to arrest you, put your feet to the fire."

"Toby did that?"

"On his own."

Toby? Huh. "What about Roy?"

"He'll be okay. We'll make him man of the hour. Give him credit with the brass for putting the kids first. We said Fay Bainbridge was planned, what you wanted." He grunted. "Roy does have a very good reason to be angry, though. I mean, you people, hell..." Lou let it trail off.

Corey shrugged. Lou wasn't supposed to like what they'd done.

Abe turned to the sergeant. "Will you help us, Lou?" he asked. "Teaser's not finished. He still has Dave, and I think he wants to kill more of us, especially Maisie."

"Why?"

"Teaser developed another version of himself in prison. Someone he calls Loki. Loki isn't interested in the money."

Lou cracked a knuckle.

"He's going to come after Maisie, again. And Corey and me, I'm pretty sure."

"Jesus" Lou muttered, again. "And how the fuck—"

"As prudently and patiently as we can," Abe interrupted, irritated.

Corey watched Lou's neck turn red with anger. She wanted to say something, try to fix this. She could see where Lou was coming from, even if he was being a hardass about it. He had to make up the story for Lieutenant Norse. If he protected them, and Teaser wasn't finished, Lou was going to get whipsawed. She couldn't think what to say. Aaron and Maisie were alive. Explaining that had turned hard for him, hard for them. So be it. She touched Lou's arm then followed Abe out the door.

❖

TEASER LEFT DAVE IN the cabin, wrapped in the old blanket, tied down to the bunk. Teaser gave him another shot of chloroform, then covered Dave's mouth again with duct tape. He'd asked Star to wait on the pier while he secured the boat; she didn't need to know about Dave. Teaser could see where Dave was bleeding through the blanket. It was cold in the cabin, but Teaser knew Dave couldn't feel the cold, even though he was naked under the blanket. Loki was okay about it. He'd be back for Dave later. Loki had plans for Dave. On the way off the boat, Star took Teaser's arm. Every time she touched Teaser, Loki burned a little hotter. It made Teaser sweat.

The condo was dark and musty. The air was stale, fouled. Star flipped on the light switch, opened the window. Teaser stood at the window, looking out at Pioneer Square. He felt the cold air. No one knew about Teaser's hideaway, his safe place. Here he was, right in front of their eyes, invisible. He could feel Loki, coursing through his veins, white-hot, molten steel. Loki was feeding on himself, getting ready. Angry that the she-bitch had fouled the plan. This time, Loki would take Maisie. And Loki was unstoppable, like a raging fire. The cold air felt good on Teaser's face. A man slept on a bench, the snow flurries settled on his coat. The homeless man couldn't feel the cold, Teaser was sure of that.

It was after midnight. Soon, it would be time.

Star touched his shoulder. "I'm confused, baby. My head hurts."

Teaser turned, adjusted the bandage on the corner of her mouth.

"You're sweating." Star touched his forehead. "Are you sick?"

"It's okay. Not to worry. We have the money, Star light, Star bright. I can see the beach, feel the hot sun."

"That's so fine. Oh baby, that's so smooth. That's the shit."

"We leave in the morning. South, to the beach. To the future."

"What about the past, Teaser? My head still hurts... what about my parents? Can you tell me about that?" She touched his hot cheek. "Please baby? Pretty Teaser baby...some of what they said was true, wasn't it? Did you know me?"

"Only in Seattle."

"They said you took care of me in California."

"That's a lie. They would have said anything to turn you against me."

"What about the rest? Who are my real parents? They got me all fucked up about it."

Teaser held Loki down, threatening him, while he wiped the sweat off his face with his shirt sleeve. He'd been thinking about this, preparing, and he was ready. So long as Loki stayed out of it. He'd threatened Loki, told him he would jump through the fucking window before he'd let Star know the truth.

Teaser took a slow breath, ran his tongue between his teeth, feeling the ridge, just barely. "I did some checking on that. It's a sad, bad story. But I'll tell it. I'll tell it, Star Light, Star Bright, if you'd like."

"Tell me, please."

"Okay. Okay then." Teaser could do this. He knew that. "Star, your mother was a foster child. And if it's truth you want, she was mentally not right. Her foster mother got her out of a mental hospital at twelve. She was fourteen when you were born. After you were born, her foster mother sent her back to the mental hospital, then she sold you on the black market."

"Sold?"

"Her foster mother was in it for the money. She'd find messed-up girls, like your mother, then she'd pay guys, like your father, to make her foster girls pregnant. After, she'd sell the babies to a black market baby broker."

"Who was my father?"

"Some drifter. He went down before you were born." Loki was getting restless, hot in his chest.

"What happened to my mother?"

"She died back in that same mental hospital before you turned two." He watched her. It was working. He was relieved. Loki wouldn't wait much longer.

"How do you know this?"

"In prison, I knew a guy got pretty good on the computers. He pieced it together from files in California." Teaser put Loki down, touched Star's face. "I'm sorry. I have it all for you to see, if you'd like."

"I knew what they said was wrong. I knew that." She snuggled against him. Loki shuddered. "You're The Man."

"Put this behind you. This is over. We won, Star light, Star bright. We have the money. And we have the future."

Star took his hand, put it between her legs. "Take care of me, baby, I'm so hot. Please, Teaser baby..."

Loki trembled. She could feel it, Teaser knew, but she didn't stop. She was rubbing up against him, unbuttoning her jeans. Loki was rising. Teaser couldn't stop him. Loki was in his chest, in his throat. Reaching for Star. Teaser pushed Star away, against the wall. "Get away," he gasped, his voice raw. "Now."

She watched his face change, watched Teaser's little smile turn to something cruel.

She ran, throwing open the bathroom door before he could reach her. She locked the door behind her. It was dark and the smell was almost unbearable. She could hear Loki, pounding on the door. "What did I do to you?" she cried. "Teaser, help me. Please," she cried out. "Please."

Loki kept pounding.

Star stepped back, terrified. The foul smell was making her sick. Star turned on the light. Saw the lifeless little girl, lying in the bathtub. Teaser's "baby," the girl she'd found for him, was lying dead in her own blood. Loki's work. She screamed. Over and over.

The door flew open, breaking off the hinges, and Loki was there, holding her arms so tight she thought she'd faint, yelling at her, calling her a slut, a she-bitch, a bloody cunt. She saw his lips curl up, his pleasure, before he slapped her face. As her head swung back she felt his strong fingers grab her crotch, then her neck. Without a word, he lifted her, throwing her onto the living room floor. Loki's face was red. "You're mine, now." He reached under his jacket, took out his knife. "You're Loki's."

"Teaser, please. Stop him. Teaser—"

"Teaser's dead. You killed Teaser," he hissed as he straddled her. With his knife, Loki cut the buttons off her blouse, exposing her chest. He cut her bra at her breastbone, exposing her ample breasts and her large, brown nipples. He drew the blade along her breast, making the thin red line, then pressed the knife to her throat.

She willed herself to stop feeling. He was a trick. A vicious, dangerous one. And she knew how to handle tricks. She put her hand behind his head, then she raised her nipple, as if responding. She pressed against him.

Loki raised his head. She locked onto his eyes, ran her tongue between her lips. He smiled cruelly, pinching her nipple now. "Yes, Loki, yes," she whispered in his ear, fighting the pain. "Thank you, Loki," she whispered, pressing against him. "Thank you."

Loki raised his head again. He stuck the buck knife into the carpet, imbedding it in the floor. With both hands, he tore at her jeans, then her panties.

When he'd ripped them off, Loki slapped her face so hard it brought tears to her eyes, then he showed her his enlarged penis.

Star took it in her mouth, knowing what he wanted. When he was ready, she helped him inside her. She knew the look on his face. A vicious trick in heat. For Loki, she sensed, sex was just the beginning of killing.

When she knew he was ready to come, she tightened her vaginal muscles. She could feel him tense up. "Let me take care of you, Loki," she whispered, as she rolled on top of him, taking him deeper still, holding him, then rising up. She watched as he closed his eyes. "I'll take care of you," she whispered in his ear, then, as he reached orgasm, she raised the buck knife and drove it through his neck.

Star watched him, dying. Tears were flowing down her cheeks. She knelt beside him, lowered her head to his ear. "I didn't kill Teaser, she whispered. "I loved Teaser...you killed Teaser."

He gasped, blood coming from his neck and mouth. "I killed Loki," she whispered.

It was the last thing he ever heard.

❖

COREY WAS SITTING IN her grandmother's chair, a short-barreled twelve-gauge shotgun resting on her lap. Abe slept on the couch, a similar weapon lying on the floor beside him. She couldn't sleep. The adrenaline was still pumping. She was worried about Maisie and Aaron, even though Lou had put men at each of their hospital rooms. If Teaser turned Loki loose, they'd have to kill him to stop him. She hoped a couple of good cops could do that. She wasn't convinced that they could. And she was upset. She'd heard from Lou. The higher-ups were unhappy. They wanted Teaser. They wanted the money.

It was like some macho asshole ritual. She was sure the FBI hot-shots and his Seattle Police Department bosses were all over him. Even though the kids were okay. She shook her head. They hadn't even guessed about Star. Lou had put it together, the only one. And he'd covered for them. He'd told his bosses that Star slipped through their net, he didn't know how. Shit, if she and Abe hadn't taken Star, the kids wouldn't have even been there. There was no way Teaser was going to trade the kids for the money. Ever. Corey was startled when the phone rang. She checked her watch: 1:43 a.m.

She picked up the phone on the second ring, listening. "Star?" Abe sat up.

"Help me, Corey Logan," Star whispered, between gasps.

Corey could hear her crying.

"Where are you?"

"Pioneer Condos." She paused, trying to catch her breath.

"Which one?"

"Redstone..." Star took a long breath. "Please help me." She hung up.

Abe was already at the door with their coats. He handed Sam the shotgun before they left. "You know how to use this?"

"In my country, I was a bird hunter. Golden pheasant."

"Right. Of course." He saw Will at the head of the stairs. "Will, you and Sam go down in the basement. Take the cell phone. Double bolt that steel door. Don't open it for anyone until we're back."

Corey handed Will her twelve-gauge. "You know what to do?"

Will nodded, grim-faced.

In the black pick-up, Abe turned toward Corey. "Lou?"

"I don't know. It could be a set up." Her face was hard as she replayed the call, weighed this. "No, I don't think it is. Star's scared. I'm not sure what she wants. Maybe a deal. If Lou shows up she'll freak." She frowned, unsure. "I don't—"

"Lou can't help us anymore," Abe interrupted, decisive. "It's better if he isn't there. For us, and for him."

She didn't like where this was going. Lou was covering for them, and they were cutting him out. It might be in his interests, but he wasn't going to see it that way. Un-unh. Not Lou. "Can you handle him, after?"

"Probably not," Abe said.

Corey turned to look at him. He was staring at the night sky, his face set in a dogged expression. By now, he'd be anticipating the worst. She thought he looked awfully good.

❖

PIONEER CONDOS WAS A high rise, not far from Pioneer Square. At 2:15 a.m. the snow covering the square was still white. In the lobby they checked out the names in front of the buzzers. When Corey saw Frank Redstone, 604, she pressed the little white button. She heard the static when the speaker came on. "Corey Logan," she said.

They were buzzed in without a word. The sixth floor hallway was covered with a new pale green carpet. Corey thought it looked like the fairway on some golf course. Corey stopped at 604. She could smell death through the door.

The peephole opened when Abe pounded. Then the door opened, just a crack. They saw Star's face before she let them in.

Star was wearing nothing but her black panties and a torn blouse. Tear stains ran down her bruised and bandaged face. Behind her, Teaser lay pinned to the carpet, a buck knife sticking through his neck like a stake. Blood had pooled around his head. Corey gasped. It was, she realized, a sound of relief. She turned to Abe. He was moving slowly, deliberately, taking everything in.

The stench was coming from somewhere else. Star pointed them to the bathroom. They stepped past the broken door. Inside, they saw the girl who had bled to death. It was horrible. She was wired to the bath tub. Corey cried out, then she turned away, gagging. She could hardly breathe. Abe opened the window, helped Corey catch her breath. She slowly regained her balance. When Corey was able, they led Star to the couch.

Star lit a cigarette. "You were right," she said, before they could speak. "About Teaser."

"What happened?"

"Loki killed him. I killed Loki."

"Did he hurt you?"

"He raped me." Star exhaled, wiping her face with the back of her hand. "But I've had tricks that did a lot worse. And this time, I got my payback."

Corey watched her sigh, noticing, for the first time, the dark-blue star tattooed on her thigh. She liked the tattoo. It was careful, delicate work. Somehow, it made Star seem softer, more vulnerable. It was quiet. She turned to Abe, who was waiting, revealing nothing. "Why did you call?" she finally asked Star.

"I don't want to go back inside. If I run with the money, they'll come after me. Big time. Without Teaser, I won't have a chance. By myself, I'm not smart enough." She shrugged. Corey recognized the gesture. Like Corey, she knew what she knew.

"You're smart enough to ask for help," Abe said, handing Star her jeans. "That's very smart."

Star looked at her torn pants. "Then help me. Please?"

"Where's the money?" Corey asked.

"In the closet there." She pointed.

Corey stood, opened the door and took out the blue duffle. She checked the money. She hesitated, looking at Star as she considered this. She turned to Abe. He nodded, just barely. "Here's what I'll do," she finally said. "I'll give you one hour. I'll cover for you. Say that you tipped me off. That you helped me make the switch. That you turned in the money. With any luck, they won't look too hard for you. Either way, I'd leave the country, start over."

Star slipped into her jeans, covering her tattoo. "Thank you." She put on her jacket, opened the door. At the door, Star turned back. "You were right."

Corey flipped her a packet. $20,000. "Luck," she said.

Star pointed a finger at Corey, bowed her head slightly, then she was gone.

When the door was closed, Abe saluted Corey, too. Just a little nod and an admiring smile. She reached out to hold him when she felt a tremor in her lower lip.

CHAPTER TWENTY-ONE

OREY AND ABE GAVE Star an hour, as they'd promised. They went to a hole in the wall, just off Pioneer Square. The room was long and narrow. An old formica counter ran along one side, a row of tables lined the other. There was a well-cared-for juke box in the back corner. Abe called Sam and Will from the payphone beyond the empty counter. He told them it was over, Teaser was dead. He asked Sam to stand by, explaining that he'd almost certainly have to bail them out of jail.

He sat back down next to Corey. She turned to him. He could see she was on her way back, not so wound up. Her face was softer, more lively. Her freckles rose on her cheeks when she smiled at him. It made him feel lucky, pleased with who they were, what they'd done. Abe sipped his coffee, watching her as she made her way to the juke box.

Teaser was dead. He let out a breath. Aaron and Maisie were safe. Corey's work. Why was it that no one

ever saw how able she was until after the very worst
was right there, unavoidably in plain sight? And why,
even then, was it only the victims who got it? The
powers that be were anything but pleased. They were
going to use them for their purposes. What they had
to do now was stay out of jail. Obfuscate. And Lou
was going to be very unhappy, really angry. He had
reason to be angry, though. Abe was still figuring how
to deal with that. He had to step back, fit these pieces
into a larger picture. She sat beside him. "I love you,"
he whispered in her ear, as Patsy Cline sang "Crazy"
on the juke box. She kissed him, hungrily. An old
man at a corner table clapped.

Corey called Lou at 3:25 a.m. "Star called...meet us
at Pioneer Condos...she said he's dead...right now."

Lou used the super's key to open the door to 604
twenty minutes later. On their way up, Corey had
counted six policeman in the lobby, tracking snow on
the carpet. Lou entered with his gun drawn. A minute
later he waved them in. When he found the dead girl, he
bit the back of his thumb.

They sat in the living room near Teaser's corpse.

"Tell me. All of it," Lou said.

They looked at him, uncertain.

"You've been here," he said. Matter of fact.

They didn't answer. Abe found a corner of the
ceiling.

"Where's the girl?"

Corey shrugged. Abe shook his head, side to side.

Lou's tone changed. "One more time. Tell me exactly what happened here."

. "Star called me at home. I made a deal with her, before the switch. I told her that if she got me Teaser, and the money, she could walk. She delivered."

Lou stood pacing. "She said all this on the phone?"

Corey and Abe didn't respond. Corey glanced at Abe, unsure how to handle this.

"You were here. You saw her."

"Why do you say that?" Abe asked, soft, polite.

"Answer the question, damnit. What happened here?"

Abe stood. "It's better if you don't know just what happened here, Lou. Aaron and Maisie are alive. Teaser's dead. And the money's right here. That's enough to know. That's truly enough."

"Let Star go," Corey said, relieved at what Abe had done. He wasn't lying, or even misleading. He was just sticking to the things he thought mattered. She would, too. "She's paid her price, believe me. She's not going to hurt anyone. And if you put her in prison again, her life will be over." She touched his arm. "The important things are okay on this. Just let the rest go. Please."

Lou's neck was red, a bad sign. "Tell it to the Lieutenant." He pointed toward the door.

❖

SAM WAS WAITING WHEN they arrived at the station. They were booked for withholding evidence, bail was set, and they were released—first Abe, then Corey. They were on the street by 10:00 a.m. The problem was that Corey had to see Lieutenant Norse at 4:00 that afternoon.

In the burgundy Olds, Corey turned to Abe, "Norse is going to throw the book at me. What do I do?"

"I've been thinking about it," Abe said, rolling down the window to let the pipe smoke out.

"Thinking about it?"

He turned. "Today, just show up at 4:00. He'll lean on you. Hear him out. I've talked with Jason. I'm seeing Lou at 11:00. Don't worry about this. We'll handle this," he told her, then he adjusted the window.

Don't worry? Corey looked at him, wondering if he was kidding. He wasn't. She considered asking, "'Handle this' when and how, babe?" but she didn't. She fingered the scar on her neck.

"That turtle you left in my office," Abe said, out of the blue. "Just after I met you, when I didn't get it when you were in trouble...you made your point. I told you then that it wouldn't happen again."

That turtle? Jesus. She hadn't thought about that in a long time—a year at least. Weeks after he'd finished her evaluation, she'd barged into his office after a so-called violation of her probation. He was with a patient, who was showing off a vanity license plate that read NOMODOE. When he wouldn't see her until he had an opening, hours later, she'd left a turtle on his waiting room couch with a note taped to its back. The note said, "Hi, my name is NOMOHARDTIME, I can wait as long as you like." Of course she remembered that turtle.

Corey watched him, staring out the window. Huh. She felt better, she had to admit. "Okay," was all she could say.

"Uh-huh," he replied. Abe emptied his pipe, missing the ashtray with a hot ash. Sam put the ash out with his shoe as soon as it hit the floor.

❖

ABE DROPPED COREY AT their house, then he had Sam drive him to Belltown, to the Grill, where Lou was in the back booth, nursing a bourbon and seven. Abe was surprised to see him drinking at 11:00 in the morning. The Grill was dark, hardwood floors and black booths. Abe ordered coffee. Lou sat there, silent.

"Lou..."

Lou waved him off. "Here's the deal. Five people are dead. I'm about to be shit-canned. Norse can't wait to serve Corey's head on a platter. When he's finished, you may be able to practice in Las Vegas, or Korea."

Lou was steaming. Abe ignored it, sipped his coffee. "You ever see that movie, *To Kill a Mockingbird?*" he asked.

"Don't fuck with me."

"You know the one with Gregory Peck? Takes place in—"

"Fuck you, Abe."

Abe raised a palm. "In that movie, the crazy guy, Boo, saves the kids' lives. Then, in order to keep Boo from going to trial—a trial that will surely ruin his life—the police chief says the victim fell on his own knife. He said that because he understood the situation and it was the right thing to do..."

"I don't want to hear about any fucking movies."

"You're like that guy Lou. You're a hero. I believe that." And he did, though at the moment, Lou didn't seem to care.

Lou frowned. "Tell it to the Lieutenant."

He considered this. "What does Lieutenant Norse want?"

"He wants to be Chief."

"Uh-huh." He nodded. "What do you want?"

"I want to be a captain." He smiled meanly. "And I want pigs to fly."

"I can't do that, yet." Abe was taking pipe paraphernalia out of his pocket, setting them on the table. "Captain, I mean."

"Not yet, uh-huh..." Lou let it hang, watching the pile grow—pipe tools, a handkerchief, a dog-eared, empty match book—shaking his head. "Abe, how often you catch your dick in your zipper?"

"Well, it's funny you should—"

"Never mind," Lou raised both hands.

"I owe you." Abe frowned, filling a pipe. Lou was angrier than ever. "I know that."

"Is that some kind of shrink insight, supposed to make me feel better?"

"No, I meant what I said. And I intend to do something about it."

"Right. Who you gonna kidnap this time? Norse's new wife?" Lou's neck was red, again. "You're running out of time." Lou looked at his watch. "In six hours your wife's gonna be back inside."

❖

COREY WAS SHOWN INTO Lieutenant Norse's office at 4:00. His office was Spartan: forest green walls, green felt blotter on the oak desk, brown wooden armchairs. The Lieutenant was tall, unexpressive, with grey crew-cut hair and gold rimmed glasses. He looked the same to her as he had when he'd questioned her about Nick Season's death less than two years ago. As he got older, though, she thought he looked more like a colonel than a cop. He stood, rigid. The lieutenant did not extend his hand. "Ms. Logan-Stein."

Corey nodded. "Lieutenant Norse."

He pointed out an armchair. After she sat, he slowly looked her over, a kingfisher silently marking a rising fish. "I've asked Sergeant Ballard to join us."

"Okay." Corey frowned. This was bad.

The lieutenant lifted his phone, said something to a secretary. They waited in uncomfortable silence until Lou arrived. It took less than a minute.

"Thank you for joining us, Sergeant," the lieutenant said, formal.

Lou stood, ignoring Corey. She thought he looked as uncomfortable as she felt.

"You both know why we're here?" The lieutenant turned to each of them, waiting until they each said yes, then he went on.

"I've given this matter considerable thought," he paused, looking first at Lou then at Corey. "Two children were kidnapped. There have been five murders."

"Five?"

"Luther Emerson." He stared at Corey. "Your friend, Franklin, who was stabbed in the alley; the as yet unidentified runaway girl who bled to death in the bathtub at the condo; the man, Dave Dickson, who died from his wounds and exposure during the night; and finally, Theodore 'Teaser' White, who was stabbed in the neck with his own knife.

"I didn't know about Dave Dickson." Dave, Maisie's real dad. She'd never know him.

"He was found on Teaser's boat this morning."

"I see." Five murders. Shit. He was going to bust her for anything and everything, then see what she had to trade. Abe had said not to worry, they'd handle it one way or another. Well, she was worried. Even the idea of a trial made her want to cry.

"The woman, Sharon "Star" Goodwin, has disappeared. According to your story, she killed Teaser defending herself."

"Yes, she said that's what she did."

"Do we agree then, on the facts as we know them?"

Lou nodded; so did Corey. She was getting upset.

He looked at Corey. "The last time we met, I was investigating the death of Nick Season, an accomplished county prosecutor, a prominent labor lawyer, and a promising politician. You, your husband and your mother-in-law took his reputation, and his life." He rapped his knuckles on his desk for emphasis. "I still miss him."

Corey took a breath. Jesus. She felt like throwing up on his desk.

Another rap. "I will not be played for a fool. Consider my question carefully. Do you have anything more to add?"

Another breath. Her face showed her decision before she said, "No, sir."

Lieutenant Norse adjusted his glasses.

Corey was already thinking about jumping bail, running her boat up the Inside Passage.

"As we know, Ms. Logan-Stein has cut corners before. This time, she lied, she withheld evidence, she obstructed justice. This time, one of the perpetrators escaped. This time, the FBI is extremely aggravated—hostile, in fact. They're especially angry with Sergeant Ballard..." The lieutenant hesitated.

Lou coughed, looking at a corner of the ceiling.

"The FBI says we've missed the forest for the trees. Incidentally, we recovered the missing $20,000. Rather odd really. Never mind. I'm forced to act..." He let it drift off.

The lieutenant was looking out the window, musing. Corey was so afraid she was sure she couldn't move, even if there was a fire.

"Forest for the trees, yes..." He turned, displeased. "We saved the children, recovered the money. The kidnapper is dead. And Sergeant Ballard's role in this hasn't even been acknowledged." The lieutenant turned back toward the window, visibly irritated, and then, mostly to himself, "His work could be recognized."

Lou shifted from one foot to the other, bewildered.

The lieutenant went on, to the window, "Perhaps this could lead to advancement." Norse turned back, eyeing them, standing ramrod straight, so tense his tight lips were white.

Corey waited for the other shoe to drop.

Lieutenant Norse cleared his throat, hard eyes glaring at her. He hesitated, then abruptly, "I'm afraid I'm late." He waved a hand toward the door.

"Uh—" she felt Lou's firm grip on her arm, and before she could say word one, she was out the door.

Outside, Corey turned to Lou. "Did you..."

Lou didn't answer. He was looking out the window.

Corey held her hand out in front of her, it was shaking. She let out a slow breath. "That's it?" she asked, disbelieving. "Uh, Lou?"

Lou still ignored her. He was mumbling something to himself. She stepped close enough to hear him. "That sonofabitch kept talking about some damn movie." Lou said. "Spaced out, like he was tuned into some Martian radio program." When she touched his arm, twice, he turned. "Hell. You know what he's like."

Corey was confused. She'd never seen Lou like this. She caught a one-damned-guess look. "Abe?"

Lou let it hang, plainly enjoying her confusion. Finally, he took pity; she'd suffered enough. "A thing like this? Who else could even think of it? Someone went to work for you, Corey. For us. They gave Lieutenant Norse the moon. And they came up with twenty grand. Though that was just the icing." He shook his head.

Her smile, when it came, was open and warm. "Abe," she said, mostly to herself.

"How—"

"Jesse," Corey interrupted. "This is her kind of deal. Jesus, I'm afraid to ask Abe what he did. I mean, she hates me."

Lou rubbed his bald spot, what a world. "Well, you owe her. And her son. I can tell you one thing, the lieutenant couldn't give a shit about the money. He just needed it to turn his back on this thing. And he won't lose any sleep if I make lieutenant, 'cause one way or another, I know he'll still be my boss. No, it was you he wanted. And Jesse. She did one whole hell of a lot more than pay twenty thousand dollars to make this go away. Had to be something the lieutenant…uh…coveted. Yeah." He grinned, pleased. "Is that a word?"

"Coveted? I think so, yeah," Corey said, a little giddy. "Jesse could do that."

She hesitated. "Lieutenant Ballard," Corey said, lightly hitting every syllable. She touched his arm again. "It suits you, Lou."

❖

IN THE OLDS COREY turned to the back seat, where Abe was cleaning one of his pipes. The snow was melting, and Sam was driving too fast in the slush. "Okay. Let's have it."

He looked up.

"What did you do?" she asked.

"Regarding?" Abe's big face was expressionless.

"Regarding?" Corey made a face. "What an asshole... Sam, is he an asshole or what?"

"All psychiatrists are assholes." Sam weaved between two trucks. "Unrealistic, like children, and they can't drive."

"Right. You're right, Sam." Corey leaned over the seat, took Abe's pipe, waited for his smile. "Okay. Lou could be a lieutenant. I'm out of jail. No charges. None. This was not a miracle. Jesse did something. You made her do it." She shut her eyes. "Just give me the bad news."

Abe sat up straight, sober. "Norse should make captain. He's on track to be an assistant chief." Corey's lower lip slid between her teeth. "Jesse owes the mayor. She's out twenty thousand dollars. And we're tied up on Sundays for quite a while."

She stayed still, letting this sink in, then Corey opened her eyes. "Assistant Chief? That's," she caught herself, "okay...okay." Corey took a breath. She watched him, off somewhere, looking out the front window. "Was it awful?"

His expression changed to something more complex. "I told her Norse would rather have her than you. That I'd make that deal. Even if I had to lie about her to Lieutenant Norse. I threatened to 'reconsider' her history with Nick Season..."

"No..." It came out slowly, in a whisper. "It's her nightmare. Her affair with that monster Nick back on page one."

"I said I'd give Norse whatever he needed." He leaned forward, focused. "I was speaking her language. At first it made her angry. Before it was over, she was actually smiling. She knew she had a hold on me, a way to reach me."

"Uh oh..."

"I know. But she stepped up. We'll have to see what that means for us." Abe sat back, finished.

Corey smiled ruefully. "She's a pistol. I gotta give her that." And Abe was perfect. She reached back and took his hand.

Sam turned. "I love this fucking country," he said, nodding at them. He swerved to avoid a snowplow and sideswiped a Cadillac.

❖

TWO PATROL CARS WERE idling by the hospital entrance when Abe and Corey arrived. They found the waiting area, where Toby was sitting in a corner by himself. He turned when Corey touched his shoulder then made room on the couch for her to sit beside him. "Aaron's asleep upstairs." Toby hesitated. "I'm really glad to see you," he admitted, self-conscious.

"Likewise," Corey said, touching his forearm. "How is he?"

"Some young doctor, who didn't want to talk with me, put sixteen stitches in the cut on his head, but that's the worst of it, physically. He's still pretty upset."

"Is he getting any help?" Abe asked.

"Could you see him?"

"No, I can't. I'm sorry. I'm working with Maisie. But I'll get you a good person."

"I'd appreciate that," Toby said. "I'd like to see this person, too."

"That shouldn't be a problem."

"Thank you. This is new for me." Toby made a wry face. "As you undoubtedly know." He raised his hands, a gesture Corey had once hated. "Nora finally called. When I told her, she screamed at me for ten minutes. Mostly, though, she blames herself. She's on her way home. Nora's a good person. She wants to be with Aaron, and with me." Toby hesitated. "I feel fortunate, and grateful."

Corey sensed something had shifted for Toby. He looked sad, even stoic.

"I've made serious mistakes..." Toby collected himself. "I hope to turn it around with Aaron. It'll take time. But I have to do this."

"Look out for him," Abe said. "He's going to have very hard days."

"We're going away. Aaron and I, and Nora, if she'll come. He wants to go to China. Is that a good idea?"

"Yes." Corey said it warmly and without hesitation.

Toby turned to her, tears starting in his eyes. "Please forgive me," he said.

❖

ABE LEFT COREY WITH Toby, and went upstairs to see Maisie. At the desk he was pointed toward a small meeting room. Through the glass window he saw Amber and Verlaine, sitting silently, on opposite sides of a table. Something wasn't right. It was in the air when Amber opened the door. Abe wondered if the fear of losing a child lingered on, like the smoldering remains of a spent fire. Amber looked low. Her eyes were red. Verlaine didn't get up from his green chair when Abe came in. He stared at the tabletop. When Amber offered Abe a seat, Verlaine looked up. His expression, especially the glaze in his eyes, was remote.

"How's Maisie?" Abe asked.

"Physically, she'll be fine," Amber said, hushed. "Emotionally, we don't know. She's gone. She doesn't talk at all. She lies in her hospital bed, eyes glazed over, staring out this little window. She won't even look at us."

"Is she heavily sedated?"

"No. It's something else. I think she doesn't want to come back to the world."

"She'll come back. She's a fine girl, and she has caring parents. She'll make it back." Abe could see that Amber was working hard at thinking clearly, carefully.

"She hates us," Verlaine said, in a monotone. He went back to staring at the tabletop.

"Give her time," Abe said, "then let her decide if she hates you."

"Maybe she'd be better off away from us," Verlaine suggested.

"No, she wouldn't." Abe took a beat, kept the lid on his frustration. "Verlaine, it's about Maisie now. What's best for Maisie."

"I'm sorry," Verlaine turned, sad. "I can't do this now. Can you excuse us?"

"No," Amber said, sadly. "I'm sorry, but he stays."

"Don't I have a say in that decision?" Verlaine asked.

"Don't make me choose between you and her." She put her hand on his. "She needs me now. And Abe. And she needs you, too."

Verlaine went back to staring at the table. "I'm sorry," he murmured.

"May I see her?" Abe asked. He was sorry for Maisie, and for Amber, that Verlaine wasn't more helpful. Still, Verlaine would wake up, particularly if Maisie improved. And Amber had come through: she was taking on this responsibility; she'd be there for her daughter. It gave him hope for Maisie.

"Of course," Amber said to Abe. Amber put a hand on Verlaine's shoulder before leading Abe out of the room.

❖

MAISIE WORE A RED flannel nightgown. Her hair was brushed, and her face was clean. She was leaning against two large pillows, staring out the small hospital room window. The room was yellow, with a Monet print on the wall. Abe stood at the door, watching her. When Abe drew a chair beside the bed, he saw that her eyes weren't focusing.

"I brought you a note from Will," Abe said. He set the envelope on the bed beside her. "He's hoping to see you soon."

Maisie didn't respond.

"I've been thinking about you, too. I'm hoping you'll keep working with me. I'd like to see you every day."

Maisie looked out the window, impassive.

"I know something about how you feel. I know it must seem like you can never come back." He touched her cheek. "You can though, Maisie. I believe you can." He paused, trying to imagine what it was like for her. He leaned in. "Please try and hear me. What I have to say is simple. And Maisie, I mean what I say, as you know." He gave her a minute. "I can't undo what's been done. No one can. The pain, the shock, the terror—it's real, it really happened." He waited, took her hand in his. "The only thing I know how to do is help you get past it. Move on. It's hard, careful work. It's work you and I could do, if you're willing. All I can promise is that I'll be there for you, and I won't judge you." He leaned closer. Her eyes were vacant. "But Maisie, I know that if we do this right, one day you'll be a young woman who smiles when she thinks about who she is...I think we can do that together, Maisie. I believe we can do that. You and I."

Abe looked out the window, wondering what she was seeing. Maisie squeezed his hand, held it tight. When he turned back, her eyes were on him, deep, dark pools. She worked to focus. A single tear ran down her cheek.

❖

COREY AND WILL WERE on the front porch, sitting side by side on the rocker. They were watching the sky and the drizzling rain, trying to figure which way the wind was blowing. The trouble was that the clouds seemed to be going one way, the rain another. They talked about it for a while before deciding that wind currents could be blowing in different directions at different altitudes. Then they shifted to the Storm, and play-off possibilities. When they'd worked that out, Corey slipped her arm around her son. "I'm sorry, Will, that I had to butt in."

"I'm the one who's sorry. I tried to butt you out." He looked around, making sure no one could see him, then he leaned back, resting his head against her arm. With his fingertips, Billy traced the tattooed bracelet on her wrist. "You saved my friends' lives, mom. I mean—jeez. Jeez, you know?"

"I still made it hard for you. Hard to be like your friends, anyway."

He sat up, looked at her. "I'm different from my friends. They feel like they have to try things, do things they don't really want to do, be a certain way—you know?—even though they don't really feel that way. What I'm trying to say is that I don't have to be any way. I feel like I know what to do when things happen. I know what to do."

Corey took Will's hand as the burgundy Olds with the neat white trim careened into their driveway. Abe got out, lumbered up the steps. He was looking at the sky, trying to figure something.

The corners of her mouth turned up, just a little. They'd forded a river of fire to forge this little family. No regrets.

ACKNOWLEDGEMENTS

Julie Albertson, Linda Alexander, Jennifer Biberman, Tyson Cornell, Dorothy Escribano, David Field, Brendan Kiley, Patricia Kingsley, Richard Marek, David Miller, Marianne Moloney, Carie Olsen, Kate Pflaumer, Brian Phillips, Amy Prestas, Mike Reynvaan, Avery Rimer, Robert Rohan, Elizabeth Trautman, Andrew Ward, Ben Weissbourd, Emily Weissbourd, Jenny Weissbourd, Kathy Weissbourd, Richard Weissbourd, Robert Weissbourd, Sophie Weissbourd, Laura Wirkman